THE GLASS HAMMER
K. W. Jeter

Author of the controversial *Dr. Adder*, K. W. Jeter has created a future—quite possibly *our* future—in this new novel. With a deft hand he places one man in the center of a struggle to control society; through Schuyler, we are shown the forces which vie for control not only of him, but of all who live in the eerily familiar strangeness of Jeter's twenty-first century.

A media cartel in the business of selling violence and risk; a church looking for a good martyr; a government that rules by misdirection and deception. Separately, they are making Schuyler very paranoid. Collectively, they unwittingly strike a blow in the world, a silent stroke of fate.

Matt Howarth has rendered fourteen black and white illustrations for this edition.

"Has the brain-burned intensity of his mentor, Philip K. Dick."
—*The Village Voice*

Books by K. W. Jeter:

*DR. ADDER
* THE GLASS HAMMER
  MORLOCK NIGHT
  SOUL EATER

* denotes a Bluejay Book

THE
GLASS
HAMMER

K. W. Jeter

BLUEJAY BOOKS INC.

A Bluejay Book, published by arrangement with the Author

Copyright © 1985 by K. W. Jeter
Cover art © 1985 by Barclay Shaw
Interior illustrations copyright © 1985 by Matt Howarth

Text design by TPM, Inc.

Manufactured in the United States of America

First Bluejay printing: July 1985

Library of Congress Cataloging in Publication Data

Jeter, K. W.
    The glass hammer.

    I. Title.
PS3560.E85G5   1985   813'.54   85-6213
ISBN 0-312-94173-0

One of the most extraordinary things about seeing yourself a lot on television is you dream about yourself in the third person. Civilians don't do that. What is ultimately scary is when you dream about yourself, and you're walking away from you, you know what the back of your head looks like. This of course is schizophrenia.

Gore Vidal, interviewed by Adam Mars-Jones
The Sunday Times, London, September 16, 1984

As the glorious sun penetrates glass without breaking it . . . so the Word of God, the light of the Father, passes through the body of the Virgin, and then leaves it without undergoing any change.

St. Bernard of Clairvaux (1090–1153)

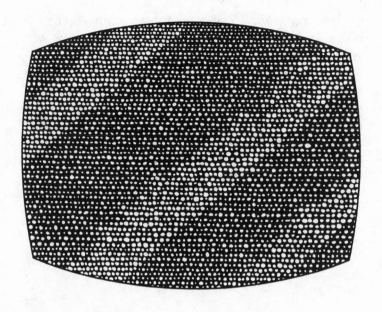

Opening

Video within video. He watched the monitor screen, seeing himself there, watching. In the same space, the warehouse, that he sat in now. There were more objects held in the space inside the screen: the sleek mass of the sprint car, the mattress and blankets against one wall, scattered beer cans, and all the other evidence of his past. Now the warehouse was empty, swept bare, those things gathered up and placed beyond his reach, inside the screen. Only the chair, and the monitor and playback unit they had given him, existed now. And the tapes stacked beside him.

1

"Do you want to go straight through them?" A voice spoke behind him. He had forgotten there was someone else in the empty warehouse with him.

After a moment, he nodded. He reached down and pulled out the tape he'd taken at random, returned it to its place in the stack, then placed the top one in the playback unit.

He watched the screen, waiting for the images to form. Everything would be in the tapes, if he watched long enough.

Segment One

The man is the heart of the burning car.

"Shit," said Norah Endryx. She sat forward, elbows to knees, and dropped her cigarette stub to the bare concrete. On the monitor screen, as she watched, another figure runs across the sand, tearing off his fire-mask. The missile trails skein above the night desert. She ground the stub out under her boot.

VIDEO: CLOSE-UP of the rescuer's face as he tugs the limp, goggled body free of the wreck. His eyes, flame-reddened, narrow in puzzlement. Then the shot blurs. In SLOW MOTION grace,

arms splaying wide, he is lifted backward by the
bullet's force. He strikes the wall of the warehouse
and slides to the angle of the floor.

"Christ, what a mess." Through the zipped-open sleeve
of her jacket, Endryx punched the keypad in her forearm.
On the monitor, Schuyler's face freezes, the expression of
surprise caught at the moment of fading beneath pain and
blackout.

"Something wrong?"

She looked over her shoulder. The monitor's glow threw
her silhouette across Wyre as he bent over Schuyler's car.
Using the hood as a workbench, he probed with his thin
chrome tools in the co-pilot's access door. The light-panel's
glare above his eyes hid his face from her when he looked
up from the metal box's innards.

"Nothing." She pushed her sweat-damp hair from her
forehead. The thick Los Angeles heat, even this far through
the night, pulsed blood-like outside; the air inside the
warehouse synched in with it. The fibers of her shirt went
through their simple program, drawing sweat away from her
skin and dissipating it in air. She felt as if she were being
sucked dry by little vampires. End up like one of those
pruney leather guys you see scuttling around downtown,
she thought. That's part of the price you pay for coming to
work in L.A. She managed a tired smile. "What could go
wrong after a day like this?"

Wyre shrugged and went on poking inside the co-pilot.
"Tape's what counts, I guess. Long as you got good
footage." He drew out a cracked circuit board. His probes
plucked out the flattened bullet embedded in the center.
"Pierced to the vitals. Poor Amf—an innocent bystander."
Wyre rooted in his satchel for a new board.

"Will he be all right?"

"Amf? No problem. It didn't hit the main processor or
any of the memory boards. He'll be his old nasty self."

Across the back of Wyre's hand the red numbers crawled like ants as he logic-checked the new board.

Endryx turned back to the monitor and Schuyler's face. She tapped out CANCELSEQ on her forearm, then hesitated. The scramble of images and time sectors that had popped up on the screen—Schuyler dragging his fellow sprinter from the missile-struck car on last night's run, overlaid with the Godfriend assassin's bullet lifting Schuyler like a rag doll just a few hours ago, but already subsumed into the tape world—all that was the result of her fingers tapping on the keypad while her mind had been running through its own tapes, gray cigarette smoke drifting over a blank screen.

God knows what I punched in, she thought. A hash, most likely. She had every Schuyler file she'd done still banked in her shadow's archives, from the first interview to the parameds loading him into the ambulance, buried under pumping life-supports.

Poor Schuyler, she thought as she gazed at the electrophores arranged into his face. Have to go see how he's doing. Her watch read minutes to go before she'd have to leave for her meeting with Urbenton, the head of Speed Death Productions' L.A. office and thus—ostensibly—her boss. On impulse she punched in RUNSEQ. Wasting time, she knew; that was all there was left to do at this hour. RETURN and the electrophores shifted, no longer Schuyler's face, forming other images.

VIDEO: LONG SHOT, a car burning on the desert, tires smoking as they melt into the sand, a circle of flaring light catching the other shapes speeding by in darkness. DISSOLVE to

TRACKING SHOT, a motorcycle skids out of control and falls, wheels losing grip in a patch of gray slush, sparks as the motor's edge digs through the ice and finds the asphalt beneath. The rider thrown in snow banked against a wall, arms flung wide

(—*cross-cut memory to Schuyler held in air by the bullet*—) black leather against white as if melting into the snow's soft crucifix. CUT to

CLOSE-UP of the rider's helmet, motionless, the dark-tinted faceshield reflecting the camera lens. DISSOLVE to

MEDIUM SHOT, SCHUYLER, silent, watching the monitor, video within video; on the screen within the screen, the motorcycle rider sprawled in snow. SCHUYLER points to the screen and says something. DISSOLVE to

REVERSE MOTION, fire gathering into a ball, condensing into a missile, and tracking a streak of light back up to one of the pursuit satellites hovering over the desert. CUT to

CLOSE-UP of a figure in barbarian's furs and iron-studded leather, the warehouse's bare walls and metal door behind. The figure's hand pushes back the rough cowl and reveals a woman's face. CUT to

REVERSE ANGLE, the expression on SCHUYLER'S face changes from bored resignation to amazement. He starts to speak, his mouth moving in silence. The bullet hits. CUT to

LONG SHOT, huts half-buried in wind-driven snow, metal blackened by long-dead fire. DISSOLVE to

Night and desert. CLOSE-UP of SCHUYLER's face reflected in his car's windshield as he looks up, tracing a streak of light in the sky. DISSOLVE to

Snow. DISSOLVE to

Fire. DISSOLVE to

SCHUYLER, locked on some revelation, lying crumpled against the wall, shirt leaking blood.

Endryx squeezed her hand hard on her forearm, shutting off the blood and the flow of images on the monitor. Behind her eyelids, as she kneaded the small ache between her brows, Schuyler's face remained.

"Very avant-garde, that."

She opened her eyes at the sound of the voice and cut from her thoughts to Wyre standing next to her, gazing at the blank screen. Amf's box shape was cradled in one arm as he worked with an old-fashioned handheld soldering gun. "I didn't know Speed Death was interested in that sort of thing."

"They're not." She erased the sequence out of memory, the shadow's archive, at least. She watched her hand zipping shut the jacket sleeve over the control pad. "They just want the straight stuff like usual. Nice, clean linear sequences." *They* were Speed Death Productions and beyond them, Hombre Mejor and Stan's CutRate—the indie rebroadcast satellites—and the international audience they served. Images for the hungry eyes of Asia and the Americas—the thought dug in by its own sharp edge. Let 'em eat TV. And all in straight lines: the sprinters' cars

8 K. W. Jeter

across the desert, the missiles tracking and falling toward them, the video signal out of the induced visual field via Urbenton's editing desk and to the satellites, and bounced back to the eager audience. Nothing but straight lines, she thought. Like a bullet.

"There." Wyre's voice brought her out of her reverie again. He turned Amf's box around to show her. The patch he had soldered on covered the hole where the stray bullet had pierced the metal. "That gives him a nice scar to brag about at the bars."

Endryx nodded and began folding up the monitor. Obediently, unbidden, the shadow rose on its spider legs and stepped toward her, a thin aperture under the lens turret sliding open. When the monitor was stowed inside she twisted around again on the chair. Wyre was gone, in his overly spooky way. He had left the mended Amf sitting on the fender of Schuyler's sprint car.

The shadow followed her over. She stopped and flicked Amf's power switch to ON. The small LED above the speaker grille glowed red.

"Leave me alone," grated the familiar synthed voice. "God, I feel like shit."

"Are you all right?" Endryx bent close to the box's mike.

"Hell, no." The voice flattened and twanged. "I suppose I'm fixed now, huh? I feel a new board."

"Wyre put that in."

"It sucks. It'll take a week to get my protocols straightened out. Some bargain-basement cheapshit replacement—I know that guy." The LED flared brighter. "And who let those loonies in here, anyway? Goddamn dykes, with their furs and spears and shit. And that broad with the gun— Great. Just great."

"Nobody knew that was going to happen." Least of all me, she thought. Some major consultations with the New York office would have to take place, and soon, to factor this into their plans.

"So just your luck," sneered Amf, "to be here when it did. Did you get it on tape all right? Me getting plugged? How nice—immortalized at last. Five minutes on the early morning wrap-up. Shit."

Endryx shrugged. "I got you. Both you and Schuyler."

"Schuyler? What's wrong with him?"

She laid her hand on the box's power switch. "He caught it too. The first shot."

Amf's speaker went silent for a moment. "He did? That jerk—"

"Good night, Amf." The red LED died under her hand.

Outside, she drew the warehouse's rattling door back down to the ground. A couple of vibers, Schuyler's neighbors, with the low harmonics rumbling out from the doorway behind them, glanced at her and went back to preening each other's shining hair. Endryx thrust her hands deep in her jacket pockets and began threading her way out of the district's alleys. Her shadow picked delicately through the layered rubble and trash, following her toward the downtown's dark outlines.

VIDEO: CLOSE-UP of SCHUYLER, his eyes still open in bewilderment, gazing at the warehouse's ceiling. His hands grope toward his reddening chest.

Endryx had told him about the accidental jumble of images she'd made. For some reason she hadn't deleted it and it had shown up here in the archive of all the other tapes.

He hadn't seen it before. Or any of the straight footage of the shooting. He looked at the image on the screen, of himself lying broken against the warehouse. I should feel something, he thought. Seeing this. He'd come that close to death; but the others went farther. A certain numbness sets in.

He reached down and picked up the next tape.

* * *

The indies were doing replays of last night's run. Above the night desert some of the stars shifted and crawled into new positions: the pursuit satellites readying their missiles, and Hombre Mejor and Stan's CutRate beaming the ritual pre-run show to all points. By mutual agreement between the sprinters and Speed Death Productions, the area around the Phoenix factory manholes was out of the induced visual field's range, making it a backstage area safe from the audience's view. The band of sprinters, eighteen with Schuyler missing, clustered around a fire built in a discarded radar dish, warming their hands and watching the tape of a car burning.

Dennie pointed with his cast to the flat screen propped up on the trunk of one of the cars. "I could feel him grab me under the arms and start pulling." The stiff foam binding the broken arm tapped at Schuyler's tiny face under the screen's glass. Dennie had ridden out with one of the others, so as not to miss the nightly gathering. "I figured it was him, 'cause he'd been trailing on my right all the way back."

A few meters away, Cassem scuffed through the sand mixed with ash dumped from the fires on all the nights before. The sharp-edged wind had smeared the black into ragged patches beneath the circle of cars. She glanced over her shoulder at the screen's blurred flames, then drained the last flat beer from the can and threw it clattering onto the other discards. The beer, still cold despite her holding it for so long, worked its chill down her throat.

"You could've gotten out, couldn't you? On your own?" Paul Sim folded his arms tight over his chest as he watched the replay, as if to keep something buttoned tight under his jacket from leaping out and screaming. Fuckin' pansy, thought Cassem, watching him.

"I don't know, man." Dennie wiped the sweat of the beer in his uninjured hand across his brow. "I was pretty out of it. The shockwave hit me square on."

"Out of it, my ass," piped up Zister, Dennie's co-pilot. "You were *unconscious*. You don't remember Schuyler pulling you out; *I* told you about that." The metal box had scorch marks on it from the wreck. Its insides had been saved by the automatic vapor system Wyre had built in.

"Damn straight," agreed another co-pilot, followed by a jumbled chorus from the other boxes sitting on the car hoods. The sprinters ignored them, and whatever point they were making out of the superiority of metal over flesh.

"Schuyler told me in L.A. that he didn't even get it from Amf to stop and pull you out. He just took a chance there wasn't going to be a follow-up missile."

Cassem closed her eyes, but could still hear the voices going back and forth.

"Lucky for him."

"Yeah, and where does it get him? That wacko broad shows up and plugs him."

At the same time Cassem found the case of beer was empty, the last cargo came up. With a box of RH chips cradled against his chest, one of the underground factory ruins' denizens cleared the steel rim set flush with the desert sand. The burly mole placed the load of pre-war micro-circuitry in the last open car hatch and slammed the lid down. "There you go," he said, scribbling out the invoice. He tore off a copy for Popejoy, this night's organizer, stuffed the rest in the front pouch of his overalls, and started back down the ladder to the moles' dens far below. "Bon voyage." Out of the sprinters' sight, his voice echoed hollow over his boots striking the metal rungs.

"Time to hit it," said Popejoy, tucking away the pink slip of paper.

Dennie went on watching the video. "They didn't say anything about Schuyler. About his getting shot." One of the indies' color men filled the screen, sitting in front of a blow-up of Dennie's arm being set in its cast.

"They're probably still figuring out how to handle it."

Popejoy picked up McHertz, his co-pilot, and carried it by the handle on top toward his car. "So as not to freak out everybody in Brazil or some place. Come on. It's show-time."

Cassem folded up the empty beer carton and threw it on the fire. The thermal foam shrank and bubbled over the embers of scrap wood. She watched Dennie switch off and stow away the video as the other sprinters split up to their cars.

"You're drunk," said Iode disgustedly as Cassem wedged herself into the driver's seat.

"No, I'm not." The LED above Iode's speaker grille dimmed as she plugged the I/O cable into the car's sensor relays. Cassem drew the seat straps around herself. "That's the problem."

The elevator went to the 32nd floor and died. Endryx got out in darkness and climbed the next seven stories to Urbenton's office. She switched on the shadow's range-finding beam, and the stair ladies scuttled out of its light, retreating to the doorless hallways that branched off the stairwell. The walls glistened black with the layered soot of their cooking fires.

Urbenton swiveled his gaze around from the bank of monitors when she let herself into the office. The screens were old phosphor-dot models, dug up from God knew where, instead of the standard multi-plane electrophoretic displays. His desk filled the blue pool of light cast by them. "It's, uh—Endryx," he said, squinting past the shadow's beam. "Turn that damn thing off."

The building's darkness folded closer around them as she sat down and pressed the fat CANCEL button through the leather sleeve. "You're turning into a mushroom up here," she said, digging out a cigarette. The small flame of her lighter danced Urbenton's wide silhouette across the monitors. "Or one of those cave fish—live their whole life out of the sunlight. Pretty soon you won't be able to see anything if it's not on those screens." She snapped the lighter shut.

He shrugged, the lift of his shoulders tightening his shirt over his paunch. "Speed Death doesn't pay me to look at anything else. That's what *you're* for. So I can look at what you look at."

Leaning back, she gazed across the monitors. The isolation shots of last night's run filled all but one of the screens; that one held the overview of the induced visual field, each blip a sprinter racing across the cathode-ray desert as it scrolled left to right, Phoenix to Los Angeles. The open circles that stood for the pursuit satellites drifted on a slow diagonal, readying their aim.

This room, unlit except for the monitors, constituted the western nexus of Speed Death's electronic nervous system. From here, the induced visual field between Phoenix and L.A. was run, the feed from its multiple viewpoints reduced to one signal for the indie satellites. An action director's dream; no wonder, thought Endryx, that Urbenton never left the room. Miles of flat desert, scraped even barer by the war, and every inch of it wired for vision. No worry about camera set-ups or lighting, no bothersome tech crews to fool with: a one-man job from the editing desk. Inside the field, a view of any point could be generated from any other point. Any angle; track, zoom or pan shot. And all for the sprinters and their nightly runs: a show covering such long distances and high speeds that no other way of taping it was possible. And thus Speed Death, she told herself, in a small space at least, sees all. There was, apparently, no other version of God between Phoenix and L.A.

She watched her exhaled smoke, a blue cloud, pass between herself and the screens. "I've got something interesting for you," she said.

"That shooting down at the warehouse? I know all about it. Cathedra Novum security were all over the place a

couple hours ago, running all the lead tapes, looking for
more."

"Find anything?"

"Just the rest of your stuff." Urbenton flattened his hands
across his stomach. "Why you're chasing around that—
whatever his name is—"

"Schuyler." On the overview screen one of the drifting
circles centered on the blip of a sprinter's car.

"Whatever," said Urbenton. "Why you're bothering,
why Speed Death sent you out here at all, it beats the hell
out of me."

"The indies want color." Endryx shrugged. "Schuyler's
an interesting character." That was the cover Speed Death
had given her, the line handed out to Urbenton even before
she'd arrived in L.A.

"Bullshit on that. He's a sprinter, for Christ's sake. A
high-velocity drunk. That's all. And bullshit on this whole
color jazz, as far as I'm concerned. You really think anyone
in São Paulo or Newhonk is interested in one of these
schmucks' private life? They don't want that—they want
the pure uncut horizontal, straight shot through the desert,
around the nasty missiles, and every once in a while a near-
miss, like last night, just to keep the adrenaline up. That's
the whole trip right there."

She listened and said nothing, having heard it before.
Urbenton was a classicist, an action director of the old
school. Essence of Peckinpah and Needham, simmered
down in the cool blue ovens of the induced visual field
monitors up here until nothing was left but the pure straight
line of event and motion. A century-old film such as
Sarafian's *Vanishing Point* was like sacred writ to him; she
knew he had a copy of it, and other classics in the genre,
safely locked away. Cars seen from a distance, cutting their
knife-edge through the exploding landscape. To drag her
little tapes in here, she knew, video full of faces and audio
of their voices, was to muck up that flow, slow the pace—

and that's a little death for him, she thought as she gazed at Urbenton's blue-lit face. From fast to slow, the grave the end of that spectrum. She had never seen him anywhere else but this room, bathed in the light from the monitor screens like windows far underwater rather than on top of one of L.A.'s decaying towers. Living for action, the high-speed progress of the sprint cars through the pursuit satellites' hail of missiles, with an occasional near-miss—such as that ending in Schuyler's rescue of his fellow sprinter Dennie—being as close as the field ever got to actual death. She wondered whether Urbenton would be happier if the real world could be fast-forwarded and he could see the changes that were coming.

Endryx shrugged. "People in factory dorms are still people. They're interested in other people. That's the theory at least."

"People weren't ever interested in other people." Urbenton settled lower in his chair, as though his outburst had bled off some internal pressure. "That's why video."

No point in arguing, or going over it again; there was no way he could see it. In Schuyler you had a guy who had managed to wangle his way out of a dead-end post in the Cathedra Novum's dreary Northernmost Parish, a post he'd been born in and by rights would have been expected to die in, only to get shafted by the Church and wind up in an even worse hole in the snow. From there, after explosion and fire and charred bodies lined up in the drifts, he'd made his way south through the white landscape with his Godfriend buddy, the woman Cynth. A hopeless trek; they'd only been rescued by the violation of the numero uno taboo in the Godfriend canon. Which was how Schuyler, schlemiel-like, had come to be regarded as the Father of God by the Godfriends and others farther south. And—after becoming a sprinter in L.A., one of the new video cowboys for the world's viewers—the object of the yearly pilgrimage and ritual mock-assassination by the Godfriends. Which ritual had become actual when Cynth, the despised Mother of God, had shown up this day; no shattering dagger then, but a coldly efficient gun. Tough luck for Schuyler, thought Endryx; the simulation became real inside his battered rib cage.

Urbenton found none of this interesting, only tedious and messy. It lacked the clean lines and grace of high-speed motion. Speed Death had thought otherwise, though, even before this day's events had brought a new bright-red episode to Schuyler's odd career. The benighted audiences in the Latin American factory dorms gobbled up the nightly broadcasts of the sprinters' runs, and any other scrap of image or word about them. Thus the surface reason for her coming out from New York to do the video bio of Schuyler. If Urbenton couldn't comprehend the reasoning behind that much, what chance of his understanding the darker, subtler strategy beneath? That was why he hadn't been told that part. He'll find out soon enough, thought Endryx.

A red glow against her knuckles; she drew her focus back to the cigarette. "You want to see the footage or not? Speed Death can send it up through New York as easily as through you."

Urbenton made a show of resignation, a sigh that lifted his chin on his collar. "Sure. Go ahead. Access the overview there." The middle screen went blank as he thumbed a desk switch.

The tape came up on the screen at the last few seconds, the sound of the gunshot filling the room.

Urbenton grunted as he swiveled about to watch.

VIDEO: MEDIUM SHOT, SCHUYLER slumps down the warehouse wall, his chest oozing between his fingers.

AUDIO: Garbled echoes of gunshot against concrete walls.

"Overloaded the mike," said Urbenton.

Another shrug. "We can fix that in post," said Endryx. She fed another command to the shadow from the control pad in her forearm, rewinding the tape back to the start, then punched the RUNSEQ light when it flashed red.

VIDEO: MEDIUM SHOT, SCHUYLER in his warehouse home-cum-garage. Looking as if he's just awakened: hair tousled and standing on end, one hand slowly rubbing the stubble on his jaw. The other hand dangles a beer can by its rim. Late afternoon: the sun slants the grille pattern of the skylight against the wall he shuffles past. He pushes open a door; CLOSE-UP of his face in the mirror over the bathroom sink. The probing lens of the shadow can be seen reflected in the distance beyond his shoulder. SCHUYLER winks at the camera's reflection, then exchanges the beer for an electric razor.

AUDIO: Three sudden loud knocks, metal on metal, a second of the warehouse's air echoing between each blow.

VIDEO: SCHUYLER's eyes in the mirror start wide at the first knock, but no other reaction. He goes on running the razor over his black-stubbled jaw.

180 DEGREE PAN, a quick blur; FREEZE on LONG SHOT of the warehouse's high open space, trussed with steel framework below the skylights, SCHUYLER's sprint car silent at rest in LOWER LEFT FRAME, the windshield a dark mirror with the shadow's stalky, goggling form in it. CENTER FRAME: ENDRYX, seated with her back to the car, leaning forward, the faint silver radiation of her

editing monitor on her face. Beyond her the wide steel door of the warehouse. She turns away from it as the knocks fade on the AUDIO track, and toward SCHUYLER and the camera lens. HOLD.

AUDIO: ENDRYX: "You want me to see who it is?"

Urbenton lifted his hand from the buttons on the desk and scratched himself. "You oughta keep yourself out of the frame. Very unprofessional."

"So edit me out." The red tip of Endryx's cigarette blotted out the gray image of her face on the monitor as she brought her hand to her real face and inhaled smoke. "Just a rough-cut anyway."

"When's the good stuff start?" With a bored expression, Urbenton chased the itch under the fold of his gut.

"Hang on."

VIDEO: Motion and time pick up again. ENDRYX's lips form words.

AUDIO: "You want me to see who it is?"

VIDEO: CUT to CLOSE-UP of SCHUYLER's face in the bathroom mirror. He lowers the razor, shakes his head and says something.

AUDIO: (Silence).

"What's the deal?" Urbenton jabbed his hand at the monitor. His interest jumped at spotting a flaw. "You didn't catch what he said."

"It's that machine they sent me out here with." Endryx raised her thumb at the the shadow behind her chair, silent and dark except for the one red light on its display panel flickering as the Schuyler file accessed out of its archive and onto the screen. "It's been fucking up all along. Especially audio. Microphone's been cutting out, missing its range— all sorts of things. You want better results, give me better equipment."

"That's why you got what you got, sweetheart." Urbenton's sick smile eased. "Don't sweat it. We'll dub it in post. God knows you got enough tape to work up a synth. Should we have him say something clever or dumb in that gap?"

"Deathly." Endryx blew the ash off the cigarette.

"Fine." Urbenton scribbled a note as the tape started again.

VIDEO: PULL BACK, SCHUYLER's face doubled in the mirror.

AUDIO: His voice snaps the silence, a clean knife edge to the first word jumping audible: "—what day it is. I always forget." Three more blows split the air.

VIDEO: The reflected SCHUYLER shimmers as the echoes lap up the mirror's glass. He turns and sets the razor down on the edge of the sink. PULL BACK as SCHUYLER turns and enters the warehouse's open space, then PAN; quick glimpse of ENDRYX at the monitor screen as SCHUYLER walks past her, heading for the warehouse door. CUT to

MEDIUM SHOT, SCHUYLER's back to the camera. The frame floods with light as he stoops down, then straightens, rolling the door's sections onto their overhead rack. SCHUYLER's thin silhouette is washed over with the white glare of the L.A. sun outside.

"Christ," said Urbenton as

VIDEO: The warehouse door rattles up and out of frame.

"How long does that piece of junk take to iris down?"

VIDEO: The light-blurred edges of SCHUYLER's silhouette become solid as the glare darkens into color and forms. Figures can be seen past SCHUY-LER. The narrow X shape of his body, hands still raised to grasp the door's bottom edge, shifts as he leans his weight forward into the sunlight. The camera TRACKS FORWARD, shifting to one side. SCHUYLER's arm and trunk fill one side of the frame, as though shading the face—round, pink, perspiring—at the front of the group. The other faces beyond watch silently, ranged down the concrete ramp sloping from the door.

AUDIO: SCHUYLER's voice: "What do *you* want?" —low, mocking the answer it knows already; the smile heard but not seen from this back angle. Then a sharp squawk of static, its crackle fading into the open air.

VIDEO: CLOSE-UP of the other's face, the mouth flapping shut. TILT to his chest, the pink hands fumbling at the cheap government-issue voke strapped inside his coat. A green light flashes as the voice-altering device switches on. The shot goes back up to the round face reassembling its dignity.

AUDIO: Static, silence, then the flat bureaucratic voice-tone, all emotion-betraying harmonics and subvocal tremors filtered out. The voice of a machine wrapped in flesh: "Mister Schuyler." (The sizzle of electronics beneath the voice, threatening to break out again.) "You were notified. As usual. By my office. Every year we go through this zicchh howow. Zaf. Through this with you. How could you forget—"

SCHUYLER interrupts: "How could I forget a face like yours? I don't know, Wolden. But I've tried."

VIDEO: While WOLDEN, the leader of the group at the doorstep, scowls and further prods the malfunctioning voke, SCHUYLER's face turns away from him, through PROFILE to THREE-QUARTERS toward the camera. Against the outside glare, enough detail can be seen of the shaded face to make out his slow wink to Endryx inside the warehouse. He turns back to WOLDEN, pointing with his lifted chin to the figures ranged beyond the other man.

AUDIO: "How many did you bring with you this time?"

WOLDEN's electronics-smoothed voice replies: "Seventeen, Mr. Schuyler. That's all."

"That's *all?*" SCHUYLER's words choke into a laugh of put-upon amazement. "Great fucking Christ, what do you mean, *that's all?*"

"Krif. Krifter Schuyler. Shit. Mr. Schuyler—there— Mr. Schuyler." The minimal voice stabilizes and grinds on. "We only ask this of you one day each year. PrimRelCom would appreciate your cooperation."

"They would, huh?" The mike barely catches SCHUYLER's snort of disgust. "Let *them* get seventeen knives stuck in them. See how they like it." The last words resigned, weary; complaining of what is already recognized as inevitable.

VIDEO: The camera TRACKS closer as the two men speak. It swings around and ZOOMS past SCHUYLER, dropping him out of frame, drawing the other figures outside to be seen. Bright sun, narrow aperture and a long depth of field—they all can be seen as the camera PANS across the group. Seventeen women: barbarians, Amazons against the flat background of gray buildings and angled street perspectives. Ragged-edge furs crossed with straps of leather fastening the knife sheathes and pouches covered in swirling interlaced patterns picked out and stained black. Thick skin boots webbed with knotted straps; hoods of coarse-woven cloth, thrown back on all but a couple of the women. The faces revealed are young, luminous with sweat—the furs and leather suited more for the wastes of snow to the north than standing beneath the heavy L.A. sun. Dark hair braided, framing jaws sharper and cheekbones higher from times of hunger. Some of them are beautiful.

The first woman of the group, just behind WOLDEN, holds an iron staff, one end resting by her boot. A bright scuff on the metal head shows where it knocked its ritual blows against the warehouse door.

PULL BACK to SCHUYLER's profile. He drops his hands from the edge of the door above him. He jerks his head toward the warehouse's dark interior.

AUDIO: "Come on." Resignation set solid now. "Let's get it over with."

VIDEO: WIDE ANGLE as the women file past, headed by WOLDEN mopping the perspiration from his pink face. A few of the women glance at the camera lens as they pass from light to shadow, and for a moment vistas of night and ice telescope behind the soft dark lashes.
The last one has her rough hood up. The camera HOLDS and ZOOMS closer, prying toward the hidden face. Nothing can be seen.

"That's her," said Endryx. "That's the one."
Urbenton froze the screen. He leaned closer to it, studying the phosphor pattern. "Could you tell already—I mean, you picked her out. Was there something about her?"
She shifted in the chair, looking away from the hooded figure on the monitor. "No," she said.
Urbenton gestured for her to start the tape rolling again.

VIDEO: MEDIUM SHOT, SCHUYLER facing the camera; shoulders slumped, hands dangling at his sides, weary expression. A few feet behind him, the bare concrete-block wall of the warehouse, as though he were lined up and waiting for execution. A leather pad, much scuffed, is strapped to his chest, over his shirt.

AUDIO: "Bring 'em on," says SCHUYLER.

VIDEO: The first of the group of women steps up to face SCHUYLER; the camera sees the back of her head, the glistening braid dropping over the edge of her fur cloak and down her back. TRACK to the Godfriend's left to show her somber expression in profile; SCHUYLER, waiting, fills the other side of the frame. The measured pace of ritual: the Godfriend draws a knife from under her cloak, raises it and drives it into SCHUYLER's chest.

AUDIO: Bright sound of shattering glass.

VIDEO: The blade shatters against the leather pad. The Godfriend's fist with the hilt clutched in it stops against his chest.

AUDIO: The Godfriend's voice: "Thus, Father-of-God."

VIDEO: SCHUYLER nods, the corner of his mouth twisting in a sour grimace. The next Godfriend steps up, taking the place of the first. SCHUYLER sighs, resigned to the loop of circular time as this woman raises her glass-bladed knife in turn.

Endryx tapped out a fast forward command on her forearm. "The same thing," she said, "sixteen times. No wonder Schuyler got tired of it. Until the last one—that's Cynth." She stopped the tape and hit RUNSEQ. The screen Urbenton gazed at filled with the warehouse interior again.

VIDEO: The last woman stands in front of SCHUYLER. The rough-woven hood still hides her face, until she reaches up and pulls it back; her face is a few years older than the ones before her, and many years sadder.

PAN and ZOOM to CLOSE-UP of SCHUYLER's

face. His bored expression changes, his eyes widening in surprise. Lips move, the mouth forming unheard words.

AUDIO: A gun's sharp roar.

VIDEO: The bullet hits, and SCHUYLER's face blurs as if jerked away by an unseen hand. QUICK PULLBACK. The body flies back against the wall, lifted in air by the impact from the gun in the woman's hand at the edge of the frame.

Endryx stopped the tape. On the monitor screen, Schuyler's body hung against the warehouse wall where the bullet's force had pinned it. "That's it," she said. "The shadow was just a couple of feet away from her; soon as I realized what was going on I sent it right into her. Knocked her second shot wild. Then the other Godfriends were on her and got the gun away from her."

Urbenton nodded. "He said something." One thick finger pointed at the screen. "That the mike didn't pick up. But you can see him say something, when he recognizes who it is." Against his usual taste, Urbenton had been drawn into the tape's small story.

She shrugged. "We could run the visual through a lip-read scan, maybe. It's only a couple seconds, though."

"Not worth it. It's no big deal." Urbenton pulled on his lower lip, mulling over the tape. "It's just kinda striking. You can really tell how . . . surprised he was. Even kinda happy for a moment. Like he never expected to see her again, or something. And there she was."

"There she was, all right." And then the real surprise, thought Endryx. Poor schmuck.

Urbenton turned away from the screen. "If Speed Death wants to go with it, fine. Can't hurt the real show. The audience'll be watching the runs long after this guy's cold meat. If he isn't already.''

She pushed herself up from the chair. The shadow tagged after her as she headed for the door. "I'll let you know. From the hospital."

Urbenton's gaze followed her. "Why hang around there? Nothing happening—the guy's gonna be out for a while."

From the doorway, she looked back at him. "I like the little green TV's they hook on to you there. That go *blip blip blip* along with your heart. It makes a nice image."

"That's cool." He swiveled around to the monitors. "If you're sure it's just image you want."

"I'm sure." She pushed the door open to let the shadow step into the corridor. "That's all I need."

On the bank of screens the machines went on moving across the night desert.

Wyre stood in the hospital corridor outside the room they had put Schuyler in. With his shoulders against the wall, head tilted back, he watched from the corner of his eye as the shambling figure approached, like a bear dressed up in jacket and baggy denim pants. "Dolph," he said when the other man was in hailing distance. "So you heard about it."

A nod that brushed the other's gray beard close to his barrel chest. "That woman," said Bischofsky. "Endryx. She called and told me." He looked toward the room's door. "How's he doing?"

"All right." Wyre shrugged. "He should be okay. There's going to be a lot of reconstruct done, though." He straightened up, easing a knot out of his back. "I'm bushed, man. The doctors are going over the tests; they're supposed to come back any time now with some kind of definite on him. If you want to hang around and maybe give me a call when they do . . ."

"Sure." The older man laid his hand on Wyre's arm. "I'll let you know."

After Wyre had disappeared down the corridor, he carefully opened the door and went in. Underneath the tubes and dangling cords, Schuyler's form could be seen motionless on the bed, his face illuminated green by the slowly pulsing line on the screen above him. Bischofsky folded his arms and looked down on him, taking a post to watch and wait.

Segment Two

Time had passed, even in the slow universe of the
hospital. For which Schuyler was grateful, finally. Anes-
thetic no-time, which had stretched the margins of the
sterile bed out to infinity, the white flesh of his arms on top
of the sheets like disembodied fragments washed up on a
distant beach, had yielded to the ticking and slow drip of the
machinery whose varied hoses and wires fed into him.
When he had at first regained an edge of consciousness, he
had fought against the process that would rejoin him to the
rest of the universe, had swum away into the warm, still
world behind his closed eyelids, all sight and hearing fallen
away. Away from where time went on in its normal way,

beyond the door of the hospital room, with its guns and roaring, tearing noises.

Now I'm back, he thought as he leaned against the pillows. For better or worse. As pleasant as that other world had been, with the constant light overhead filtered into red and orange by his eyelids and the anesthetics reducing the regenerated flesh of his chest into a dull, comforting ache, this one had reclaimed him. His arms were his, connected to him again, wired into his nervous system. Mere thought could cause one hand to pick up the plastic cup from the little table beside the bed and bring it to his mouth to rinse out the chemical taste, drug side effect, that collected under his tongue. For which we are truly grateful, he thought. Simple marvels. Done even more easily now, since the last of the encumbering wires and tubes had been detached yesterday.

The arm and its movements were part of the world of time. That was a small realization, but enough. You couldn't have both that and the timeless semi-death's comfort. He closed his eyes and lay back, flexing his hand into one fist after another, pumping the blood in and out of his heart.

"Hey, Schuyler. How you doing?"

He opened his eyes, lifted his head and saw Endryx looking around the door. She pushed it farther open and the lens turret of her shadow became visible behind her.

"Great," he said. "Can't you tell? Come on in."

"Nurses tell me they're about ready to spring you out of here." She half sat on one corner of the bed, elbow propped against the end-rail.

Schuyler regarded her elongated, pared-down image, the black-denimed media gypsy's uniform in high contrast against the white hospital linen. Her dark hair, close-cropped at her brow but trailing longer at her neck, feathered the collar of her multi-zipped jacket; her small breasts all but hidden by the frayed workshirt beneath. Eyes

dark as well, with a cool, unwavering gaze, miniatures of
the shadow's all-absorbing lenses. It had stationed itself
some distance from the side of the bed, its wide-angle lens
swiveling into position to record the scene. The two
entities, it had struck him before and now again, woman
and machine, were alternative versions of the same concept.
Stalk and observe, he thought. They see it and it happens.
And in some ways, beyond the calculating and recording
optical apparatuses, they had evolved together, coming to
resemble each other. The shadow, despite its spidery tripod
legs and rotating lens turret, was recognizably human, or as
much so as a lot of things stalking around in L.A.; you
could imagine talking to it, buying it a drink perhaps. Might
as well, thought Schuyler. And the woman was becoming
more machine-like, perhaps consciously so. Lean and
functional, but machine-like without the old pejorative
notions of programmed, unvarying activity; machine-like as
we've come to know machines. Tougher and smarter than
us, he thought. With their different ideas—different from
human—on what's valuable and worth doing. And without
the factor of doubt; that's where they've got us. He had seen
that identical hard recording head behind the watching eyes
and lenses. That's what they share between them.

"So they tell me," he said. To escape their gaze, he
looked down and undid the buttons over his chest, spreading apart the cloth to inspect the reconstruct surgeons'
workmanship. Above his head, he was dimly aware of
Endryx and her shadow also leaning closer to look. He ran
his fingers over the smooth scars, the visible tracery of the
hidden repairs to the damaged flesh, bullet-torn lungs and
case of bone. "Good work they did." He started redoing the
buttons. "They took some tissue samples this morning. If
the tests all read OK, then I'll be out of here tomorrow."

"Going out on runs again?"

He looked up at her. "Sure. That's all a sprinter does."

Endryx nodded. "Glad to hear it. We can have the indies'

color men announce it on the next update. It'll make a good
lead-in; the first episode of your bio gets broadcast
tomorrow night."

"Do it however you want. Doesn't matter to me."

She tapped the controls on her forearm and the shadow
moved closer to the bed. "Feel like going over some more
tape? We weren't quite finished when your . . . friend
showed up."

The thought of his reconstructed past wearied him. Better
it should remain buried, only the scars showing, the same as
his flesh-and-blood heart. Reverse surgery, he thought. The
doctors cut to heal; this is something different. But he had
known it for some time, from the beginning, in fact. He
only had to summon up his previous resignation. "Sure,"
he said. "Fire away."

She was already unfolding the monitor screen from the
shadow's interior. "This is pretty much down to the final
edit. Not much time left before it goes on the air. So don't
ask for any big changes."

"What episode is it?" He drew himself up against the
pillows, readying himself. Even before Cynth's bullet had
landed him in the hospital, he had lost track of what sections
of his past had been unreeled before him.

The screen's electrophores danced as static and resolved
into a crawl of reference numbers. "This one will be the
fifth and final," said Endryx. "It picks up right when they
first brought you to L.A., and Wyre recruited you to be a
sprinter." The screen blanked, then opened into other time.

"What goes before that?" He felt too tired to reassemble
his own history.

She gave him a sharp glance, then ticked them off. "First
episode covers when you were back at Northernmost
Parish, and you wangling your transfer out. The second
broadcast will be when you were on the train heading south,
and your running into Cynth and Bischofsky aboard. Third's
Eureka Station, including the explosion and you and Cynth

starting out on foot. Then fourth is the trek and the rescue. And bingo, like I told you, you're in L.A. in the fifth."

He looked away from her. "Neat little pieces you got there." Cut and dried, he thought.

"We do our best." She coolly fielded the comment. "People live in episodes. On video, at least. So that's what we give them."

Schuyler said nothing. He gazed at the shadow's extruded monitor, waiting. Beside him, he heard the motion of Endryx's fingers on the control pad in her arm, and the screen filled in response.

VIDEO: CLOSE-UP of SCHUYLER's face. He appears a few years younger, but weathered. The planes of his face are hollowed by hunger and exposure. His gaze drifts off to the edge of the frame, as if distracted or listening to something not heard by others.

AUDIO: "Schuyler," says an off-camera voice. "Look at me."

VIDEO: PULL BACK to MEDIUM SHOT. SCHUYLER turns his distant gaze to the lens. He sits in a small office, a crowded desk between himself and the person who spoke to him.

"You know what this means, don't you? What we're doing here?"

Schuyler looked up at the Cathedra Novum official on the other side of the desk. Pay attention, he told himself. They're probably screwing you over here; you'll want to remember the details, for later. "I'm sorry," he said. "Could . . . could you go over it again?" He rubbed his forehead, as though trying to draw his thoughts up to present time.

"You're being excommunicated, Schuyler," the official said patiently. Maybe he had repeated it already; Schuyler couldn't tell. "Kicked out of the Church, in effect. All the sacraments are closed to you. Forever. Your soul is forfeit to this world; the Church takes no further interest in it."

"Oh." Well, shoot, he thought vaguely. He wasn't sure of the extent of his own interest in the matter. Nor what the sacraments were; back at Northernmost Parish he had never gone to anything except Wednesday evensong, finding the tape-recorded choirs echoing against the concrete walls to be a soothing soporific on top of a six-pack. Now that was gone, he supposed, along with everything else. Reduced to a sad file in memory.

"I'm aware of your scorn." The official plowed on. "However, there are some practical considerations attached to this action that even someone in your depraved state might consider important."

Schuyler nodded. Lay it on me, he thought. He had no recall of coming to this room. It was as if he had woken up in it, with the rigid face of the CN official, reminiscent of old Lembert up north, lecturing him even when silent. No air conditioning in the shabby office, and a dry, desert-like heat—matching an imagined desert, the only one he'd known before—pulsing through the window, the view a brick wall baking in dazzling light. A silky dust coated the arms of the chair and the papers on the desk—he could see the official's fingers draw sweaty trails across every piece he shuffled. It must mean I'm in L.A. now, Schuyler supposed. Confirming what he had been told by the Cathedra Novum guards that the Godfriends had handed him over to; nothing else had been said to him during the long train ride south from Victoria Base. That journey had given him uninterrupted hours to lie on the bunk in the sealed-window cabin and trace, and retrace, the parallel routes of event and distance that had finally brought him here.

A bare image of shapes—buildings, the straight-edge

angles of a city—silhouetted in air that was warm even when dark. So we got here at night, he thought. That was what he had seen, his first glimpse of L.A., when he had been taken off the train and pushed into a basement room with cot in the basement of some Church administration facility. All that just to get to this. To another Church sub-ascendant laying out what a shit I am.

"Your membership in the Church is ended." The official picked up one of the papers. "Records show that you bartered all of your Church credits before you left Northern-most Parish; you would have been entitled to only the minimum benefits. That is, if you hadn't violated Church ordinances regarding respect for other religions. Now you have no right to the bottom-level stipend from the Church, no right of entry to a Church dormitory or dining hall, no right to employment at a Church-operated facility. Do you understand what I've told you?"

"Sure. I suppose."

"Sign this, please. It's an acknowledgment that you've been informed of the Church's position regarding yourself."

He took the offered pen and signed without reading, then handed the paper back to the official. "So what am I supposed to do for a living now?" That much of the fog-like sheath of memories had worn away.

The official folded the paper and stowed it in the desk. "That's of no concern to us, Schuyler. The Cathedra Novum was always an inconvenience in your life. I've read your file, the reports on your attitude. Well, now you're free of all that; you don't have to bother with the Church anymore. This is what you wanted. I hope you enjoy it."

"Fine." He pushed himself up from the chair. "And fuck you too." The wire that ran through the memories, stringing them together, was the Church jerking him around. Me and everyone else, he thought, blood tightening his face. At least I'm not a stick-figure of ash and charred flesh lined up in the snow at Eureka Station, like all the other poor suckers the Church stuck there. "How do I get out of here?"

After the corridors and stairs, he emerged from the building's lobby into the hard glare of the L.A. sun. The Church guards on either side of the doors wore dark glasses to shield their eyes. One trained the mirrored lenses in his direction, studying him; Schuyler saw his own face, doubled. The same face that smooth surfaces back at the Parish had reflected back to him, but changed now. Something removed from under the skin; the circle of bone sharper around the eyes. That's what it took to get to L.A., he knew. That's the cost. The guard folded his arms and looked away, scorn at the corner of his mouth.

Schuyler started walking, into the streets and buildings that became more and more real the farther he went.

VIDEO: LONG SHOT, SCHUYLER's image growing smaller as he walks down an empty street. The gray faces of the buildings loom over him.

Propped up in the hospital bed, Schuyler nodded at the screen. "Your make-up crew really caught that one. I mean the face you gave me. I remember feeling exhausted when they booted me out."

"Not make-up," said Endryx. She had leaned back and put her feet up on the edge of the bed. "Synth and key-in. They just went with what you told me on the pre-taping interviews."

"Whatever." He turned his attention back to the monitor.

CUT to CLOSE-UP, SCHUYLER's back. Someone else's hand appears, and claps him across his exhaustion-rounded shoulders.

"Schuyler—"
He felt the hand on his shoulder, turned and saw the gray-

bearded face, a visual spark jumping the gap between now and the last time he'd seen it. Then it had been lolling forward onto the barrel chest as the Church guards had dragged the limp body back onto the train. "Dolph," said Schuyler. He grabbed the other's arm with both hands, squeezing as if to focus him into sharper reality.

"Good to see you." Bischofsky laid his arm around Schuyler's shoulder, drawing him farther down the street, kicking through the strata of ancient litter. "Really—you made it, you turkey. I knew you would."

"It took a while," said Schuyler.

"Yeah, well, the mill of the gods grinds slow. But it eventually grinds out justice. Which is what I'd like to believe, at any rate." He thrust his hands into his pants pockets and walked on, dipping his head, bull-like, to follow the course of some connected thought.

He looked thinner to Schuyler, as if, out of the snow and into L.A.'s heat, he'd shed an insulating layer of flesh. Though it could also be laid, Schuyler saw, to the change to a thin, open-necked shirt and faded denim jeans, rather than the padded cold-weather gear that had made him look like a quilted bear. A gray fringe of hair now just touched his collar, instead of tangling down his neck as before.

"How'd you know where I was?" said Schuyler.

"No big deal. Got my ways. Actually they informed me first about Lina being down here, in the hospital. The burn ward."

Schuyler stared at the other. "Lina's down here? Already?"

"Sure," said Bischofsky. "Since yesterday. They flew up and got her while you were still out at Victoria Base. The doctors told me she would've croaked if you and what's-her-name—Cynth—hadn't popped her into the medex capsule as soon as you did, back at the Station."

Well, shit, thought Schuyler. A certain irony to it. Lina blows the place up and winds up getting a free ride down to

L.A. While me and Cynth have to hoof it, through the snow and all the other bad shit.

They walked on. "Did they ding you up pretty bad?" he asked.

Bischofsky looked up at the question. "Hm? Oh—you mean on the train." He rubbed the side of his head. "Still got a sore spot here. Couldn't talk above a whisper till the train practically got here to L.A. Bastards had me in a chokehold on the floor. I made at least one of the fuckers sorry he ran into me, though." The last recounted with enough relish to bring his own smile up.

"I appreciated it," said Schuyler.

"Yeah, well, didn't do much good. But they were screwing you over." He shook his head. "So how you been, Schuyler?"

He shrugged. "All right, I guess. Up and down."

"I heard about what happened. Most of it, at any rate. I got a lot of contacts inside the Church. Just gave you the boot, didn't they?"

"Sure did."

"Figured they would. Father of God, hm? You really got your foot in it this time. Hit a nerve—the Cathedra Novum higher-ups are crazy about the Godfriends. I think those withered-up old celibates have some kinko B and D fantasy built up around untamed dykes of the frozen north. Ha. Or something like that." He looked sharply at Schuyler as they walked. "Got any money?"

"Not really." At Victoria Base, when he'd been told he was going to be taken to L.A., he'd realized that he'd left his small wad of cash back at Eureka Station: not so much as excess baggage not needed for the trek, but as an unconscious bet laid down against him and Cynth surviving at all. Don't know if I won that one or not, he mused.

"Don't worry about it," said Bischofsky. "You can flop down at my place. The Church keeps me on a pretty short leash—any supplies I need, I gotta put in a req order to them—but we can always water the soup down some more. Come on."

They worked their way through a thin cross-section of L.A.; under the sun's weight, Schuyler pulled his jacket off and slung it as a sweaty rag in the loop of his arm as he walked alongside Bischofsky.

"It's not a bad town." said Bischofsky. "If you don't mind people going around mumbling to themselves. Seem to do a lot of that here."

Schuyler looked around at the dust-shrouded streets disappearing into the sun's haze. Distant gray hills beyond the city's shapes. They had arrived at a zone of people, and motion and noise. Eyes focused on him, then moved on in their tracking search. Other figures shuffled away on their errands. For a moment the scene, the whole city as far as his vision reached, seemed to be vibrating at a pitch tuned to the edge of his hearing.

He turned and looked at Bischofsky, a smile breaking through his exhaustion. "It's everything I ever hoped for," he said.

"Be it ever so humble." Bischofsky pushed open an unpainted door. They had walked on into another relatively quiet zone of corrugated metal buildings. "Back here."

Schuyler ducked his head to follow him into darkness. The low-ceilinged corridor ended in a space bright and open enough that for a moment he thought they had stepped outside on the building's other side. The glare dimmed in his eyes, and he saw the wall of clear glass, divided into squares by aluminum framing, reaching up to the roof's interwoven struts.

"LTA," said Bischofsky, watching him crane his neck to gauge the height above.

"What?"

"Lighter-than-air facility. Blimp hangar. Big rubber company used to keep one here, send it out to advertise

tires. Only place the Church could give me that had enough
room."

Overhead a pigeon pushed away from a metal beam and
flapped through an open skylight. Schuyler brought his gaze
back down to survey the rest of the building. A small area
had been carved out against one wall, evidence of human
habitation: mattress on the bare concrete, refrigerator, table,
chair, Bischofsky's meager wardrobe slung over a rope
stretched between two eye-bolts. A computer terminal, its
thick cable snaking across the concrete, completed the
tableau.

"Hey, Wyre!" Bischofsky's shout was swallowed,
echoless, into the cavernous space. "Come on down—got
somebody I want you to meet."

Schuyler turned and saw a crane in front of the windows
move. The articulated arm bent, lowering the basket and the
figure at its controls. As the slow, mechanical descent
neared the floor, he saw the lanky frame and sharp-edged
face, one eye magnified by a lens angled down from a
headband.

"This is my buddy," said Bischofsky. "From the train."

Wyre swung his long legs over the side of the crane's
bucket and walked toward them, wiping his hands on a rag
that he stowed in his back pocket. "Schuyler," he said.
"Right?" The lens stayed in position, as though the
magnified eye were studying him. He pushed the headband
up across his close-cropped hair. "Father of God and ex-
Church."

"Word gets around," said Schuyler. The other's scrutiny
irritated him. The lean face seemed a knife sharpened for
gathering secrets. Like an animal, he thought. A skinny
wolf scooping out its, and everybody else's, territory.
Beyond that unease, he saw that the lensed headband and
logic probe slung on his hip were stamped with the insignia
of the Cathedra Novum engineering staff.

"Don't worry about it," said Wyre, tracing the direction
of Schuyler's gaze. "I'm strictly free-lance. This is just

some equipment I wangled off one of Dolph's req orders. Good stuff—they're going to be out a few bucks when they try to get it back."

"Wyre's my main man," said Bischofsky. "Tech-wise, that is. The Church wanted me to use one of their crews, but they didn't have anybody who could do some of the stuff he does."

"Or as cheap. They're getting a bargain." Wyre turned back to Schuyler. "Don't sweat it if everybody you run into knows your story. This is a hustling town—people get angles down fast."

"How's it coming?" Bischofsky walked over to the wall of glass and looked up into the light streaming through the panes.

Wyre shrugged. "Getting there. Down to the fine tuning soon." He gestured for Schuyler to follow him over to the terminal. "Watch this. Cheap thrills." He tapped out a command line, and the light pouring across the concrete floor changed subtly.

Schuyler looked up from the terminal screen and saw that an oblong of glass, intense blue, had appeared near the top right corner of the windows. As he watched, the sound of Wyre's fingers on the keyboard beside him, the glass piece rotated slowly, first perpendicular, then parallel to the floor. The blob of color cast on the concrete shifted, following the glass's motion.

Bischofsky stepped back to study the piece. "Oh, right. B series." He scratched at his beard. "I remember this one—number four thirty-eight."

"Thirty-seven." Another quick tap at the keyboard, and the piece halted in place.

"Looks like you finally got the color down. That friggin' blue's a bitch to match."

"Lot of funny gradations there," agreed Wyre. "Something funny added to your basic oxide of cobalt there. Plus the blue was nearly all flashed glass; that transparent layer really bends the spectrum." As if remembering he was there, Wyre leaned closer to Schuyler. He gestured at the wall of windows with its one spot of blue superimposed. "What we got is an interference grid, set out from three angles about a foot in from the wall. On that we can position the image of any of the catalogued glass pieces, then rotate it through any plane—like you saw. The grid's infinitely divisible, so Dolph can get the exact positioning he wants."

"This is from the window up north?" Schuyler nodded at the point of blue. "From the excavation at Northernmost Parish? But just simulations. Why not use the actual pieces?"

Wyre shook his head. "The glass is too fragile to risk it, what with all the moving around Dolph wants to do. Besides, a lot of pieces are still being analyzed down at the Cathedra Novum labs. There's more data—spectrographs, density scans—coming in all the time. We can factor it all in as it shows up, then adjust the display as necessary. Once I finish setting it up. If all those tiny scraps had to be moved around mechanically, it'd take forever. This way, zip—whatever arrangement Dolph's theories have come up with."

Bischofsky had fallen silent, lost in study of the simulated image of blue glass far above his head. He turned around. "Can you put up the rest of the B series?"

Another command line, and a row of blue shapes appeared across the top of the windows. Most were irregular squares, a few triangles, but all with the same deep color. The outside light burnt through the glass images as ink flame. The air inside the high-ceilinged space shifted, almost cooling as it followed the spectrum. Like going underwater, it struck Schuyler. The view from beneath some ocean.

"We're definitely going to need that latitude adjustment," said Bischofsky after a moment's contemplation. "You got the glass right, but it's the light—it's the light coming through we gotta work on."

"He wants another grid set up," explained Wyre. "In front of this one. To filter the light before it goes through the glass images. So as to get light composition corresponding to different geographical latitudes, incline of the sun to the earth's surface, and so on. He's got some theories that the arrangement of the pieces may depend on the map location where they were set up to begin with. So we have to be able to vary the light coming in along those lines. That's going to be the toughest," he said as Bischofsky approached the terminal. "Can't see light—always harder to fake the invisible."

"Shut it off." The light across Bischofsky's wide shoulders shifted up from blue to unfiltered daylight as Wyre skipped one finger across the keyboard. "I got faith in you. I know you can do it."

"Whatever." Wyre leaned his elbows on top of the terminal. He turned his sharp gaze back to Schuyler. "That's what's going on around here, at least. What's your shtick?"

"What?"

"You just got bounced, you're not on the Church tit any more. What're you gonna do for cash?"

"That's why I wanted you to meet him," Bischofsky said to Schuyler. "Wyre's got a way of getting down to basics. Got any ideas?" The last to Wyre.

"Maybe," said Wyre.

I bet you do, thought Schuyler. The other's face had the sharp, feral pitch of someone holding hidden threads through a maze. Like an animal that knows every twist and exit of an underground burrow. Secret knowledge, that meant survival; the image of a fox or lean-ribbed wolf struck him again. But not vicious; there had been an actual note of kindness, barely perceptible, in Wyre's talk of all the tech stuff he was doing for Bischofsky. As though, he thought, the work's some kind of indulgence, a friend's quirk gone along with for the sake of the friendship. But still—a warning generated from inside himself—best to watch out. "Like what?"

"Different stuff." Wyre's gaze drifted over the blank windows, as if he were shuffling through an interior card index. "You're in luck, actually. Being here. It's like that old line John Doe once said—you probably don't know who I'm talking about, but I'm a big X collector; I've got a lot of stuff from before Doe and Cervenka were canonized, the original 'White Girl' acetate, things like that. Anyway, John Doe once said that L.A. was the best city in the world to be broke in. At least you don't have to worry about freezing to death. And there's things people can do for money. Might try sprinting."

"What's that?" He had heard the word before, with some other connotation attached to it, part of the vague, danger-ous constellation of images that had drawn him to L.A. to begin with. Now he realized—now that it had been taken from him—how much protection he had been counting on from the Church, that he had in fact always counted on. Which is money, he thought, a safe little bit of it. A thick glass barrier between himself and the toxic excitement of L.A., so he could see it but not be touched by it. But a single blow had shattered that glass. You're in it now, he told himself. For good or bad. Now you're in this world.

"You know," said Wyre. "Be a sprinter."

Now he remembered. "You mean that chip-running bullshit?" Some of the people he had known back at Northernmost Parish had hot-wired their Church-issued microwave dishes to bring in the scattered edge of the indie satellites' broadcasts. There had been a brief vogue for the coverge of the sprinter runs; he hadn't cared much for them, there being no attempt at plot, just the endless high-speed motion of the cars across the night desert and the fiery explosions of the tracking satellites' missiles. He'd heard the shows were popular in the high-density dorms of the Latin American and Newhonk factories, that being where the indie satellites mainly aimed their broadcasts. "Forget it. I need to find a way to make a living, not get my ass blown off by by some antique military skyware."

"Well, that's the point, see. Sprinters don't get hit by the missiles. At least, very few do. That's the talent."

"Right. And I can imagine how you find out if you have the talent or not. Tough luck if you go out there and you don't."

Wyre smiled, looking even more feral. "Naw," he said. "There's other ways." He pulled off the headband and unslung the logic probe from his hip, then bent down to pack them into a cluttered leather carryall. "Hey, Dolph. We're going over to my place. So I can run some tests on Schuyler."

"You guys go ahead." Bischofsky placed himself in front of the terminal and began tapping at the keyboard. "I got an idea I want to work on."

The light around them deepened again as Schuyler followed Wyre, toting his equipment, toward the door. He looked over his shoulder and saw the same blue shapes on the window grid, slowly forming themselves into a circle.

VIDEO: MEDIUM SHOT, EXTERIOR: two men, backs turned toward the camera. Sunlight glazes a corrugated metal door. One man bends his head over the work of undoing a padlock. The other, in profile watching, is SCHUYLER. The lock comes free; WYRE looks up as he pushes open the door.

AUDIO: "This is the place," WYRE announces.

VIDEO: CUT to INTERIOR: a dark, cramped space, the L.A. glare spilling down a wooden stairway from above. PULL BACK as SCHUYLER and WYRE descend.

A row of high, dusty windows looked out onto the bare sidewalk baking in the sunlight. Schuyler followed Wyre through the cool darkness, suddenly illuminated when the other pulled the chain of an overhead utility lamp. Wyre slung his equipment bag onto a cluttered workbench and continued through the narrow corridor formed of stacked electronics, wires and circuit boards spilled in disarray, picking and gathering certain gear as he went.

"Here's the pitch," said Wyre as he returned, his arms full, to where Schuyler was standing under the swinging light bulb. "Sit over there, will you?"

Schuyler sat on the indicated fiberboard crate and waited.

"Basically," said Wyre, hands moving deftly among wires and other, more mysterious parts on the bench, "there are three overlapping fields of pursuit satellites over the spring routes. Otherwise it'd be a straight shot from the underground factory ruins at Phoenix, to L.A. No trick to it at all. But if you've ever caught any of the indie broadcasts of the nightly runs, you know the satellites make it a different picture. The pursuit satellites were really the limit of tight-focus American military tech when they were put up. The weathermods are general in effect, really were more instruments of economic warfare than the traditional run-'em-and-gun-'em; more of a nuisance, once you adjust to the new weather patterns. Nowhere near as sexy as killer trackers with optic and thermal scans capable of picking up a coyote fart out on the high desert and then zapping the poor son-of-a-bitch to ashes. That's the kind of thing that really got the military appropriations blood pumping in the old days."

Wyre's high-speed discourse bounced around the limits of Schuyler's temples. An amphetaminoid rap, he thought. Minus the drugs. In his own den here, the exteriorization of his skull's contents, Wyre had obviously connected with his own adrenaline source. A man who loves his work, thought Schuyler. "How come those things are still up there?" The question was meant to slow down the stream of words as much as for information.

"That's an interesting question." Wyre peered into a circuit-board-stuffed metal box. "Obviously, they're well-built; the pursuit satellites were the last great Hughes Aerospace production. And ammunition's no problem; 'missiles' is actually a misnomer cooked up by the indies for an unsophisticated audience. What the satellites shoot down is really a pulse-phase particle beam; the explosion when it hits is the struck matter coming up to synch with the beam and then destabilizing when overloaded. Small-scale nuclear reaction—takes only a microsecond. The trails you see in the sky are the same thing happening with the atmosphere's molecules. So anyway, there's no chance of the pursuit satellites' running dry. They can generate operating power and particle beams until the sun goes out. No, the real question is why the satellites haven't been taken down. They're still under the control of the American military authorities back East—why don't they shut 'em off?"

"I'll bite," said Schuyler. "Why?"

"Different theories." Wyre screwed the back panel of the metal box back onto the frame, finished with its inside workings. "After the Cowboy Soviets were broken up on the West Coast, the government back East didn't have the resources to establish control this side of the Rockies. There was a whole Korean Mafia rising around the Moonie communes in Virginia that they were barely able to put down. The Cathedra Novum's parish organization was the only structure with enough depth to fill the void. And still is, which is why we got a dual protectorate state here in L.A. Nominally, all the western territory is under the control of the American government—they could go into Phoenix, blow up what's left of the underground factories, and put an end to the chip-running right at the source. But they'd be risking a confrontation with the Church over

who's really got the power out here. Theory goes that
certain Cathedra Novum higher-ups are getting paid under
the table by the Europeans who buy the bootleg chips, for
them not to interfere. So the sprinters are operating in a gray
zone; technically, the chip-running is illegal. But it's
tolerated. Keeping the pursuit satellites left over from the
war up in the sky is the American government's only way of
keeping the trade down to a low roar. The limit isn't even
how many chips can be brought out from Phoenix to the
black market in L.A., but how many can be bought by the
big Euro-manufacturers like Philips and Neue Krupps A.G.
without being able to come out in the open and admit
they're using them—they can't risk losing the markets
controlled by the Americans." Wyre set the box upright and
switched on a row of lights underneath a round mesh grille
in front. "Of course, another theory is that the payoffs run
the other way, that certain American government figures get
paid to keep the satellites up as the official way of keeping
the chip-running down. As long as the sprinters are able to
get through with the chips, the Europeans are happy."

"What's so special about these RH chips, anyway?"

"Actually, you're about to get a demo." Wyre plugged in
a set of headphones to the box. "Sorry it's taken so long to
get this set up, but I had to tear it down last night to put in a
new chip. RH's are a little volatile; you can fry 'em out real
easy." He fussed some more with the wires. "RH stands for
'random hierarchical.' That's the distinguishing character-
istic of these chips. They have a true randomizing factor
built into them, and one that influences the subsequent
operations of the chip. In a sense, these are the only devices
that replicate an essential element of human intelligence: the
ability to make mistakes *and then draw everything that
follows into compensations based on that error.* All other
mechanical or electronic randomizers don't generate true
random events; they're really just complicated equations
that produce a long string of numbers. Once you dope out

the equation, you can predict the next pseudo-random number. Unless it's based on particle decay or something like that, and then you run into other problems. Those bullshit randomizers and their operations are thus entirely contained in this world. An RH chip's randomizing factor, however, can't be worked out. It creates a 'true error,' one that can't be predicted from inside this world. And then the chip can't admit it's wrong—it has a rudimentary ego, in a way—and so creates a supra-reality, a reality that it operates on, different from this one. And before this world can incorporate that deviation, make it a factor in this reality and thus predictable, the RH chip has already made its next 'error' and based another supra-reality on it, and so forth. Got it?"

"Christ, no." Schuyler didn't add the rest of his thought, that Wyre and the RH chip sounded equally cracked.

"Doesn't matter. A lot of this is ex post facto theorizing, anyway. All of the research that led to the Hoger/DMM process was lost in the war, anyway. Hoger himself was killed in the first raid that hit the Albuquerque factories. And nobody's been able to duplicate the manufacturing process. That fact, of course, adds to the value of the chips brought out by the sprinters. Once the Albuquerque and Phoenix ruins are mined out, that's it, no more. There's some speculation that the acid baths used to etch the RH chips were contaminated by a virus-like organism that operated on gallium arsenide rather than proteins, and that the randomizing factor is a mirror image of that organism's life cycle. Or, if you want to get further out, there's supposed to be some radical theologians inside the Cathedra Novum itself who believe that a true randomizing factor is evidence of God's intervention in this world, and that's why the sprinters are unofficially tolerated."

"Great," said Schuyler. "God's intervention does you a whole fuck of a lot of good these days." The image of Cynth waiting out her God-ordained pregnancy in her little cell came to his mind.

"I knew you'd dig it. At any rate, the important thing to
remember is that the RH chip mimics human intelligence by
misperceiving the world, and then drawing the world into
alignment with that misperception. *The theory changes the
reality it describes.* So it's truly unpredictable by normal
methods; it predicts *you*, not the other way around. That's
what makes the pursuit satellites above the sprinter routes
dangerous; they've got RH chips built into them. So the
scatter pattern of their particle beam hits can't be figured
out." Wyre patted the top of the metal box on the bench.
"This thing here is called a co-pilot. All the sprinters use
them. It contains an RH chip as well. But it's designed to
operate in synch with a human brain; it creates a double
randomizing factor. Just as the pursuit satellites' RH chips
get above this reality with the supra-realities they create,
this gets above the supra-realities and incorporates them.
Makes them predictable." He fell silent, a pleased look on
his narrow face.

Schuyler realized that the next line was his. "Did you—
what? Design this?"

"Nah." He shook his head. "Not really. I'm strictly an
applications man; just your basic pliers-and-screwdriver
stuff. You need an electron microscope for starters, just to
begin program work on an RH chip. You'd be lucky to find
a magnifying glass in L.A. No, what happens is Speed
Death sends me the sealed units their micro-designers have
worked up, plus the basic input-output codes, and I plug
'em in. But the actual hard-wire engineering of the end
device is all mine."

"But you're not part of this Speed Death? I mean, on the
payroll?"

"Strictly free-lance. Piece-work, jack. They needed a
fixit man on the spot to build and maintain the running gear
for the sprinters. I'm the best in L.A.; I do all kinds of shit,
for all kinds of people." He picked up the metal box and
turned it around. "Nice for me that these RH chips have a

high burn-out factor. A little built-in obsolescence keeps the cash flowing."

"How's it work?" said Schuyler.

"It talks," said Wyre. "It scans and analyzes the hit patterns of the pursuit satellites, then creates a verbal interface between its randomizing factor and that of a sprinter's brain. The words are nonsense on the surface, but the sprinter absorbs them—below conscious level—as data from a source not contained in this world, and then bases an evasion pattern on that data."

"So you say."

"Well, it works most of the time. There's been no more than an occasional near-miss for a couple years now."

"For anybody?" asked Schuyler.

Wyre shook his head. "No. You have to have the talent. The sprinting talent. A few people respond to the stimulus of the co-pilots' output. Most people don't."

"And you think I will. Why?"

A shrug. "Sprinters have certain . . . qualities in common. A certain fucked-up nature. As if a parallel error-generating process got lodged in their hearts."

"Thanks. I got reasons."

"Everybody does. Want to give the test a shot?"

"Why not," said Schuyler. The operating principle of my life, he thought. From this point on. "What do I have to do?"

Wyre held out the headphones. "Left channel's a simulation of the pursuit satellites and their missiles—particle beams, actually. This co-pilot"—he indicated the metal box—"has two RH chips in it. One generates a random strike pattern corresponding to how the real satellites operate. You'll hear some low rumbling sounds; that's the missiles hitting ground. Or you. Also there'll be a constant twittering sound, like birds. That's the analog data of the satellites moving around. The right channel is generated by the other RH chip. It'll be that verbal stream I told you about. The chip is scanning the events simulated by the first chip, and creating an interface based on them."

Schuyler slipped on the headphones. A trilling birdsong in his left ear, and silence in his right until a synthesized voice said matter-of-factly, "A red hut gravity. Being and the as as silkily?" He lifted the rear earpiece, the nonsense words then tinny and faint, to hear the rest of Wyre's instructions.

"Keypad's for your responses." Wyre handed him a hand-sized assembly of six pushbuttons and plugged the trailing cable into another socket on the box. "Simulates the evasion pattern you'd set up if this were real. Just listen to the two tracks and push whichever buttons, whenever you want."

He turned over the keypad, as if more instructions would be found on the soldered metal's underside. "That's all?" said Schuyler. "Am I supposed to—what? Blank my mind? Alpha state or something?"

"Whatever you want," Wyre said patiently. "Doesn't matter. If you got it, you'll know what to do." He flipped the last switch on the front of the co-pilot, and a small LCD spelled out PHOENIX. "That's your starting point. Ready to go?"

"Sure." Bullshit, thought Schuyler. There's more than one stream of nonsense words shooting through here. He settled the headphones back over his ears. The bird twittering grew louder, then leveled off. "*Glazed show omelet regard angelic,*" muttered the flat voice in his other ear. He sat with the keypad balanced on his knee. Bored. Experimentally, he poked a couple of the keys. As if in response, a bass note growled in his ear. Another, fainter with simulated distance, sounded after. Unbidden, a trickle of adrenaline fed into his heart, speeding it. "Angelic blastoma." He strained to catch the voice's next words, suddenly the most interesting thing in the world.

VIDEO: MEDIUM SHOT, PAN away from SCHUYLER
concentrating on the test, to WYRE calmly fixing
himself something to eat, and around the workshop. The passage of time indicated by return of
the shot to WYRE to show he has finished eating.
TRACK as WYRE goes to SCHUYLER, who takes off
the headphones. CUT TO

CLOSE-UP of the metal box as WYRE shows him
the LCD; it reads LOS ANGELES. CUT to scenes of
SCHUYLER starting out on his first run.

He closed his eyes, letting himself sink back into the
pillows. The LCD spelling out L.A. as his destiny remained
as an after-image. "It's fine," he spoke, without raising his
eyelids. What do I care? he thought. He couldn't recall
having had such a detailed conversation with Wyre at any
time, let alone five years ago; such a neat, precise
explanation of this little pocket of scurrying human activity.
Somewhere along the line he'd found out what sprinters
were, the value of the cargo they carried and how they
brought it across the missile-lit desert landscape. If it had
happened the way it had in Endryx's tape, fine; and fine if it
hadn't. The past was beyond his reach. Having enough
flippin' trouble with the present, he thought in the dim
hiding place behind his eyelids.

"There was some other stuff I wanted you to look at,"
Endryx's voice came to him.

Weariness unconnected with his wounds drained through
him. He lifted his hand and waved her off. "However you
got it," he said. "It's fine by me. You know everything that
ever happened to me better than I do." He brought himself
out of darkness to look at her. "Just because I was there—
that doesn't mean anything."

She smiled as she stood up from the corner of the bed and
began folding the blank screen back into the shadow, the

machine's round glass eye drawing back to record the scene. "Okay," she said. "Just remember. I don't want to hear any complaints from you after the broadcasts."

"I don't have any complaints about anything." Schuyler wondered, as he watched her deft hands involved with the machinery, if this was a point at which she had engineered his arrival. The signing over of his past to her, a malleable substance to be worked over at her editing monitor, until it achieved the proper form and consistency. Like bread, he thought. In the blue glare of her kitchen. Where you can get sliced and fed to yourself, a self-consuming transubstantiation. This is my flesh, this is my past. Fictional or otherwise; reality, he supposed, was what you made of it.

He heard the door open again and swung his gaze around. Wyre—in flesh, not videotape—slid into the room. His sharp-edged face broke into a grin.

"Schuyler, my man." Wyre leaned over the bed's endrail. "Hear you're about to rejoin the living." He looked around at Endryx and nodded in recognition.

From the bed's vantage point, Schuyler observed the glance between the two and broke it down into its various parts, or what he imagined them to be. Endryx's high-tech connections had earned Wyre's admiration from when the video-bio taping had first begun; the two of them were on some abstract wavelength not shared by mere mortals. The shadow, the extension of Endryx's existence, being the ultimate target of Wyre's attention; the gaze with which men undressed women taking in both Endryx and the machine equally. He wondered whether any loop in the shadow's archives recorded both a sexual encounter between them and a partial disassembly of their electronic devices.

"That's right," said Schuyler. "They're kicking me out."

"Figured I'd better bring you this." Wyre lifted his canvas bag, weightier than usual, up onto the bed. "Time to start polishing up your skills." He extracted a familiar metal box and held it out.

"Amf. Well, all right." He found himself oddly pleased at the sight of the co-pilot. He hadn't even though about the device all this time, while it had been sitting—he assumed—unattended in the dark warehouse. Now this little piece of that other life was here with him. He flipped its power switch and tilted the speaker grille toward him. "Nice to see you, Amf."

"Your ass." The synth voice snapped at him. "Don't give me that 'nice' crap. Because of you I got shot. Thanks a lot."

"Don't let him hand you a line." Wyre touched a soldered patch on the side of Amf's metal case. "He's as good as new. I left the scar just to give him something to brag about."

"Hands off, turkey—"

Schuyler switched off the machine. He remembered now what he had been told about Cynth's other stray shots. Though accurate enough, he thought. At least at short range. "Thanks," he said. "I missed the little son-of-a-bitch." Realizing that he had.

Wyre moved toward the door, lifting his carryall from the bed. "Gotta run. Catch you at Dolph's, maybe."

"Yeah, sure." He and Endryx were alone in the hospital room again. Plus her shadow's constant presence.

She pushed her jacket sleeve down over her forearm control pad. "Me too," she said. "Going to be a hustle to get this ready in time for broadcast. At least the first episode's in the can, ready to go."

"Sorry I couldn't help you more. Still a little tired, I guess."

"Don't sweat it. See you on the outs."

After the door had closed behind the two figures, human and mechanical, Schuyler rested the silent metal box on his stomach, then switched Amf on.

The expected saw-toothed voice remained silent. Bending closer to the speaker grille, he heard a crackle of static, the noise of circuits misfiring. Then a voice, different, that he had never heard from the device before. It sounded faint, filtered by distance. One word came through.

". . . dying . . ."

What the hell. Schuyler lifted the device to study it, peering in through the grille. So much for Wyre's repair work. *I thought he was better than that.*

The static hissed and snarled again, louder. Than the voice, in mid-sentence.

". . . dying . . . they're all going to start dying. Listen, Schuyler . . . this is important. Now they're ready . . . the sprinters—they're all going to start dying now . . . watch—"

His own name chilled him, scratched out by the fading voice. It cut off, replaced by silence.

Jesus, he thought, nothing else, no other words. This was something new, unexpected. Another new thing had entered his world, speaking its own name aloud this time, speaking of death.

Maybe it was a joke. Wyre tricked Amf up to freak me out. That must be it. Schuyler flipped the switch, killing the red LED under the grille, then set the metal box carefully on the bedside table. He watched it in silence.

Segment Three

First day out of the hospital; he spent it shuffling about inside the warehouse, reorienting himself to the spaces and objects that in two weeks had become as foreign, yet oddly familiar, as the rebuilt tissue in his chest. Home's where your new heart is, Schuyler thought as he poked through the debris drifted against the walls. He opened all the skylights so that L.A.'s dry winds could drive out the musty air. A thin layer of dust had drifted onto everything except the sprint car. That had a note taped to the side window: TUNED AND READY TO GO.—W. With his usual regard for things mechanical, Wyre had kept the car spotless in Schuyler's absence. It figured; he crumpled the paper into a ball and tossed it on the floor.

A walk to Bischofsky's studio, to kill time and thank him for time spent at the hospital. Even before he'd gained full consciousness, Schuyler had been aware of the broad-shouldered, gray-bearded figure, as if standing guard at the bedside.

He found Bischofsky slumped in his chair behind the terminal, gazing in deep depression at the floor. The small figure standing next to him broke off in mid-harangue and swung her gaze around at Schuyler. A frozen, shiny-skinned face under a slightly askew black wig—as though a store mannequin's head had been transplanted onto the woman's body. That being the limit of the facial reconstruct work Lina had received some five years ago at the Church hospital. A wax mask, thought Schuyler every time he saw her. It was somehow appropriate. His having also survived the explosion and fire at Eureka Station—which she'd caused—had somehow become linked in her cracked brain with all her subsequent complaints against the world. The hatred she bore him was entirely readable by the narrowed eyes set in the immobile face. Their separate journeys out of Northernmost Parish had both ended up in L.A. It hadn't seemed to have made much of a difference in Lina; she had just carted her lunacies along with her and earned a face to match them.

She scuttled out, giving Schuyler a wide berth. He turned back to Bischofsky, still gazing at the floor. "What'd she want this time?" An often-repeated question; he and Wyre often spent time bucking their friend up after one of Lina's blitzkrieg visitations.

"Who knows." Bischofsky sighed and shook his head. "Came in here screaming. Her usual mode. Says she's pregnant by me."

"You've been sleeping with her?" Hard to believe, but Bischofsky had a reservoir of pity for his ex-wife—usually expressed in the form of money—that had long baffled and infuriated everyone who knew him.

"God, no. She thinks I did it by telepathy."

Such were the workings of Lina's mind. Schuyler walked to the center of the studio and looked up at the rose-window simulation. That was the easiest way to break the cycle of Bischofsky's thoughts, by setting him back onto his main obsession. "This a new arrangement?" he said. "I don't remember seeing this one."

Bischofsky straightened up in the chair and made some adjustments on the terminal; the window's colors brightened. "I've been trying out some geometrical schemes. Overlays of pure classical models. This arrangement's kind of a combination of the Rose de France pattern in the Chartres north transept, where you got sets of squares on a Fibonacci spiral, and the Alchemists' Rose at Notre-Dame with the interlocking stars you get from running an endless line from point to point on the circumference." Thoughts of Lina were far away now, as Bischofsky worked the keyboard to point out the arrangement's intricacies. "You do the two patterns separately and you don't get a very high probability rating, but the interesting thing is that the rating goes up when you superimpose them . . ."

Schuyler headed back to his own place after an hour of glass talk. Endryx showed up in the evening, the shadow stalking along behind her, the points of its tripod legs picking through the littered concrete.

"They told me you weren't going out on the run tonight." She stood by his chair and touched his shoulder.

Schuyler, his spine loosened by the day's drinking, looked up from his slouch and nodded. "Doctors told me to take the first day off." He lifted a half-drained can from its perch on his belt buckle. "Ease into things."

"Tonight's the telecast," she announced. "Of the first episode of your bio."

"So I heard." He swallowed, eyes closed and head tilted back.

"Are you going to watch it?"

He shrugged. "Sure. Why not. I fascinate myself."

Endryx began rolling up her jacket sleeve. "How about if I set up, then. Catch your reactions to it." The shadow, obedient to her fingers on the control pad, spidered into position.

The red light blinking on atop the device's lens turret tapped at the corner of his eye. "Go ahead. We're in it this far." His resignation to the process was complete. He watched as she pulled out the monitor screen from its niche inside the shadow and tuned it to one of the indie frequencies. She brought another chair out of the warehouse's kitchen area and placed it to one side and behind him so as not to show up in the shadow's camera angle.

One of the color men—all equally obnoxious to him—was on the screen, hyping the bio broadcast. A blown-up still of Schuyler was behind the jabbering head. He gathered that the show was just minutes away. Glancing up at the dark sky visible through one of the skylights, he realized that it was later than he'd figured; the day had slipped away in an alcoholic haze.

"Here it comes." Endryx's soft voice sounded behind him.

The opening credits scrolled by quickly, as well as he could keep track of them. Then he found himself looking at the snowbound streets of Northernmost Parish.

VIDEO: LONG SHOT, streets covered with snow except for rutted lanes plowed through the middle. The drifts are piled high against the contrasting dark buildings. PAN to show the narrow alleyways branching off; in the distance, the skeletal form of a building crane looms over the low structures. CONTINUE PAN, then HOLD when a figure is revealed, walking toward the camera. CUT to

MEDIUM SHOT, the figure is SCHUYLER, younger by five years, hands thrust deep into the pockets of a heavy jacket, collar turned up against the cold. His breath clouds in front of him as he works his way along the narrow line trampled into slush at the side of the street.

AUDIO: The whine of a motorcycle engine, faint, then growing louder as it approaches.

VIDEO: CLOSE-UP of SCHUYLER's face as he turns toward the sound. PAN to follow his gaze. HOLD on LONG SHOT of the street; the motorcycle appears and speeds toward the camera. As it approaches, a Cathedra Novum dispatch rider can be seen. ZOOM and HOLD. His features are hidden behind the helmet's black faceshield. CUT to

LONG SHOT of street, as before. The motorcycle leans into a turn, heading away from the camera. Suddenly it loses traction in the plowed slush; it goes down. The rider's gloved hands rise from the grips as he falls into the banked snow. Sparks flare around the spinning machine as the edge of its motor digs through the ice and finds the hard surface beneath.

AUDIO: The engine sputters and dies.

VIDEO: For a moment the rider lies, arms flung wide, in the bed of snow. CUT to CLOSE-UP of the helmet's black faceshield. SCHUYLER's reflection can be seen in it as he steps toward the accident, then stops. PULL BACK to show SCHUYLER watching as the rider, unhurt, pushes himself upright. The figure brushes snow from himself, then remounts the motorcycle and kicks the engine to life.

AUDIO: The engine rasps, then fades away.

VIDEO: HOLD on LONG SHOT of street, SCHUY-LER, back to camera, at the side of the frame. He goes on watching for a few moments after the motorcycle is gone, then turns—PULL BACK to place him at center of frame—and continues walking.

"Why the hell did you put that in?" Schuyler gestured at the screen's image of himself gazing at the spot in the snowbound street from where the motorcyclist had risen and departed.

"Hey," said Endryx behind him. "You're the one who remembered it happening. I've got the transcript of you talking about it. So we went on up there and taped it. I think it makes a nice opening. Moody, sort of."

"Demented, more like it." Weird enough—as he'd felt from the beginning with these tapes—to see himself shuffling down the white-against-black streets of Northern-most Parish, as if he'd never escaped after spending the first twenty years of his life there. As though some loop had collapsed, wiping out L.A. and the long trek there, depositing him back into the same footsteps trudging through the gray slush. The reconstruction of his former self was oppressively effective; he could feel the curve of the young Schuyler's weary shoulders in his own. Back at the start of the bio project, Endryx had introduced him to the actor doing the part, an affable and colorless entity named Jerry Monmouth. The colorless quality being part of what made him Speed Death Productions' leading physical chameleon: a body that could shape itself to the set, the stance of the bones and the motions of the flesh, of anyone else. The face—Schuyler's face in this case, five years younger—was an ultra-high-resolution computer synth keyed in over Monmouth's oddly immobile features.

So now I can see myself, thought Schuyler as he watched the figure walking on. As others see me. Had they been looking.

VIDEO: MEDIUM SHOT, SCHUYLER slumped in a chair, gazing at a monitor, a cluster of empty beer cans littering the warehouse floor beside him. On the screen, an image of himself in another time stands in a white street.

AUDIO: "Demented, more like it."

VIDEO: SCHUYLER goes on gazing at the screen, the light from it sliding across his expressionless face.

"It was an omen." In the warehouse, emptied by time of the objects it held before, Schuyler watched another monitor. No shadow, but a simple tape playback unit sitting on the swept-bare floor. He leaned forward in the chair, careful to keep his weight off the leg that frostbite had left with a permanent stinging pain under the skin, and tapped the glass over the image of one Schuyler watching another. "That's what I saw."

The other person, behind him the way Endryx had always kept herself, spoke in the warehouse's hollow space. "What do you mean?"

He had become so engrossed in the tape that he couldn't remember who it was with him, and didn't care. The opening into previous time, and time before that, was all

that mattered. "The guy on the motorcycle," he said quietly. "With that faceshield. It was like a lens; like black glass. That's why I remembered it all that time. He could see me, but I couldn't see him. Just my reflection."
Silent then, he watched the screen.

VIDEO: LONG SHOT, SCHUYLER mounting the snow-covered steps of a building. CUT to MEDIUM SHOT, REVERSE ANGLE as he pushes through the glass doors. Before the doors swing shut, the words *CATHEDRA NOVUM ADMINIS-TRATIVE OFFICES—NORTHERNMOST PARISH* are visible.

Made or broken here; he knew that. Schuyler watched Sub-Ascendant Lembert's brown-mottled hands smooth the papers on the desk. A signature from the figure leaning forward from the creaking swivel chair meant the difference between a train bound for sunny L.A. and his ass staying frozen here at this cold butt-end of nowhere. Schuyler slowed one careful breath after another, waiting and noting the constellation on the balding head lowered before him, the dark splotches the same color under the gray strands as the liver-spotted hands.

Lembert looked up at him without changing the angle of his neck. "Who do you think you're fooling, Schuyler?" The hands pressed flat against the transfer application, as if the Sub-Ascendant was about to spring, yellow teeth bared, at Schuyler's throat.

"What—?" His breath caught, became a rock that he tried to swallow.

"What are you trying to pull, Schuyler?" Crepe paper folded around Lembert's eyes, until they became slits in wadded-up pink tissue.

Snow and ice formed around the rock in his chest. "I'm not trying to pull anything, sir."

"Look at this crap." The chair's plastic foam mesh sighed as Lembert leaned back and turned to stare out the window; he ranked high enough only for a view of the stacked, cut-up stones of the cathedral, and not the excavation itself. He left one hand on Schuyler's application, as if the offending words were etched so deep they could be read by touch. " 'So I can better serve the Church.' 'Greater field for my efforts.' 'Devotion.' 'Faith.' Crap."

"I don't know what you mean." *Oh, yes you do*—his own voice throttled behind his clamped teeth. *Shut up, shut up, shut up.*

"I've heard this crap from so many other guys, that even if it were true, it would still make me sick. And it's never true. Never."

Schuyler stayed quiet, hardening his face as though leaning into a frozen wind outside. He'd be thankful if he was still standing in the same place when it blew over.

"The Cathedra Novum feeds you, clothes you, keeps your ass out of the snow, and this is what it gets. Lied to. By punks like you."

Jesus, what touched all this off? Schuyler forced his voice from the wedge at the back of his throat: "If there was any way I could—"

"Could what?" Lembert swung his heavy, meat-pink face back around from the window. "Prove you're not lying? But you can't, can you? Because you've tainted your whole application, everything you say, by your actions. Didn't you?"

"I'm not sure what you mean."

One corner of Lembert's mouth screwed into wrinkles as he pulled the top desk drawer open, denting his stomach. He dumped the contents of a large manila envelope out onto the desk. "What's this, Schuyler."

"Oh." Schuyler looked at the small objects and found himself no longer leaning against a cold wind, but falling into the chill vacuum at its core. His own words sounded stupid, in his ears, obvious statement of damning fact: "You went through my rooms."

Lembert grunted, all the confirmation needed. He held up the largest object between his thumb and forefinger, as though examining a bug. "So what is it, Schuyler."

He exhaled, without lessening the weight in his chest. "It's a voke reader."

"And what does it do. Tell me."

It was obvious that Lembert already knew. Just part of the interrogation, the complete condemning of oneself. "It scans vocal patterns and timbres," said Schuyler. Might as well get it over. "To see if somebody's running a voice-alteration unit when they're talking to you. So you know if they're trying to hide something from you."

Wires dangled from Lembert's hand to another small metal box, the same gray solder smeared along the seams. "Complete with sub-vocal modification. Very thorough." The boxes clattered together as Lembert dropped them on the desk. "Where'd you get them, Schuyler?"

Silence, and the weight of the other's eyes. "I built them," said Schuyler after a moment. "From a kit I sent for."

"Christ, Schuyler, don't you think everything that comes up here on the train gets scanned? Especially packages for somebody who's got a transfer application in."

This is what they ream you out for, thought Schuyler. He gazed up at the idiot pattern of holes in the acoustic ceiling. Not for doing anything wrong. Just for being stupid. "I didn't think—"

"'Didn't think' isn't the problem. You think too much, Schuyler; that's your problem. Too fucking clever for your own good. What did you think you were doing with these?" Lembert scooped up the other objects, a half dozen tape cassettes, and let them fall clattering. "And you can turn off the tape recorder in your pocket now. Fun's over."

"I guess so." He pulled out the recorder, tapped it off, then stripped the pinhead mike from under his collar.

Lembert shoved the scattered cassettes around with a thick finger. "Every talk we've had in this office, every interview on your application—you taped them all. Then trotted home and ran 'em through your little mail-order voke reader. And what did you find?"

"Nothing." A dim light started to seep around the edges, showing the breadth of the hard flat wall he had run into in the dark. "Nothing at all."

" 'Nothing at all.' That's right, Schuyler. You didn't find a thing. Because we screwed you. You thought your little dime reader could tell you what we were really thinking about your transfer. And you thought everything was going just fine, you were just about on the next train south— because we were feeding you an overvoke all along." Lembert reached again into his desk, this time pulling out a small control pad, the professional chrome gloss of its construction set off by the cobbled-together devices strewn on the desktop. Schuyler watched as Lembert prodded one of the switches under the miniature crossed t-squares logo of the Cathedra Novum Engineering Staff. As soon as Lembert spoke again, even without taping the words and running them through the voke reader, he could tell the difference.

"Like that," said Lembert in his subtly altered voice. "Nice and smooth, all the giveaways, the sub-voke trem- ors, all ironed out. All the little words under the words taken out—so you'd go on thinking your transfer applica- tion was just sailing through like we told you, and you wouldn't be able to tell otherwise with your bitty gadgets. Didn't you know we could do that, Schuyler?"

He brought his gaze back down. "I didn't think," said Schuyler, "that this was that important. To bother feeding me disinfo like that."

"It's not." Lembert flicked the control pad off, his voice

dropping back to its overtones and biting rasp. "Don't kid yourself. Your soul is what's important to the Cathedra Novum. Nothing else. Whether your ass freezes off in the snow up here is of no concern to the Church."

"So you went and searched my rooms." He fastened on the one small grievance, grudgingly, the only one he had.

"The rooms belong to the Church. So do you, Schuyler."

"Then that's it." Schuyler gripped the chair arms, elbows angled out, ready to push himself upright, propel himself out of the room, the building, and back out in to snow-covered streets. "Looks like I'll be here a while." Probably forever, he thought. You. Stupid. Shit.

"Wrong again." Lembert folded his hands across his stomach and settled deeper into the chair, as if under the gravity of some denser ground. "Pack your stuff. You're on the next train south." He drew the transfer application across the desk, signed and shoved it back toward Schuyler. Another stack of papers spread out across the desk as he began sorting through them.

"What?" Schuyler lifted the application. The signature was the real thing, and not some obscenity as a final joke.

Lembert looked up from the papers. "You're heading out of here. Just like you wanted, right?"

Schuyler's words tapped forward cautiously, feeling for the edge of a trap deeper than the one he'd already fallen into. "I'm not sure I understand."

"Like I said, your soul is all that matters to the Church. Moves in mysterious ways. If the Cathedra Novum thinks it would do your soul good for you to leave here, then it doesn't matter what kind of jerk you are, you're leaving. So go already." His head, a heavy box of pink meat, tilted to reveal the balding crown again.

VIDEO: MEDIUM SHOT, the front of the building. SCHUYLER stands at the top of the steps, the doors closing behind him. The transfer papers are in his hands. He closes his eyes, tilting his head back with an expression of joy as he carefully folds the papers and stows them inside his jacket. CUT to

LONG SHOT paralleling a motionless train cutting a diagonal across the frame. SCHUYLER appears, laden with a green canvas duffel bag, walking through the snow at the side of the tracks.

Underneath the train the snow had melted. As Schuyler passed by the engines, a warm mist smelling of oil and steel enveloped him. L.A. smells like that, he thought. If it smells like anything, it smells like that. He yanked the canvas strap of his bag to hitch it up higher on his shoulder and quickened his steps toward the cars farther back. If Lembert and the rest of the Cathedra Novum authorities decided that the joke had gone on far enough, there was no way, never had been, that they were going to let him out of this dump—he took one hand from the bag's strap and tapped his jacket pocket, to make sure that the folded square of the transfer papers hadn't leaked away, a mirage all along—they'd have to drag him off the train. If they can find me, thought Schuyler. First they'll have to do that.

He saw something move overhead, and stopped for a moment to watch it. A way of saying good-bye to another feature of the parish; with any luck he'd never see one of the weathermod satellites again. Through a break in the clouds, the distinctive sparkle of one of the ancient weapons systems was visible, locked above in synchronous orbit. Still up and operative, he thought, meddling with winds and cloud covers, maintaining its zone of arctic cold on the territory beneath, from here to the ice-locked harbor of abandoned San Francisco; right to the sharp edge above L.A., where the southern weathermods took over with their baking heat . . . this long after the designers responsible for the satellites, and the strategists who conceived warfare by weather control, were in their graves. A legacy from the long-ago war, like a lot of things in the world. That included the muddled history, years cloaked in darkness, that the Cathedra Novum bent its whole existence to penetrate. Their problem, not mine, thought Schuyler as he hoisted his bag higher on his shoulder and resumed walking. The only history I'm interested in is my own, starting now.

The heat from the train's engines faded yards before he reached the metal steps unfolded from one of the central cars, and he was soon ankle-deep in the congealing muck, as though one of the snowplowed streets of the town had unrolled itself here. The tromping of feet in and out of the train had stirred the mire at the bottom of the metal steps into even deeper mud; Schuyler felt it ooze over the top of his boots and trickle down inside in a slow freezing ribbon as he waded through it. After he slung his bag from around his shoulder and pitched it up into the open doorway, he leaned forward and grasped the steel handrail just inside. He felt his heel lift inside his boot, the cold muck sliding under his sock with a sucking noise. At the same time, a patch of cold more intense than the surrounding muck signalled the bite on his ankle. Another left-over from the war, out of some military genetic-engineering department. One this small was a nuisance; the Parish's surrounding thermal mesh kept out the bigger, dangerous ones.

"Christ." The train's doorway invited him in, a dark rectangle opening onto further possibilities. And now I'm stuck in the flipping mud. Figures. He grabbed the handrail on the other side and strained. The mud settled firmer, as the tiny wetblanket's icy bite squirmed under his knee. Now what? he thought. They won't leave without me. The tight grip of the chill soil around his ankle squeezed a small bolt of panic up his spine. If the train started to pull out, maybe he could just hold on . . . Maybe that'll drag me out. He squeezed his eyes shut with the effort of gripping the handrails.

"Gotcha." Another grip caught him, hands wrapped under the bony knots of his elbows. "I'll pull, you bend your knees."

VIDEO: MEDIUM SHOT, the frame filled by the shining metal side of the train car, the black opening of the doorway in the middle. Two hands reach out of the darkness, grasping Schuyler's arms. He lurches up out of the mud. CUT to the close interior of the car. The bright glare of the snow barely enters the space; SCHUYLER sprawls forward on his hands and knees in the half light. The other figure, a dimly seen shape wrapped in a hooded robe of coarse fabric, rocks back into a sitting position by the doorway.

AUDIO: The other's voice: "You lost one of your boots."

VIDEO: CLOSE-UP from an angle parallel to the outside of the train. The figure leans out to retrieve SCHUYLER'S boot. The clumsy robes fall forward, and with a quick toss of the head, the figure shrugs them back. The figure is seen now, in profile, as a young woman. The hammered gold ornaments around her wrists and neck spatter the sunlight into the camera lens. Two thick braids of dark hair swing free as she bends forward, dangling just clear of the mud.

"Where did you find her?" said Schuyler. Meaning, someone who looked so much like Cynth. Somehow he knew that the young woman's face was not a synth, like his own keyed in over Jerry Monmouth's living blank.

"The bloodlines are all pretty close among the God-friends." Endryx's voice held a workman-like pride. "She's actually a sort of niece, the way they figure it, to Cynth. They don't have any religious scruples about being in a tape like this. She turned out to be quite a natural actress. I was prepared originally to dub in her voice, but we didn't have to."

Schuyler nodded, his attention drifting back into the screen. "Looks just like her," he said softly.

VIDEO: MEDIUM SHOT, the dark interior of the warehouse, the light from the monitor spilling across SCHUYLER. A young woman's profile fills the screen in front of him.

AUDIO: "Just like her."

"She was so pretty," said Schuyler. Now even farther away in time than the image of himself watching the screen-within-a-screen; he still thought so.

"Which one?" said the other behind him. "The real one?"

He nodded. "They are all lovely. But I didn't realize until now how beautiful the real one, the real Cynth, was."

VIDEO: MEDIUM SHOT, the train car's cramped interior. The woman hands the muddy boot to Schuyler, now sitting across from her.

"Thanks." For a moment, her open gaze caught him full-face as he took the boot from her. A thin row of ornamental scars, careful stitches in flesh, outlined the upper orbits of her eyes. He looked away as he set the boot down beside himself and started rolling up his pants leg.

"Don't pick at that. You'll get it infected." The woman leaned forward on her haunches and poked at the wet-blanket, a shiny transparent patch on Schuyler's leg, starting to pinken with his blood. He saw now that the dark braids

were oiled with something that glistened in the sunlight
slanting through the train's door; the end of one brushed a
sable feather across his bare ankle as she inspected the inch-
long parasite. "Hold on a second." From a leather thong
underneath the coarse robe she pulled out a small thermic.
She pumped the handle until the blade glowed red, then slid
the heated edge over Schuyler's leg. The wetblanket
clouded, blackened, then shriveled and fell off; a circle of
red pinpricks sizzled under the thermic's glow where the
tiny soft mouths had worked through the skin.

The blade started to darken, cooling, as she relaxed her
grip on the handle. "There you go," she said, tucking it
back under her robe.

"Thank you." A formal phrase; he had never been this
close or talked to one of the Godfriends before, had only
seen the small delegations of the elder women in full
military regalia striding through the Northernmost Parish
gates on the way to a meeting at the Cathedra Novum
headquarters. This one was much younger than any of
those—probably a low-ranking warrior, thought Schuyler,
stuck with some boring guard duty. Most excitement she's
seen today. The smell of sweat pungent with the same oil
glistening her braided hair caught him as she sat back
against the partition behind her, watching him tug his boot
back on. The hammered ornaments and shining skin under
the robe's folds counterpointed the muddy boot leather at
the center of his eye.

He tugged his bag over to him by its strap, stood up and
lifted its weight onto his shoulder again. The young
Godfriend stayed sitting in her easy hunker, her scar-arched
eyes regarding him.

"Pull a lot of people out of the mud here?" He nodded
toward the open doorway.

She shook her head. "You're the first. Most people get on
back at the passenger cars. This is freight." A small, lazy

smile, as she pointed with her thumb behind her. "You can just go on through. Got papers?"

He extracted the transfer. She unfolded it, then handed it back up to him a second later. "Whoever's on duty," she said, "just have 'em stamp it. Otherwise they might have to throw you off along the way. Be a cold hike back here."

"Not me. I'd just keep going."

"Suit yourself." She turned her head to gaze out the doorway, her interest in him at an end.

VIDEO: MEDIUM SHOT, SCHUYLER, his pack hoisted on his shoulder, walking down the long corridor running through the center of the train's freight cars. Without stopping, he turns his head to look back toward the camera; at the same moment, another figure steps into the corridor, and they collide. CUT to TWO SHOT, SIDE ANGLE.

AUDIO: "Sorry," says Schuyler. "My fault—"

VIDIO: He backs up a step, spreading his hands in apology. The other man is older, barrel-chested, with a thick gray beard and thinning hair brushed straight back from his forehead; inattention to haircuts and other small details of grooming show in the curls fringing the collar of his frayed and stained insulated jacket. He shakes his head in response to SCHUYLER, signifying no big deal, an accident, then looks away in the direction from which SCHUYLER came. His eyes narrow, then widen; he shakes his head again, this time in wonderment, as he speaks.

AUDIO: "Jesus. Mother of God," says the other man. "That is the *sexiest* woman I have *ever* seen."

VIDEO: CUT to LONG SHOT, past SCHUYLER turning to follow the other man's intense stare; the
GODFRIEND that pulled SCHUYLER up into the
train leans against the open doorway of the car he
just left. The light outlines her profile as she gazes
outside, turns her thick braid of hair into dark
gold. She is unaware of, or pays no heed to, the
watching men. CUT to MEDIUM SHOT, SCHUY-
LER and the OTHER looking down the corridor to
the sight that holds them. A third man, a freight
handler wheeling a stack of boxes on a dolly,
comes up behind, looks past them and grins.

AUDIO: "Forget it, man," says the freight handler.
"She'd dice your heart up over her breakfast
cereal."

The other man's voice deflates into rueful acknowledgment: "Yeah, well. Whatever."

VIDEO: SCHUYLER squeezes sideways through the
crowded passageway as the OTHER turns to
checking the labels on the stacked boxes. TRACK
FORWARD, the camera catching the OTHER's
surreptitious glance down the corridor to the
GODFRIEND.

"You caught that one right." Schuyler had slouched
down in his chair as he watched the broadcast, a succession
of beer cans dangling from his hand, then joining the cluster
around his feet. He looked over at Endryx, smiled and
nodded. "That flippin' Bischofsky. He's such a horny
bastard."

Endryx's fingers formed a cage in her lap. She and her
shadow, one of its lenses a dark circle past her shoulder,
watched and recorded Schuyler's reactions. "Makes a lot of
trouble for himself." A small prompt. "Doesn't he?"

He tilted his head back, looking up at some spot in the warehouse's ceiling where the screen's blue light didn't reach. The thought of his friend lengthened his loose smile. "That's more'n half of it right there. The more trouble it'd make, the more excited he gets." He dropped his chin to his chest, the screen drawing him back to its canned world.

VIDEO: MEDIUM SHOT, INTERIOR, SCHUYLER slumped in a chair, illuminated only by the monitor he watches; the blue light streams past him and glazes the fender of sprint car behind him. On the screen before him, the image of a gray-bearded face sneaking a look down a freight car's narrow corridor. SCHUYLER looks up at the warehouse ceiling.

AUDIO: SCHUYLER's voice is filtered through alcohol. "The more trouble it'd make, the more excited he gets."

He leaned forward. On the screen, beyond his own face, he could see the face of his friend, frozen on the other screen held in the tape's recorded past. He nodded slowly, hearing the words he had spoken in that other time.
"He was a horny bastard." A briefer smile, in remembrance. "All the time I knew him. Right up to the end."
In the empty warehouse, the space enlarged by the absence of the sprint car, the metal shape dimly outlined at the screen's edge, he watched himself watching; the layered past.

VIDEO: MEDIUM SHOT, INTERIOR, SCHUYLER stands in line with five or six others, holding his transfer papers and boarding pass ready to be examined by the Church official sitting behind a temporary desk created from a pair of boxes. As the line shuffles forward through the freight car, SCHUYLER looks over the stacked crates on all sides. He turns to the man behind him.

AUDIO: "What is all this shit, anyway?" says SCHUYLER.

THE MAN BEHIND, patient, bored: "Glass."

"What?"

"Stained-glass windows," explains THE MAN BE-HIND. "From the excavation. They finally got 'em all dug up, and ready to be shipped down to the archeo-labs in L.A. For testing, and putting back together and shit. Plus their big, fancy expert; they're shipping him back with 'em."

VIDEO: SCHUYLER's gaze here follows in the direction of the other's thumb. PAN to the freight car's open doorway; it frames a LONG SHOT down the loading dock. The gray-bearded man SCHUYLER ran into before is supervising the last of the crates, taller than the handlers wrestling the ropes and winches, being loaded aboard the train.

AUDIO: THE MAN BEHIND: "Some dude named Bischofsky."

"Never heard of him," says SCHUYLER.

VIDEO: SCHUYLER shrugs. At the head of the line, he looks back from the doorway and carefully unfolds his papers for inspection.

In Urbenton's darkened office, Endryx sat watching the end of the first broadcast. The night's run hadn't started yet; the screens around the central one showed various angles of the sprinters around the Phoenix factory's molehole, lazing up against their cars as the moles brought up the small bundles of RH chips to be ferried to L.A. In Speed Death's New York studios, she knew, the indies' color men were waiting on line with their multi-lingual replays and analyses of last night's run. Thus they'd fill the time, stringing out but not satiating the Latin American and Asian audiences' endless appetites, until Urbenton had edited down the first couple of hours' action from the induced visual field's recorders and viz synthesizers. From his editing console he fed to the satellites; and thus every night. The Schuyler bio was the first alteration in the pattern since it had been set up—in its own way a revolution. She watched the back of Urbenton's head as he brooded over the episode's final scenes. She was reminded of the transition from the Classical to Romantic eras in music: from the impersonal pure forms to the dirty, sweaty personal. So no wonder he hates my guts; she could read it under the blank pink dome of his skull. That's what happens when the times change, and you begin to suspect you're on the wrong side of the hour hand.

She had left the warehouse and Schuyler, deep in a silent alcohol-fueled meditation as he gazed at the screen, to come here. She'd come to this other silence—Urbenton's reaction. This was her own small survey of the first broadcast episode's effect. Even now, before the broadcast was over, she knew Speed Death's data teams would be filtering through the Latin American factory dorms, taking the pulse of the real audience, those for whom every image and flicker of light was intended. The reports, analyzed and summed up into the revealing psych curve numbers, would come out of New York in the morning. In the meantime she watched the back of Urbenton's head, hill-like between her and the monitor screen.

"So this is the great man's life story, huh?" Urbenton swiveled around to look at her, sensing the end of the episode approaching. "Fascinating. For this Speed Death is paying production costs. For a cute meet." He shook his head. "As if anybody cared about him and his dopey friends."

Endryx looked past him to the screen. The numbers would come in the morning; she wanted to be here then, too, to watch his face. "We'll see." The broadcast was heading into its last scene. "Wait for it."

Urbenton grunted and began flipping switches on his desk panel. "Screw this." The words a growl. "I gotta start putting together the real show." The blank screens filled with the preset angles from the induced visual field between Albuquerque and L.A.: the sprinters and the satellites tracking them from above. That life was raw, uncut, all motion and parabolas of light through the desert's night sky. For the next couple of hours he'd be editing, cutting and zooming from point to point in the field, boiling it down to the final feed to the indies. Already, within just a few seconds, he had faded into the world of his craft, oblivious of anyone else's presence in the studio's blue-lit shadows.

Poor little guy, thought Endryx as she watched both him and the central screen. He doesn't know. Not yet.

VIDEO: CLOSE-UP, a flurry of snow brushes past SCHUYLER's face. PULL BACK. He leans against the open doorway of a freight car. The train is moving, picking up speed, gradually leaving the camera behind. CUT to LONG SHOT, SCHUYLER looking back. The camera comes to a halt and PANS down the tracks to the loading dock and the gray buildings of Northernmost Parish beyond it, shrinking into distance. The camera lifts into AERIAL SHOT. For a moment SCHUYLER's uncovered head is visible, his dark hair blown across his brow. Then the black line of the train cutting through the white landscape thins, grays and fades below the wind-driven snow.

Well, well. This is your life, Ross Schuyler. On the screen—the minor credits having finished crawling across the bio episode's final blank white shot—one of the indies' more obnoxious color men now prattled on, leading into the recap of the previous night's sprint. The slow current of his thoughts damped out the needly voice as effectively as a twist of the volume knob on the monitor. I have entered the realm of the immortals; he closed his eyes, his head rolling on the loosened pivot of his neck. For all to see. Where— something something. Bischofsky would know the exact Biblical quotation. Where moth and rust and corruption don't happen.

He had gotten much more than the Warholian fifteen minutes. The brief fame promised to all the sons of man. Had seen, sharper than memory could ever serve, his own face—or the simulation of it keyed in over Jerry Monmouth's expert blank; what was the difference?—braced against the freight car's doorway, watching the little prison of Northernmost Parish fading out of his life, never to be seen again. It was a neat chapter's end. He nodded, affirming his admiration for Endryx's skill in shaping the jumbled, half-forgotten clutter of his life into something recognizably narrative. Fictionalized or not; the official truth—beer grace to the internal pronouncement—sufficeth.

"That was all right." His voice cut across the monitor's drone. "All right."

No answer came, and he realized he was alone. He drew himself up in the chair and looked around the dark warehouse. She had slipped out without his noticing. Lost in the broadcast, his own past. He'd found himself enjoying the broadcast. Fascinated by himself. Which put a light on why he'd dragged through the interviewing, and the taping, and all the other processes involved in getting to this point; never really cooperating with Endryx, always passive resistance. Because this was the ultimate trap, how they finally got you for good. By feeding the ego; pay some attention to me, and I'm yours. Gratefully, your existence acknowledged at last in the only way that mattered anymore. He had sensed that somehow at the beginning, and resistance had proved useless, anyway. They got to him, no matter what.

The cans at his feet had been emptied long ago. Their contents, transferred to his bloodstream, broke down bit by bit to less toxic, less exhilarating elements. The inner barometer ticked down the one notch necessary to bring him in sight of sobriety. He felt heavy-faced and bleak, muscles of soft lead bearing down against the chair's plastic mesh. They got me, he thought again, brooding. Or something like me. That was enough.

He got up, clanking cans toppling around his feet, and switched off the monitor. The color man's face faded into dead gray glass. The sprinters—whose numbers he would be rejoining soon; that much he had to look forward to—would be pulling across the outskirts of L.A. soon, and coasting into the after-hours marketplace and unloading zone for their contraband. The end of the line, after a long night's run. The desire, and the decision, had already formed—to go down and meet them, shoot the shit as they all stood around the softly murmuring cars, the buyers from the Euro-combines appraising the wares delivered and then peeling off the appropriate cuts from the thick-padded manila envelopes drawn from inside pockets. Passing beers around. Like kids, he thought. That's what they—we—are. Overgrown kids.

That was the other world, that Speed Death Productions, with all its high-tech-up-the-butt induced visual fields, indie broadcast satellites, shadows, Endryxes and all the rest, hadn't penetrated to. Schuyler stood head down, concentric layers of the silent warehouse and the night outside wrapped around his long thoughts. That secret fraternity of the fucked-up. After the run and all the action was over; then the party, the communion, of the world's rejects. That's us—in some way proud of it. The stones rejected by the builders.

Trailing his jacket across his shoulder, Schuyler passed the length of his own sprint car. Wyre had left Amf sitting on the rear fender. He switched on the metal box. Maybe if the device was in good form tonight, it would want to come along.

The familiar grating voice didn't sound. A faint hiss of radio static filled Schuyler with dread, a half-forgotten shot of a moment back in the hospital. That he had no wish to remember.

The other voice came on, the one he'd heard that other time, just once. As before, it faded in and out, words barely squeezing through the crackling veil.

". . . Schuyler . . . now you're going to find out— . . . told you—" A sharp electronic snarl pulsed and wavered. ". . . they're going to start dying now . . . the sprinters . . . dying now . . ." The voice faded under the static, which itself diminished and evaporated into silence.

Chilled under the L.A. night air, still warm at this point past midnight, Schuyler switched off the device. He hurried out of the lightless warehouse, heading for noise and the voices of others.

It was not a fun gathering as he'd hoped. The premonition, the small seed that the other voice coming through Amf's speaker had placed in his heart, split, replicated, grew larger under his breastbone. This at rounding the corner of the last alleyway, and seeing the sprinters' grim faces. The stood about the cars, sweating cans dangling in their hands, but none of them drinking, no voices raised. They turned to look at him when he approached; every step weighed more under their gaze.

"They got Joroff."

The seed bore its black flower. Popejoy's flat statement was all that was needed.

Schuyler looked around at the circle. Their silence in some ways an accusation: they had been on the field of death, and he hadn't. "Where?"

"Halfway out from Phoenix."

On some cue inaudible to him, the circle parted, the sprinters stepping back to reveal a monitor and tape playback unit sitting on one of the car's fenders. An image was frozen on the screen.

He stepped closer, pressing his hands against the car's smooth metal and bending to examine the screen. For a moment he couldn't make out the electrophoretic pattern, the jumble of microscopic dots held by their electrical charge against the layers of glass. Static on the optic nerve, the brain refusing to read the visual input. Then, piece by piece, the picture assembled itself. In one corner the skull-and-wheel emblem of Speed Death Productions appeared, with this night's date below it to brand the images as a replay taped off the air.

A long diagonal streak through the black upper half of the screen was the aftertrail of one of the pursuit satellite's particle-beam missiles. The destabilizing air molecules were just beginning to disperse, the trail wavering in the high desert wind.

VIDEO: LONG SHOT, EXTERIOR, a line of fire traces through the night.

The coils of light at the bottom of the screen were flames twined around a column of black smoke. Something of crushed metal was at the center of the fire.

VIDEO: LONG SHOT, EXTERIOR, the burning car.

The electrophores dissolved into scrambled visual chatter

as Popejoy ran the tape back. At the stop code he'd inserted the screen froze into the night desert from above. A staggered row of sprint cars was motionless until Popejoy hit the PLAY button, and they flickered into motion, the sand blurring under their wheels.

VIDEO: TRACKING SHOT, the missile hits the car. For a brief moment light streams out of the car's windows, as though everything inside had been made luminous. Then the light breaks into churning red and orange as the metal tears apart, jagged pieces pinwheeling over the desert, to let out the ball of flame. The viewpoint's motion slows as the eroding wreckage loses speed, coming to rest in smoke-wrapped ruins.

"Finally," said Urbenton. He gazed at the monitor screens with rapt satisfaction. "Action at last. The real thing. With death, you get real interest factors." He swiveled around to look at Endryx. "Maybe it's a good thing you came out here. Maybe you brought me luck."

Endryx smiled at him. "Oh, I've brought you luck, all right." She started gathering up her small paraphernalia. "Believe me. Nothing's going to be the same for you."

When she went back to her place to sleep, she found Wyre watching one of the old Schuyler tapes.

She kept a small apartment, halfway between Urbenton's studio and Schuyler's warehouse digs. The first week she'd been out from New York, half her spare gear had disappeared while she'd been out taping with the shadow. Speed Death had recommended their L.A. free-lance contractor in things electronic. Wyre's homebrew security system had done the job: things had stopped disappearing from the apartment. She soon accepted that Wyre appearing in the apartment was part of the price paid for the service. And not

unwelcome—Wyre was connected to Schuyler, another
input on him. If nothing else, Wyre had the latest read-out
on the state of Schuyler's running equipment. She just had
to be careful not to leave any hard-copy communications
from Speed Death lying around the place.

"Why don't you catch it off the telecast?" Endryx
directed the shadow to a corner of the room and shut down
its power. She peeled off her jacket and hung it over one of
the blank lenses.

The monochrome glow from the tiny playback unit's
screen was the only light. Wyre's profile turned in it,
smiling. "Can't stand those color men the indies use. Drive
me nuts." He gestured at the monitor. "You got some good
stuff here."

She stood behind his chair. The monitor showed an out-
take, a segment edited out of the broadcast feed. Wyre had
pressed the FREEZE button on the playback unit; the image
of Schuyler's face lay unmoving against the hospital bed's
pillow, his eyes shut, in sleep or anesthesia.

The smoke she exhaled blurred the screen. She brushed a
speck of ash from Wyre's shoulder, then let her hand rest
there. "That's not worth watching," she said.

He looked up at her. "Why'd you tape it, then. I went
through the file. You got hours of this stuff. Just the face."

She brought her other hand up as she stood behind him.
Her thumbs traced the curve of his shoulder blades through
the shirt fabric. Looking past him, she watched the still
image on the screen. "What's it to you?" she said quietly.

"You know me. I got a professional interest. In how
things work."

She dropped her hands and walked away from the light
shed by the monitor. "Stick to things, then, and you'll do
all right." She started to unbutton her shirt. "Think you
could wrap up your private screening for now? I gotta get
some sleep sometime."

When Wyre had gone, leaving the playback unit still

switched on, she looked across the room at it for a few moments. Then she stepped back into the monitor's dim glow. The screen's color tinted her small breasts blue, like curved snow seen at night. The image of Schuyler's face went on sleeping in its frozen segment of time.

The electrophores' light streamed through her fingers and across her bare arm, as she pressed her hand against the cold glass of the screen.

Segment Four

Schuyler checked out Wyre's work. He rolled up the warehouse's metal door to let the night air flush out the exhaust fumes. The pressure pads of the vintage recaro seat, salvaged from the rusting corpse of a Porsche, sighed and flexed around his spine as he leaned back from the steering wheel and flipped on the ignition.

The engine coughed, then filled the warehouse space with its muffled square-wave murmur. Foot pressing the accelerator, he ran the noise up to the shrill peak of the afterburners kicking in, then backed it down again.

Every switch on the dash console brought up the green glow of one of the sensor displays. He studied the row of cross-hatched scopes—the nearby viber commune registering as massed blobs of heat on the infra-red scan, a dense line of overlapping frequencies on the sonic—then blanked them. The engine muttered, then died to silence when he switched it off.

Next, Amf. He fetched the co-pilot from the worktable and set the metal box on the sprint car's fender. A moment's hesitation stayed his hand before he was able to switch on the device.

Fear rewarded: Amf's familiar voice didn't come from the speaker grille, and he realized he hadn't expected it to. Not now—that being the point he had reached.

Silence, then a hiss of static swelling in volume, as though the metal box wasn't stuffed with gallium arsenide microcircuits but ancient radio tubes slowly warming up. Then the new voice, fading in and out behind the screen of noise.

". . . they're all going to . . . one by one—that's the plan . . . but not you . . . all the sprinters are going to be hit, Schuyler, except you; you're protected . . . a couple more every night . . . but not you—"

The voice broke off, without even the crackle of static following. A few seconds silence, then: "Schuyler, you turkey."

It was Amf's voice, loud and clear. The other voice was gone, fallen back into the airwaves, actual or bound by his skull.

"So answer me, schmuck. We going on the run tonight?"

He roused himself to speak. "Yeah," he said. "We are."

"Terrific," Amf rasped sourly. "You're so fucked-up these days, you'll probably get us both killed. Like Joroff last night."

"No," said Schuyler slowly. "I don't think so."

Before the run, everybody at the Phoenix loading zone did a private head count. Sitting on the fenders of the cars, working through the first of the night's cases, beer sweat in the warm air tinged with a sharper acridity, an element injected as of last night. All the counts started with minus one, permanently subtracted in a burst of fire. The total going on this run would depend upon the subtler calculations of fear.

Twelve, down from eighteen, thought Cassem. She derived a certain pleasure from the dwindling number. She had already decided that—if Joroff's death was the opening round in the sequence they had all along been waiting for— she'd be the last one running. Dead or scared off, preferably the former.

Waiting in line behind the fuel tanker, she turned at the approach of another engine note. "Well, well," she said, setting a beer can down beside her co-pilot Iode. "He made it." She re-counted, came to no different total, and realized she'd been counting him all along, in absentia.

Iode's sneering voice came out of the speaker. "Schuyler? So what were you expecting—he's a big star now. Can't disappoint his fans."

The car slid through the alley in low gear and pulled up behind Cassem's. She watched, eyes half-lidded by the beer's pull, as Schuyler got out and exchanged cool minimal nods with the others leaning against their cars. The hydrogen-booter walked over from the valves of the tanker. Schuyler signed the chit on the extended clipboard.

"Full charge?" asked the booter. Schuyler nodded.

Cassem pushed herself away from the fender as the booter dragged the high-pressure hose over and clamped the nozzle onto her car's port. She handed a fresh can to Schuyler. "Ready for action?"

"Sure." He dangled the can without opening it. "Why not?"

"Thought maybe you'd just stay home and watch yourself on the tube." She nodded at the monitor on the hood of one of the circle's cars, a cluster of sprinters watching expressionlessly as the indies' color man pitched the upcoming episode of the bio.

"Why should I?" He smiled thinly. "Think I'm that much in love with myself?"

She measured and aimed. "No," she said. "Safer that way."

Something pulled a reflex tic in his eyes, but not what she expected, or anything that she could read.

Engine noises built around them, layer by layer. The night's coordinator had begun waving the fueled cars out onto the road, and thence to Phoenix.

Schuyler's gaze drifted away, across the cars drawing into a line, and beyond. "You worry about it."

The opening credits for the second episode came up on the screen. Urbenton looked back from his chair. "This one got any more action than the first one did?"

Endryx shrugged. "Depends on what you mean by action." She knew what he meant; it would be a while before the sprinters entered the fire zone. In the meantime, Schuyler's past, rather than his present, filled the central monitor.

VIDEO: MEDIUM SHOT, TRACK FORWARD to follow SCHUYLER as he makes his way through the narrow corridors of the train.

He heard voices raised in the car ahead of him. Or one voice, a woman's, squalling in a high-pitched, drill-like monotone. A few muffled replies in a man's voice, which quit before Schuyler got there. He had contemplated turning back, giving these people whatever privacy they deserved, but finally pressed on his way. In a train there was only one route to wherever you were going.

In one of the baggage cars, the big, gray-bearded man he'd run into before was seated on a crate, wide shoulders slumped under the force of the woman's voice, a weight pressing him into the tracks rolling under the train. The woman was small, a skinny child's body, with a narrow face contorted with idiot anger. Schuyler could make out only a few words.

"Your fucking glass!" the woman shouted. "You don't owe those fuckers anything! You owe me, you owe *me!*" She whirled around and started tugging on a steel pry-bar that had been half-buried in the splintered side of one of the crates, with the obvious intention of smashing it some more. Unable to pull it free, she again confronted her victim. "You asshole!"

They didn't see Schuyler standing in the car's doorway. He had stumbled upon a little section of looped time, destined to run forever, over and over. There seemed no limit to the woman's malice, no limit, short of death, of the man's endurance. They were locked into it.

Shit, thought Schuyler. His bunk was on the other side of this scene. Right now he didn't feel like watching an endless rerun of whatever acid-woven cord had been strung between the two. On a sudden impulse he stepped forward and grabbed the woman by her collar and belt. Easy enough; she seemed to weigh nothing. Her mouth gaped open, drawing in an outraged breath. Before she could say anything, he had carried her to the doorway, tossed her into the next compartment back and slid the door shut. He expected her to start pounding on the other side, but the silence held. Maybe she went catatonic, he thought. A relief to all.

The other man, blinking as if waking from a dream, looked up at him. "Well." He peered down the corridor to the shut door. "Thanks."

"Anybody you know?" said Schuyler.

"Eh. My ex-wife. Her name's Lina. Is that a surprise, or what." He spread his hands, pleading his case. "I get my transfer out of Northernmost Parish, the Church is shipping me down to L.A. for my work, I get on the train, and who do I find's aboard? My demented ex-wife. There's no escaping. Somehow she weaseled her way on." His voice turned even more bitter. "She gets whatever she sets her little rat mind on. That's the thing about being nuts—it gives you great determination."

Schuyler dredged up a fragment of memory. "You're the, uh, the stained-glass guy. Right? Bischofsky."

The other nodded. "Complete with glass." He gestured at the crates stacked around them, then reached over and easily pulled the pry-bar out of the one his ex-wife had attacked. "I've been working on this for twelve years. Just getting it dug up and sorted out. My magnum opus, restoration-wise."

"I think I did some of the data log-in," said Schuyler, looking around. "All those little tiny pieces."

"Oh? You have an interest in stained glass?"

He shook his head. "Just numbers to me. Just a job."

"Wish I could say the same." Bischofsky gazed at the crates. "This thing's just about driven me crazy."

"What is it? I mean, what exactly?" He'd evidently pushed some button in the other's head; he could stick around for a while to hear about it.

"It's the rose window. From the cathedral excavation. Or at least as far as we've been able to determine. That's why everything, me included, is being shipped down to L.A.; the testing and analysis equipment is better down there. There's a limit to what we can accomplish in terms of putting it back together up at the Parish."

"Why?" said Schuyler. "You got the pieces. Stick 'em back together. Like a jigsaw puzzle." Twelve years for a flippin' window, he thought. It sounded typical of the Cathedra Novum's penchant for useless, navel-gazing work. The Church was obsessed with its own buried past; every human effort was dragged into that obsession.

"Not that easy," said Bischofsky. "The glass pieces, the stone framing, the leadwork, everything was jumbled up

and scattered over a couple hundred meters. Enough of a
job just finding the pieces. There's some indication that the
cathedral may have caught a stray missile at some point
during the war; that would account for the dispersal pattern.
Plus there was apparently some soil creepage during the
period it was buried. But the problem's deeper than that.
There's no record of what the rose window looked like when
the cathedral was standing. We don't know if the window
was originally created for placement in the cathedral, or
whether it was an older window taken from someplace else,
maybe somewhere in Europe, though the *Corpus vitrearum
medii aevi* archives don't record any such transfer." He was
completely lost in the exposition, as if Schuyler were no
longer there. "Also we don't know, if it is an older window,
whether the original pattern was recreated at the cathedral or
whether the pieces were used to make a new pattern, like
the Bishop's Eye in the York Minster; technically, that's not
so much a pattern as a random assemblage. Same principle,
though. Or perhaps what seem like old glass are more recent
recreations, using the old techniques. Maybe that's why
there was such a mixture of styles: you got muff and crown
pieces, pot metal and flashed glass, all mixed together.
Some beton-glass. Even some stuff that looks like the old
claustra technique, though this would be about the first use
I've seen of it outside of Mohammedan art." He shrugged,
bringing his gaze back to Schuyler. "Quite a mystery. We're
not sure of what the original faith of the people who built
the cathedral was, before the Cathedra Novum took over the
area. So I don't even know what their beliefs, their
symbols, were. Half my time's been spent in straight
theological research, trying to match possible arrangements
of the glass pieces with every religion that's come down the
pike since the world began. I'm working both ends of the
problem toward the middle. Maybe when I get down to the
Church labs in L.A., I'll make a little more progress on
it."

That had been Schuyler's introduction to Dolph Bischof-sky and the rose window. It was a slow train, and a long haul; plenty of time to hear all about it, and the other details of Bischofsky's life.

The next time he saw her, the young Godfriend had exchanged the coarse robe with furs beneath for baggy denim jeans, snugged tight around her boots with leather thongs, and a short-waisted military jacket. The last might have fit her a few years ago, something she'd worn as a child—now the sleeves were too short, showing her forearms with the hammered gold ornaments slid down to her wrists; the threads at the back of the seams were pulled loose by the width of her shoulders.

Schuyler stood in the passage to one of the freight cars, watching her unnoticed. He gripped the metal rim of the doorway to steady himself against the train's motion. She sat on the car's floor, back against one of the crates, and worked with something propped on her knees. When he craned his neck, Schuyler saw that it was on old-fashioned folding terminal—the characters on the tiny gray screen inched across as she tapped the keypad.

Her attention held on the device's screen as he walked toward her, threading his way through the corridor of strapped-down crates and boxes. She only looked up when he was standing right beside her.

"It's the mud man." One corner of a smile, and a nod of recognition. "Did that heal all right?" She took one hand from the keypad and prodded his shin, his pants leg covering where she had removed the wetblanket.

"It's fine," he said. "And it's Schuyler. Not mud man."

" 'Schuyler?' " she echoed. The other corner of her smile matched the first. "You mean your name? You want me to know your name? Is that it? And now I suppose you want to know mine."

Jesus, he thought. Not even out of the *gate*. What's the

deal? Not worth it, whatever it is, he decided; her smile nettled him. "No," he said. "Not really."

"Hey, no, it's okay." She lifted her palm, fingers spread, placating. "They told us that some of you might try and talk with us. It's okay. It's Cynth."

"Cynth?"

A shrug, the white thread at the sleeve seams tautening. "There's more, but it's private."

"Yeah, well—"

"Hey, don't go. It's not against the rules or anything. Just to talk, that's all right."

He had turned and taken a step toward the doorway. Her hand had grabbed the cuff of his pants, and now she pulled him back.

"Come on." She slapped the freight car's floor beside her. "There's a ways to go—you got plenty of time."

The rhythmic vibration of the tracks traveled up his spine as he sat down, sharing the crate for a backrest. Beside the Godfriend, the smell of her sweat, shining on her face, came to him. It's too warm for her, he realized. Inside, with heating and stuff, she's used to the snow. The thick braid of her hair had been coiled and pinned to lift it from her neck. Drops of perspiration dotted the few stray wisps of hair trailing to jacket collar.

He pointed to the terminal perched on her knees. "Figuring out how long it's going to take to get to L.A.?"

She shook her head. "Naw. It'll get there when it gets there. Besides, I could care; I'm not getting off there, anyway. I'm just along to guard the train with the rest of the detail." She gripped the sides of the keypad to steady it. "This is just . . . stuff. Religious junk. That's all."

He leaned forward to look at the small screen. Six horizontal bars, a couple broken in the middle, formed a square. "Oh," he said. "The what's-it. That Chinese stuff."

"The oracle." She tapped the ENTER key, and a

different pattern of six lines formed, the response to what she had been inputting when he had interrupted her.

There were people back at Northernmost Parish who used it; he had seen it before there. An aura of faded hipness clung to the device, with the more determinedly antiquarian using coins, and a book with all the hexagrams in it. He remembered the rattle of the three coins thrown upon a flimsy plastic table ringed with the empty bottles of a party back at one of the Parish dorms, and then the flutter of pages as some cryptic Confucian jive was looked up. He was surprised to see a Godfriend using it, even if it was on a computer rather than with coins and a book; nonsense either way. He had always thought the Godfriends much more serious, grimmer, than that. But this one's so young, he thought. Maybe that accounts for it.

"Is this something you do a lot?" He leaned back against the crate.

Cynth looked up from the terminal. "It's different with us." She had matched his tone of voice with the look on his face, and figured out what he was thinking. "We all do it. All the Godfriends. This—" Her hand slid along the terminal. "This is hooked up to a random number generator at Victoria Base, running on isotope decay; so everybody's on the same wavelength. It's a sacrament."

Some diplomatic remark was called for, he knew. A thin layer of ice had drawn between them. You gotta be careful, he told himself. They had a reputation for touchiness. Indicate respect, he told himself. "So it's—something you love, then."

The screen went blank with a sudden stab of her finger. She turned and looked at him. The complete dark behind her narrowed eyes pulled the ice up under his skin, freezing his heart. "No," she said. "We hate it."

"You don't know?" Bischofsky turned and looked at him with amusement. His gray beard and moustache sparkled with his breath turned to ice by the chill wind curling at the end of the train.

Schuyler gripped the metal rail with gloved hands and watched the track unreeling, curving north through drifts of snow. "No," he said. "Why should I know something like that?"

"You mean you spent all that time, your whole life, in a Church Station and you didn't learn anything?"

"Not about religions. Not about any funky Godfriend hoo-hah, at least." The rail's cold had worked through to his palms; he tucked his hands in his jacket pockets to warm them back up.

"Admit it. You're just bone-ass ignorant." Bischofsky's frosted smile widened.

"So why do you know so much about it?" Schuyler assumed, at least, that the older man did. He had come across him in one of the freight cars, rummaging through crates of books: Bischofsky's own research library, packed up for shipment to L.A., and all ponderous theological titles. Not a lightweight among them, Schuyler had noted. Which was why he had asked about what the Godfriend Cynth had said to him. "It's not like you got any reason to know. All you do is muck about with that stained glass and stuff."

"'Muck about.' Hmm." Bischofsky's merriment deflated. He gazed off at some private vista overlying the white landscape. "You're right about that," he said glumly. "Anyway, the Godfriend thing. They're Gnostics. They think the world's a shit place. Granted, it's easy enough to come to that conclusion when you wake up in the morning, you got frostbite up the wazoo all the time." His own gloved hand gestured at the snow drifts.

"So?" It seemed a reasonable conclusion to Schuyler; his own, in fact. And thus L.A.—which will at least be a warmer kind of shit, he thought. He wondered if there was a way he could move the discussion back into the train and out of the wind, but Bischofsky seemed locked on his own track, sunk in rumination.

"So the fact that the oracle works—the Godfriends think it works, anyway—that's a sign that the Gnostics' world view is correct. That the world is a shit place. If the world was a nice place, then the oracle wouldn't work. You wouldn't be able to predict stuff, or tell what the best thing for you to do in a given situation, by using it. But you can— so they think—and that rankles their collective ass."

Schuyler studied the tracks passing rapidly under the train. "Why?" he said.

"Why what?" Bischofsky looked annoyed at being drawn back to the conversation.

"Why does the oracle working—why does that mean the world's a shit place?"

Bischofsky sighed. "Your ignorance is appalling."

"Jesus. Sorry I asked."

"Listen up. The theory—the Godfriend theory—is that the oracle is a system. It interprets another system, which is the world. And that system is a prison system. To them, the whole universe is a big clanking construct of iron bars and grinding machinery, run by completely inflexible guards, machines who answer to a warden who is nothing but a machine itself. The oracle tells you how to keep out of the way of the steel doors slamming shut, how to say yessir/ nosir in the politest way so the guards beat you up the least—survival stuff. But it doesn't tell you how to get out of the prison. Because there isn't any way out, at least, not in the Godfriend theology. All right? Got it?"

"You believe that?"

Bischofsky's sigh was wearier than before. "I try not to. Actually, I don't know what I believe. Maybe if I did, I'd be able to put that damn window together."

Schuyler nodded, thinking of the look Cynth had trained on him, like an icicle to the heart. My way with words, he thought. "So that's why they hate it."

"That's the straight shot. Christ died to save us from the *I Ching.*"

"He did?"

"So the Godfriends say. That's their religion; part of it, at any rate." The back of his hand rubbed the ice-speckled beard. "And He'd come back and be with us if He could. Just so there'd be a little light inside the prison. Comfort all the prisoners, that sort of thing."

"What's stopping Him?"

"Stopping Him what?"

"You know." Schuyler smiled; other people's religions struck him whimsically. With none of his own, he could take a superior attitude. "From coming back."

Bischofsky stared at him, no longer amused. "You don't know anything. Nothing at all." He shook his head. "The Godfriends—that's what they believe. That's the whole point of their religion. They're the ones who keep Him from coming back."

"You could get a book on this, you know." Cynth dangled her legs off the bottom sill of the freight car's door, her thong-bound fur boots kicking at the bank of snow beyond the steel rail. The train had come to a halt while the tracks ahead were cleared of some impediment. She leaned forward, hands gripping the sill, and turned her head to look back at him. "I mean, if you're so curious about the subject. That'd be easier than shuttling back and forth between your friend and me, asking a lot of dumb questions."

Schuyler squatted on his haunches, back against the open door. He had gotten used to the degree of cold that the Godfriend found comfortable, even preferring, as long as the train wasn't moving or a gale wasn't stinging his face with ice crystals, to sit and talk here rather than in one of the passenger car's stuffy heat. "But what Bischofsky said— about what the Godfriends believe—that was true?"

She shrugged. "In a way. Simplified—for your level."
The same one-cornered smile appeared.

"So you tell me then."

"It's like this." Cynth turned away from him, no longer
smiling. Her gaze stretched off into the snow.

Schuyler sat watching her, the cloud of his own breath as
it met the cold air outside the freight car matching her
white, visible words.

"We know who we are. Almost nobody knows who they
are, except for the Godfriends. That's because there's one
less barrier between us and God. So we see more, because
there's more light for us; not all the light, just more. Much
more than you—people like you—have, Schuyler." She
looked around at him and for a moment he saw himself,
side-lit by the glare off the banked snow, reflected in the
dark centers of her eyes. "The revelation came to our blood
a long time ago. Generations ago. That we were the ones by
whom God would reenter the world, to finish what He had
begun so long ago. And that's the knowledge that is passed
on, from mother to daughter, among us. That to us the
reincarnate deity, God made flesh, would be born, a child to
one of us. And it's true. The truth that is told to us is just a
confirmation, a putting into words, of what every Godfriend
already knows inside herself. Jeez." Cynth shook her head,
smiling to herself. "I sound like some goddamn catechism
manual. Can you believe this shit?"

"The question is," said Schuyler, "do you believe it?"

"Oh, yeah—that's not a question at all." Cynth looked at
him, offense that was only half-mocking clear on her face.
"This isn't a religion like you guys and the Cathedra
Novum, where you got a choice about believing it or not.
And you don't. For Godfriends, this is like believing in
gravity or not, or believing in taking another breath. I mean,
I could be a jerk and deny it, say it's all just bullshit if it
would make you happy, but I'd have to be crazy to believe it
really wasn't true. Because it is. Simple as that."

He sat face to face with a belief equal to his own, admiring it. But I don't believe anything, he thought; he was somewhat proud of that, proving as it did that all the years from infancy on with the Church's funnel stuck into his brain, with their convoluted garbage poured in, tamped down with a stick in some Ascendant's hands, still some part of him had remained un-fucked-with, free of bullshit. And if one part was free, then the whole thing was. Like Lincoln or some other ancient he had read of, saying that as long as one person was a slave, then he wasn't free, either. That wasn't supposed to work in the reverse, thus failing a certain logical rigor, but still. No such thing as partial brainwashing, he told himself. Either you are or you aren't. So—roundabout—he did have a belief after all: that it was all bullshit.

And Cynth sat looking at him, a small amount of silence between them, the right-angled frame they sat in a doorway between the boxes and crates of one world and the cold, rolling landscape surrounding them, and he knew that she believed something else. And that Something had been proved to her the same way his belief had been proved to him. By the simple operation of the universe, which gleans truth from bullshit, gravity from a lot of airy-fairy nonsense. Which wasn't such a simple operation after all, he realized now, having proven two different things, two beliefs to two different people.

"So—let me see if I got this right." Schuyler shifted himself, his knees stiff from squatting in the cold. The edge of the freight car's doorway had sunk an ice rod along his spine. "You're going to give birth to God? Not you, necessarily, but one of the Godfriends? The whole Second Coming thing?"

The smile again, sadder this time: a certain fond pity. "Not will, Schuy. Could. The Godfriend blood is the medium, the genetic material capable of receiving the seed by which God reenters the world; His flesh can become incarnate only through ours. Christ, you ask me these questions, and I don't even hear my own voice telling you the answers—I hear one of the mothers back at Victoria Base telling me all this stuff when I was a kid. And it makes sense to me. But that's a Godfriend thing. It probably all sounds like nuts stuff to you, or heresy or something like that if you're heavy into the Church. That's okay."

He shrugged. He could tell she wanted the conversation to end. It had ventured into the semi-private, things the Godfriends kept, if not to themselves, at least away from some scoffing punk atheist. She doesn't want me to laugh at her, he thought. Or worse, go away and laugh about what she told me. Is that it?

"Okay, 'could,'" he said. "So when would all this happen?"

"God coming back into the world? How should we know? That's up to God. All we can do is provide the opening, the genetic material to receive the seed. Whether He enters or not through that opening is His decision. And anytime a Godfriend has sexual intercourse—here goes the catechism again—with a male—any male; it's not his seed that counts—that opening is created. That's how He came the first time. That's how He would come again, if He could."

"So why doesn't He?"

Cynth rolled her eyes, exasperated. "Because the opening is never created. He doesn't have the chance of entering the world again. Your friend Bischofsky is right. We—the Godfriends—stop him from returning. You know that much, don't you? I mean, Jesus Christ, you're not actually hanging around here exchanging light conversation because you think you've got a shot? You don't think I'm going to all of a sudden say, 'It's cold outside, I'm horny, you're horny, let's get it on?' You do know, don't you, that Godfriends don't have sex with men?"

"Well, yeah," said Schuyler. His discomfort came not

from the subject matter, but his slowness in understanding it. "I just didn't make the connection before. They didn't tell me all this other stuff, or they did but I wasn't listening, back at Northernmost Parish. I just assumed you were all—"

"Dykes, right? That's the word, isn't it? Look, Schuyler, you're a nice guy. I'm glad I'm able to save you from going through life with a bruised ego. We wear the furs and stuff because it's cold here. We carry weapons because there are lots of things here that would like to eat us. The gold and stuff is because we think they're pretty. Decorations, stuff like this—" She touched the row of small scars outlining the bottom of her brows. "We think those are pretty, too. Or sometimes they mean something. And if I don't sleep with you, it's because Godfriends believe that's how they keep God from coming back into the world."

"But why? I still don't get it. If you're the so-called friends of God, why don't you want Him to return?" Now I'm starting to talk like I believed all this stuff, he thought. So much for hypothetical discussions.

"Schuy—think about it. You know, what your pal Bischofsky talked about. If you were in prison, the worst prison possible—and yeah, I remember everything you told me about Northernmost Parish; think of something even worse than that—if you were in that prison, would you want your best friend, who was still out in the sunlight and the open air, would you want that friend to come join you in prison? To suffer and die in darkness that smells like rotting flesh? Every disease, every slow piece of death—would you let him come, if he wanted to? If you really loved your friend, would you let him?"

His head pressed against the door frame behind him, as if the sudden fervor in her voice had grasped his chin and forced it back, forced him to listen without scoffing. "But I thought this was God we were talking about." He was, for this moment, entirely on her ground. "I thought He was supposed to get us out of this prison."

"What makes you think He could? He wasn't able to the last time He came; and that was thousands of years ago. Just because your friend's love for you is so great that he would voluntarily come and join you in the filthiest of prisons, just to be with you and comfort you any way he could, that doesn't mean he's also got the key to the iron gates in his hand. That's just wishful thinking. God doesn't come into this world in order to get us out; He can't do that. This world, for whatever reason—and the Godfriends don't claim to know everything—it's beyond His power. Maybe there is a reason for that. Maybe this is the cosmic sewer where all the rest of the universe drains into. A shit place, as they say. Whatever—if God enters this world, He becomes flesh. And flesh suffers. It dies here. That's the nature of the place. And God would die here, too, just like He did before." Her fingers had scraped up a splinter of wood from the floor; now she flung it with sudden vehemence out into the snow bank. "End of sermon. Take it or leave it."

"But you stop Him," said Schuyler quietly. "Because you're his friends."

"That's it. Bingo. You're a full-fledged theologian now. You've earned your wings."

He ignored the veneer of her sarcasm. "Very admirable."

A trace of her smile returned. "We're a touch bunch. Everybody knows that. It's okay for everybody else to whine and cry boo-hoo for God to come and pick them up where they fell down. I guess we've just learned to get by without Him."

"'Him?' I meant to ask you about that?"

"A word. Means nothing. Plus if we went around saying 'Her,' everybody would make the obvious assumptions about what the Godfriends believe. Not that we care."

"Wait a minute." The thought just struck him. "Where do the babies come from?"

"What babies?"

"Baby Godfriends. You know, your little sisters."

Cynth looked exasperated. "I know everybody thinks we all sit around at Victoria Base gnawing raw meat off of bones, but we really are a little more sophisticated than that. We got gene-engineering equipment. We can get done what needs to be done." She lifted her legs, putting her boots on the sill of the freight door. "Any other questions? I got duty in about five minutes."

Schuyler shook his head. Back where I started, he thought. Bullshit on one side, me on the other. An uncertainty lingered about where Cynth, and all the other Godfriends, stood.

Distant shouting, from up toward the front of the train. Cynth turned her head to the calls, then got up and jumped from the freight car's doorway. Schuyler lowered himself to the ground to follow but quickly fell behind her loping run through the narrow space between the snow banks and the train.

He saw what the obstacle on the tracks had been when he came up within a few meters of where Cynth had halted. Beyond her, the gelatinous bulk of a full-grown wetblanket had fastened onto the tracks in front of the lead engine. The shiny skin was spattered with dull gray, the patches growing as the tissues broke down in rapid decay: one of the Godfriends ringing the creature had managed to root the heated point of her long spear into the nucleus.

Another flurry of shouts, sharper in pitch. Sighting between the backs of the nearest Godfriends, Schuyler saw a sudden movement, as though a bank of snow had lifted, then collapsed. The Godfriends rushed in closer, blocking his view.

Then silence, after the shouting and cries. The Godfriends drew back from the wetblanket, its surface no longer smooth but hacked apart, lumps of the graying tissue scattered about. Two of the Godfriends bent low, dragging something out from under the dead bulk. When he saw the red leaking onto the snow-covered tracks, he realized what it was.

A bloodless face gazed up at the sky. The Godfriends looked down at the one of their number who had been caught in the wetblanket's last convulsion.

VIDEO: LONG SHOT of the Godfriends clustered about the corpse, the white landscape around them divided by the black diagonal of the train. PULL BACK to reveal CYNTH at one side of the frame, gazing at the scene. PULL BACK to SCHUY-LER, another watcher. CYNTH turns and looks at him. In her face, set with a furious grieving, a confirmation: the dimensions of this world.

Schuyler lifted the metal door, got back into the sprint car and eased it forward into the warehouse. Through the side window he saw Endryx sitting a couple of meters away, watching the shadow's monitor. She looked over at him, easing back in the chair and waiting.

He left the engine on, as the videotaped image of the night desert slid across the windshield before him, cast by the monitor's glow. Bursts of flame counterpointed the murmuring idle as he smoothed the steering wheel's rim with his hands, knowing the missile hits were taking place on a track where even less evasion was possible.

Silence after he finally switched off the engine; Endryx had been watching the tape with the audio off. He left the door up to let in the last of the night air—the dark already thinning beyond the alley's buildings—before the day's heat began.

Beer in hand, he stood by Endryx, gazing with her at the monitor. The night's run, reduced to layered electrophoresis, flowed by on the screen. "How'd you get in?" he said.

"Wyre was here." Endryx took the can from his dangling grip and drank from it. "He left a little while ago."

"The ubiquitous Wyre." To whom all the world was at least semi-permeable. Whatever annoyance he had felt at Wyre's fox-like slipping in and out was gone now. What invasion of privacy was possible to somebody with his whole life being broadcast around the world? I've got no complaints, he thought. Not about that, at any rate. He took his beer and knocked back half.

"Got pretty rigid out there tonight." She froze the screen on the image of one of the burning cars.

An engraved wheel cover, caught in mid-spin from the incandescent wreckage clued him: Dennie's car. A hit that for Schuyler, at the other side of the sprinters' wing going through the fire zone, had only caught at the corner of his eye in real time. Pulling Dennie out from his overturned car before—back in that other life, right before Cynth's shot and the hospital—had only delayed this moment. Or perhaps that made it worse when it came round again: he looked at the contorted silhouette at the center of the stilled flames (memory FLASH CUT to the same image surrounded by snow rather than desert) and knew no hands could reach through and again drag Dennie to safety. Safety's somewhere else now, thought Schuyler, a vanished concept.

"Might say." A self-generated anesthesia, deeper than the hospital's, had set in.

"Five hits," she said, pointing to the screen. "That's the record for one night, even going back to the old pre-co-pilot days."

"No kidding." He was beyond calculation. A distant image of counting charred bodies laid out in snow unreeled in his memory. "That should give the color men something to talk about."

"All fatals."

He shrugged. "There's not much left after a direct hit."

This had been demonstrated to his weary satisfaction this night.

"Are you going to keep on with it? The sprinting?"

He pondered the question. Behind him he could hear the car's hood creak, shifting to a new balance point in the differential between the engine's heat and the cool pre-dawn air. He pondered her question: Go on with it? I suppose so; but what if she asks *why*. Then he'd be stuck for an answer. Because a little voice told me I'd be safe? *Auf den Pfaden, auf der Welle/Ewig ängstlicher Geselle*—he'd picked that up from Bischofsky's store of German poetry, straight from the heavyweight *Faust*. And *always fearful companion* describes it all right, thought Schuyler. Screw that safety shit. You can't have your friends going up in big whacking balls of flame all around you without your own skin's shrinking in the heat. No little voice coming out of a square metal box where it shouldn't be is persuasive enough to beat that. Not even worth listening to. So why, then?

Because what you want is out there, thought Schuyler, looking down at the monitor's desert with flames. And you don't care if death is there, too.

Or else that's the thing you want.

Schuyler drained his beer and threw the can, the wet rim spattering his hand, into the unlit spaces of the warehouse. It clattered and rolled to a stop against the far wall.

"Are you?"

He looked at her for a few seconds before remembering the rest of the question. "Sure," he said. "Why not?" Good a reason as any.

"That'll make a lot of people happy."

"What?" He stared at her. "What's that mean? Speed Death—the show's over if the rest of the sprinters quit. That's it, right?" *Happy*—the word alone had triggered his anger.

"Forget them. You haven't heard any of the reports yet?

About how the broadcast of the first bio episode went down?"

"Why should I?"

"Hey, check it," said Endryx, smiling. "You're more than a star now—you're part of a religion."

"I've been there before. With the Godfriends. It's not worth it. What are you talking about?"

"The audience survey, in the Latin American factory dormitories. They went wild for you. The first episode of the bio had a nearly ninety-eight percent audience penetration—that's ten points better than the sprints themselves do. The indies test-blanked part of São Paulo, and riots broke out when the signal was cut off—three dead and seventeen injured."

"What's that got to do with religion? People down there used to kill each other over soccer games."

"This is different," said Endryx. "That level of interest merits sending out the whole army of probes. And the verbals they got out of the dorms were completely consistent. There's a new religious movement sprung up in the factory worker population. It's gone through all the dorms. It's centered around your son Lumen. Somehow they've learned all about him, and they agree with the Godfriends that a five-year-old boy is the incarnation of the deity. The true savior, destined to lead them out of bondage. Destroy the oppressors. And so on, and so on. It's a popular movement."

Schuyler grunted and shook his head. "And—what? They know I'm the kid's father, I suppose. So the bio broadcast picks up some kind of spin-off interest from this new religion?"

"This is more than spin-off." Endryx reached out and tapped the monitor screen. "This is a visible miracle. To them you're the rolling confirmation of their faith. You have come back from the dead—they know about your getting shot; that was on the color reports, anyway—and now you ride through a field of death, and while others all around you are getting snuffed, you emerge unscathed. Because you have numinous protection."

"I have what?"

"Numinous protection. You have encountered the godhead in this world—being the holy child's father, and all—and now no mortal hand can harm you. Or the various extensions thereof, such as guns and pursuit satellite missiles."

"Great." He turned away in disgust and stared out the open doorway. This is what you get, he thought: no end to lunacy, once it gets started. It spreads, infects, and now people I don't even know have looned-out ideas about me. Bad enough, that being the case with people I do know. The thought of the poor suckers in the factory dorms bore down on his heart. Who would disabuse them of these notions? Not Speed Death Productions or the indie satellites. If a ninety-eight percent audience penetration requires a new religion, then all hosannas to some five-year-old sitting thousands of miles away from these true believers in the snowbound Godfriend encampment. Where they also worship him, now that he managed to elude their barricade around this world.

Outside, the buildings lining the alley had gained the angles of shape and form, the light reddening toward morning. If people elsewhere wanted to worship his son—a son he had never even seen—then let them. No stopping them, in any case. But leave me out of it, he thought. Numinous protection, my ass. Here he felt, for the first time, the invasiveness of the millions of distant eyes examining the reconstruction of his life, or what his life was supposed to have been. Not the flat observation of event, but the conjuring of ideas about you. That was where the intrusion began. So that one's own death, or the pursuit of it in any of the fire zones of this world, was no longer yours, but theirs: their re-edit to fit their frame.

"Speed Death would like some more material on you."

He turned around, out of his silence. "What, you don't have enough already? For Christ's sake. I thought you had the whole bio in the can."

Endryx shook her head. "For a follow-up. After the bio broadcasts are done. The New York office called me, said they want to keep this audience level up. Naturally. They thought some kind of business in a current time-frame would play."

"It doesn't play, it sucks." As far as he was concerned, all the events of his life except the last one were over. And they already had the rights to that, apparently. "Tell 'em to forget it."

She lowered her chin to her forearms folded on the back of the chair. "I had a couple of ideas that I thought might interest you. For the follow-up."

"Like what?"

"Thought we could fly up to Victoria Base, do some taping there."

"What the hell for?" Schuyler's irritation became rawer. "Nothing but snow up there. Would've figured you had enough of that."

She coolly laid out her high cards. "I already talked to the Elders' Council. And the PrimRelCom. I got clearance for you to see Cynth. And your son."

"Really." Schuyler's anger drained away in the shift of ground. Bemused, he weighed her words. The offer was obviously a bribe. The only one that would work, he thought. She scanned me, and found the button. Once it was pushed, he had to respond. He felt a certain uneasiness when he looked into her gaze, as watchful and absorbing as the lenses of the spidery contraption that always accompanied her. Lenses that focused and recorded, and analyzed. He wondered if there were other buttons that had been deduced, ready for her to press them, the same as she operated the controls in her forearm.

"All right," he said. "When do we go?"

The shadow was already retracting the monitor, preparing for travel even as it continued taping the scene inside the warehouse. Endryx tapped out a few more commands on her forearm. "Get some sleep," she said. "We can head out before noon, do the taping, and get back in time for your sprint tonight. Deal? I'll come by for you."

Segment Five

He woke up slumped in the chair, spine a stiff curve, mouth stale from breathing in and exhaling discomforting dreams through the night. Gray light seeped through the warehouse's windows; it matched the monitor screen so exactly that it took him a few seconds to realize the tape playback unit was still on. A barely audible high note died when Schuyler pressed the switch. The gray light faded across his wrist before he drew his hand back.

Ah, wretched life. That's what you get for dozing off like that. Massaging his neck, he drifted around the warehouse, chewing on a half-dried French bread heel from the corner that served as kitchen area. The heavier weight of his dreams slowly separated out from the night's actual events, falling back into darkness to be forgotten.

The broadcast of the second bio episode; more of the staticky spook voice coming through Amf; going out on a run again; and five deaths, five hits on the field. So much for a return to the old life. You could return, but it wouldn't be the same life. He ground the last crust between his teeth.

His dreams had been of a run that never ended: where cars were battered into flames that did not consume, where speed was not lost. He needed a shower to wash away the dried sweat. He checked his watch: there was time to kill before Endryx came by for the flight up to Victoria Base and the Godfriends.

The street was abuzz as he made his way to Bischofsky's studio: two of the neighborhood vibers fluttered into step with him. Their extravagant hands, birds darting on either side of him as he walked, sketched their emotions.

"*Loved* the bio. So interesting!"

Schuyler nodded. The vibers were quite sweet—he had always got along well with them.

The one with the spade goatee widened his kohl-rimmed eyes in remembered horror. "And *then*—we heard; we didn't watch it, but we *heard*—one of your friends was *killed*."

"Yeah, well." Schuyler shrugged. "That's the chance you take."

"It is?" The other viber looked puzzled. "Since when?"

Good question—it went on repeating itself in his head after the vibers had peeled away from him, strolling back to the steady hum of their compound. Joroff's death put a new light on the whole business of sprinting. Lethality had entered the playing field. An element that, once (always?) in existence, spread from one sector to another. Until we're all dead, thought Schuyler as he paced along. Sprinting, before this, being on the level of an old-time video game, the omnivorous blips and creatures made of no more than light projected on the screen of the sprinters' windshields. Given the ability to play, the talent to interpret the co-pilot's chatter and act upon it, you could have some high-speed fun and make back just enough to go on playing. Now the change that had hit the zone of dealing with the yearly Godfriend contingent had infected this other. Simulated violence had become real; you died, or came close enough to it. Now I don't have to go home to get killed—the thought tagged along down the last stretch of heat shimmering concrete. Now death is everywhere.

It was cool inside the converted hangar, the Wyre-installed machinery rejecting the heat from outside so that all the rest of the Wyre devices could operate smoothly. As Schuyler stood in the doorway of the vast space, he watched the simulated cathedral window shift its colors. A depiction of robed prophets adoring a geometric rose became, each piece sliding to a new position, a shoal of fish, one crowned, penetrating the lace-fringed waves of Japanese engravings.

Behind the terminal in the middle of the bare concrete floor, Bischofsky gazed up and brooded at the new glass arrangement. "That really sucks." He didn't look at Schuyler as he approached, but instead leafed through a ream of densely numbered printouts. "I don't care if it's got a probability factor up in the gamma range. It's stupid-looking. That's all there is to it."

"What's it supposed to be?" Schuyler stood beside Bischofsky's chair to get a better angle.

"Who knows?" The gray-bearded face scowled in disgust. "Looks to me like some mutant version of the window Wendling did for—Aachen, I think." He punched a FILE SEARCH command into the terminal, and a rapid series of colored patterns flipped across the screen. "Yeah, right—the baptismal chapel." One pattern held. Schuyler glanced at it and saw fish, stylized, simple blues and reds, no crown but a crucifix reaching up from the mouth of the largest. "About 1950—the original was one of the best twentieth-century windows. But this pseudo-Orientalia . . . who needs it?"

"You tell us. You're the doctor." Wyre had materialized from the shadows and now stood on the other side of the chair, a set of screwdrivers bundled with his logic probe in his hand. His wolf smile flashed over Bischofsky's head to Schuyler. "Smile for the camera."

Schuyler looked behind himself and saw the reflection of his face distorted in a circle of dark glass. Unheard by him, the shadow had stepped close and focused its wide-angle lens on the three of them. "Endryx here?"

"Naw." Wyre slapped the tools into his other hand. "The thing's on auto. She's been sending it over to get more footage of ol' Dolph here. For the broadcasts."

Schulyer mulled over this information. He stepped away from the terminal, watching the shadow from the corner of his eye. It turned from the others, its lens turret swiveling a close-focus lens into position to follow him. Which means it's got a preset on me—he looked up at the dark clear curve regarding him. I show up and it switches from taping Bischofsky to me. Which means Endryx was expecting, or hoping, that I'd come here.

The shadow's presence formed a damper on his original plan, to talk to Bischofsky about the new voices he had heard coming from Amf's speaker. The voices were still his secret, perhaps the only one he had left. And one which, any suspicions of Endryx aside—and the shadow haunting about did trouble him—he wasn't ready to share. His reason for wanting to discuss the voices with Bischofsky had been that the older man, with his parade of loony wives and girlfriends, and Bischofsky's own shuttling in and out of therapy and the bin back at Northernmost Parish, had made him something of an authority on cracking up. He was better than a psych tech, having seen it both at close range and from the inside. He could tell, if anybody could, if the voices on Amf were actually the sound of Schuyler's brain cells breaking free of each other, the connections corroded, as might be expected, by recent events. As long as I can keep him from going off on some religious tangent to explain it, thought Schuyler. Such as the voices being the Holy Ghost on a shortwave set. An explanation like that wouldn't get him anywhere—who'd be able to tell who was crazy then?

At any rate, he didn't want it to be picked up by the shadow and forwarded to Endryx and points beyond, the world at large. Maybe it's ego, thought Schuyler. This is the star trip that comes from having every boring detail of your life made the subject of a camera's attention. You start grooming your image. But he knew that wasn't it. There was a deeper reason: to admit insanity, even the tinge of it, was to lose control of one's world, to fall under the so-called care of all the white-jacketed machinery created for those fucking up in a major way. And when death is perceived as part of the environment, all the smart creatures, the sharp-nosed ones who hunker down in their burrows and survive, hang on to as much control as they can. The alternative was to roll over and wait for the teeth from above.

"Well, that's what you get." Schuyler looked around from the shadow to the simulation of the cathedral window. "How many years you been working on this—and you get fish." The topic that had brought him here being ruled out, he tried for the joke.

"Shut the fuck up." Bischofsky looked up at him with eyes red-rimmed with fury. "Just get out of here."

He stepped back, fending off the other's sudden anger with an upraised hand. "Sure—whatever you say, man. Catch you later." Screw this, he thought, turning and walking.

"Hold up a second," called Wyre after him. "Try it now, Dolph."

A couple meters out of range, Schuyler watched as

Bischofsky, head lowered, bear-like, glared at the terminal keyboard, than hammered out another command. The light pouring into the hangar from the simulated window changed, moving along some spectrum of place or time that Wyre had programmed.

"Yeah, that's better," muttered Bischofsky, not even looking up.

The shadow, as Schuyler had expected, tagged along after Wyre and himself, to the bar closest to Bischofsky's studio, a frequent locus for picking apart the events of their friend's world.

"So what's the deal?" said Schuyler, "with Bischofsky?" The shadow stationed itself at the end of the booth to line both of them up into a two-shot, the bar's gloom requiring a wide-open aperture. Not the sort of place where a metal spider studded with lenses drew more than a couple glances.

Wyre shrugged, gazing into his beer glass. "The window. It's always the window."

That was the center of their friend's life, a center that had grown almost to the periphery, swallowing everything. Obsession as cancer, though Schuyler—a verification of some of the conversations he'd had with Bischofsky a long time ago. Maybe when they talked about Lina, back on the train. The idea enters into the person's thinking, and keeps on growing until the idea *is* the person. Irony to prove it with your own life. That the process is the same whether it's a rat-like scrabbling onto another's neck for sustenance—as with Lina—or whether it's some grand religious investigation. The result is the same. "The window."

Wyre drank and set the glass down in the middle of the table's overlapping wet rings. "It's reached a certain stage," he said, "that you're not quite up on—a quantum leap in his thinking took place while you were in the hospital. Whole different theories came out of some of the new lab data."

That's how it goes, thought Schuyler, sipping his own beer. Check out for a week, and even the little worlds go on without you. "Like what?"

"The Church labs came up with something called meson bleed factors." A tinge of excitement crept into Wyre's voice, his usual response to tech talk. "Completely new scans. You see, they started working on the lead moldings that were dug up. Inasmuch as they'd run out of tests to do on the glass itself, at least for the moment. Anyhow, they worked out a rate of influence between the glass pieces and the metal surrounding them—an actual subatomic warpage. Every piece with its own signature, and you go layer by layer through the metal, and you get a history of every piece that came into contact with any section of lead. Even, supposedly, past the lead being melted down and remolded. A *very* subtle effect—only traceable over a span of centuries, and you wind up with these tiny gradations, just the least cut above the best equipment's error margin. Completely disputable—the theory alone's got Church physicists punching each other out." Wyre nodded sagely, judging not. "But it did come up with some wild readings— some glass arrangements I don't think Dolph ever expected to see."

The best possible arrangement, thought Schuyler, would be meter-high letters spelling out, GIVE IT UP, BIS-CHOFSKY. With a phalanx of saints, perhaps, giving him the finger. A 100 percent probability, to boot. That might break the spiral into madness and death. GO OUT AND PLAY, in luminous blue tinged with scarlet fire. THY LORD BROOKETH NO SHIT.

Probably not, though—more's the pity. "Such as?" he said. His own concerns he pushed to the back of his mind, the advantage of talking about absent friends.

"Visual aids time." Wyre drew one of his messily soldered devices, a palm-sized flat box this time, from his jacket and pointed it at the shadow. "C'mere, spook."

The editing monitor was already extruding from the shadow's thorax as it stepped closer. Sucker's been hot-wired, thought Schuyler. That's what Endryx gets for leaving it around where he could get at it.

Wyre fiddled with the home-brew control box, and the screen came to life. It showed the interior of Bischofsky's studio, in a long shot that encompassed the simulated cathedral window and, in the foreground, Bischofsky at the terminal. The figure on tape, with his back to the camera, seemed to have forgotten the shadow's presence in the hangar, as he looked down from the window to the keyboard and back up again, every alteration in the window playing in the light around him. Watching the monitor, Schuyler was aware of Wyre's hands working the control box; the shot froze on the screen.

VIDEO: ZOOM IN to the window, the circle of colored light filling the frame. HOLD. The glass pieces depict a man sitting cross-legged, a tree arching over his head to shade him. The man's face is broad, Oriental, a slight smile tugging at the corners of his mouth; he raises the palm of one hand to the onlooker.

"Buddhism?" He wasn't bone-ass ignorant; this much he could recognize.

Wyre nodded. "This one got a really high probability. Threw Dolph for a complete loop."

"I didn't know there were any Buddhist stained-glass windows."

"Who knows? Maybe there aren't." Wyre worked the control box again. "Wait till you see some of the other new arrangements."

VIDEO: CLOSE-UP of the window, as before. DIS-SOLVE to another pattern of light filtered by

colored glass: a star and a crescent moon. DIS-
SOLVE to another star made up two triangles
intertwined. DISSOLVE to a sinuous dragon coiled
around a pearl divided into curved teardrops of
light and dark. DISSOLVE to a swastika; DISSOLVE
to a hammer and sickle. DISSOLVE to a man
hanging by one foot from a star-laden gibbet.
DISSOLVE and DISSOLVE again, the images coming faster and faster upon each other until they
blur in visual memory.

Wyre blanked the monitor screen, his rummaging
through the shadow's archives finished. He leaned back to
drain his beer.

"There's a problem here." Schuyler had been able to see
that much as well.

"True enough. Up till now, Dolph's always been working
within a basic Christian framework. Which suited him fine,
really; he might crab about the Cathedra Novum, the
officials, even some of the minor doctrines, but he still fit
right in. Drudging away in his little workshop, like those
anonymous craftsmen of the Middle Ages who built the
cathedrals in the first place, carving the backs of gargoyles
and shit that nobody would ever see anyway. All for the
glory of the Church, right? But now it's a different deck of
cards that's been handed to him, a much bigger deck. *And
one that possibly invalidates everything that he's thought
and done before.*"

I know the feeling. Schuyler kept the thought to himself.
Instead, aloud: "I imagine that would get to you."

Wyre glanced sharply at him, then shrugged. "You could
say. At any rate, there's some basic questions raised. About
the nature of the window itself—not just the particular
arrangement of the glass pieces inside it. Some new
possibilities. One, *the window may never have existed at*

all. A mistaken assumption based on a pile of glass pieces found all in one spot. That might be all there is to it."

Schuyler turned the idea over. "But what about the arrangements? All those computer analyses of what the window might have looked like?"

"Ah—now we get to the scary part. Scary for Dolph, that is. The theory changes the reality observed, right? You work that line yourself. All the sprinters do. That's how the RH chips in the co-pilots get you around the missiles falling out there on the desert. Good for you, but too bad for Bischofsky. Because that line invalidates the whole process of inquiry itself. The probability of any glass arrangement that the computer analyses come up with being the true arrangement might be a probability relative to all other possible arrangements, and nothing more. But that doesn't face the issue of whether any of them at all is true. Or whether anything is true; Dolph's dopey bits of glass being a subset of the world at large. As above, so below. The basic tenet of mysticism. Because if the computer analyses are creating—not finding, but *creating*—patterns out of meaningless data, then Dolph has worked himself into a hole that a lot of other people have fallen into. Maybe all of us, without knowing it. The world we perceive is the result of what we analyze of what we perceive; what then did we perceive in the first place, and what did we analyze? Nothing we can be sure of. Nothing but the inquiry itself. Not even existence. No answer, just the question." Wyre tilted the glass over his mouth, the last drop of beer sliding down the side, then set it down again. "When you reach that point, when all your efforts have brought you there, then you're on a cold edge, all by yourself."

"Is that so?" There are other ways to get there, it seemed to Schuyler. "Hey, is that really the case? I mean, all that lab work, and computer analyses and shit—that's what it adds up to? Nothing at all?"

"Beats me," said Wyre. "That's a philosophical question. An old one, at that. Me, I just make the machines work."

As long as the machines work. Schuyler studied the bottom of his own glass. Machines were the reference point for Wyre. As long as the machines around you kept doing what they were supposed to be doing, then you were all right. People could screw up—you expected them to—but machines are made of finer stuff. They're not supposed to begin talking, in a new voice, out of the blue, about death and weird shit like that. Schuyler's own problems, briefly pushed under the horizon of consciousness, hit a tangential link with Bischofsky's world. When the machines begin talking like that, he thought, you know it's *you* that's screwing up.

And screwing up was this problem's label. His thoughts returned to Bischofsky, to what both he and Wyre had seen; he had a specific reference to match to the sudden flash of anger back at the hangar. It was years ago, on the train from the Parish, all that time spent shooting the breeze, killing the hours while the snowbound miles of rail clicked underneath them. One meandering conversation, him and Bischofsky and one of the freight handlers with nothing to do until they got to L.A., had as its topic How Would You Know You Were Going Crazy? It was a subject inspired by Lina, there being a real concern on the part of Bischofsky and anybody else who came into her deranged line of fire, to avoid becoming like that oneself, to know the warning signs in oneself and thus be able to nip the whole devolving process in the bud, before one became a weasel-brained lunatic. Presumably, one would do this by seeking professional help; by icing oneself if necessary. (Bischofsky, in his crisis-ridden personal history, had tried both approaches, with limited success in both cases.) Schuyler, his back against one of the crates in the freight car, had volunteered that his personal warning sign was a deformation in his visual field: three-dimensional objects, especially distant ones such as mountain ranges, appearing as flat as a painted backdrop. This had happened to him one time when he'd been particularly depressed about being stuck in Northernmost Parish. The self-administered therapy, administered before he started *believing* mountains were painted on canvas, had been to start laying his plans for getting out of the dump. Louie, the freight handler, after much thought, had stated that he would know he was going crazy if he found himself lying in bed all day, pissing and crapping on himself.

"Jesus," Bischofsky had said, appalled. "That doesn't mean you're going crazy. That means you *are* crazy. It's too late by that point!" And later, when Louie wasn't around, he'd gone through a whole number about how the statement had meant that, to Louie, a generally cheerful part-time inebriate, everything short of pissing and crapping on oneself was to be considered normal. A certain amusement there.

But Bischofsky's own self-designated sign of impending madness had been sudden flashes of anger. The overture to one of the downward spirals that had landed him in the Northernmost Parish bin had been his hurling a coffee table through the window of his apartment when his current girlfriend had left the toilet unflushed. That was the sign, the warning that the world had become too much with him.

A joke had been made of it, back in the freight car. "Really?"—Schuyler had fed him the straight line. Bischofsky had glared back below a thunderous brow: "Boy, it really pisses me off when somebody says that!" They had all laughed then. Now it wasn't so funny.

The question now was, has Dolph spotted his own warning sign? And is he willfully disregarding it? He can't give it up now, thought Schuyler; that was the grim part. And if the answer to his quest, the solution to the window's puzzle, lay beyond the gates of madness, then—Schuyler knew it—Bischofsky would follow the line to its bitter end.

The window having become his life sure enough, what else was he to do? Could he give it up, and spend the rest of whatever was left of his life shuffling around in the cavernous space of his studio, a blank gray wall where the vivid lights of the simulated window had once played, as he noodled about on inconsequential little restoration projects sent over by the Church? While the big one, his magnum opus, was boxed up and stored away on a shelf somewhere, like a Christmas jigsaw puzzle with too many pieces—or perhaps the One, without which no other pieces would fit, missing? Because if that's the alternative, then madness is preferable. Bischofsky would beat the gray-covered skull holding his stubborn, bear-like intellect, so much like his barrel-chested physical being, against the problem until the skull cracked. As it might already be doing.

Such was life in this world, Schuyler reminded himself as he finished his own beer. One of the advantages to the Gnostic outlook on life—an outlook he'd adopted formally in his heart, since his education in it from Cynth and subsequent events—was that, once the blinders were removed as to the basic shitfulness of this world, you didn't have to look far to find somebody having an even rougher time of it than you were. All I've got to worry about is getting killed, one way or another. That appeared to be the intention of large segments of the world toward him; he took the introduction of the lethal element into the sprinters' runs as aimed at him personally: a slow-moving bullet, but one that would arrive eventually.

"Of course"—Wyre's voice broke into his thoughts—"there are other explanations about the window. Explanations other than an epistemological black hole that swallows up all human inquiry processes, leaving us to wander in a cheerless empirical void."

"That's a comfort," said Schuyler.

"The window might be a fake. A deliberately concocted puzzle. Concocted by whom? Perhaps the Cathedra

Novum, to drive Bischofsky crazy. That's the short-range paranoid explanation."

"Jesus." Schuyler didn't want to think about it any more. The effect was that of mirrors facing mirrors, an infinite regression blurring down a corridor of nonexistent space. "What would be the point of driving Dolph crazy? Or crazier?"

"Maybe it's not just Dolph." Wyre's face, in the bar's dimness, became even slyer and more animal-like. "The Cathedra Novum spends a lot of money, not just on Dolph, but a whole army of researchers and reconstruction experts. Archaeologists, linguists, historians—essentially, they employ every available person, anybody who can dig two potshards out of the ground and put 'em together."

"And they're all working on supposedly concocted projects, like Dolph? What's the point of that?"

"If everybody's digging into a concocted past, then nobody's digging into the real past. If you've got something to hide, you can't just forbid people to dig it up—that just tells them where to look."

Well, shit. The next question, Schuyler knew, would be, what does the Cathedra Novum have to hide? But why bother to ask it? The process of concealment implies the unpleasant nature of the thing concealed. To hold power, to be an empire in a world like this—he could imagine Cynth, the version of her he had known back on the train, explaining it to him—was to be of a piece with this world, a stain that couldn't be eradicated.

And if that's true, then we are all mightily screwed. Not just Dolph, but all of us. And so back to the window—it's preferable to go on believing it's real, and just needs figuring out, than to arrive at the place its falsity gets you to.

"Or"—relentless, Wyre went on—"possibility B, the window was faked by whoever built the cathedral up in Northernmost Parish in the first place, to drive whoever came after them crazy. More of a historical conspiracy approach there. The implications being—"

"Enough. Please. No more." Schuyler started to slide out of the booth, shaking his head. The relief that had always been found before in an excursion into the Bischofsky world, a world that had provided those tuned to its wavelength with regular bulletins and progress reports as interesting as the most exciting novel doled out a page per day—that relief was gone, dissipated. Death, spreading from sector to sector, had entered here as well.

"Lemme show you one more thing." Wyre flicked the shadow's monitor back on. Schuyler, dully bound, sat back down and looked at the screen.

VIDEO: CLOSE-UP of the simulated window, as before. The colors are arranged in a simple geometrical pattern, no apparent symbolism. The light filling the frame is brighter, though: some of the spaces outlining the straight-edged figures are empty, letting the white light from behind pass through unfiltered.

"That's his latest kick." Wyre nodded at the screen. "That the original design of the window may have incorporated actual blank spaces, where no glass was fit into the framework at all. So there'd be no coloration there, just pure light coming through. Some religious significance to that, no doubt."

"This is something that came out of the lab analyses?"

Wyre shook his head. "Something Dolph came up with on his own. A hunch. That's all; just something he felt."

Why not. Schuyler gazed at the pattern of light until Wyre blanked the screen.

Wyre had other business to take care of; the shadow went the opposite direction, picking its spidery way down the

sidewalk outside the bar, a signal from its master overriding
its auto settings. So Schuyler was alone when he returned to
Bischofsky's studio and stood silent in the doorway.

Bischofsky didn't notice him there. He sat behind the
terminal, gazing up at the simulated glass. More blank
spaces in the window now, white light streaming through at
least a third of the window. The light falling on him was
brighter than Schuyler had ever seen it before.

Segment Six

Schuyler leaned close to the helicopter's curved glass, the seatbelt tautening against his hip. His breath clouded against the transparent sphere, the thin shield that separated him from air and the fall to the distant, snow-covered ground below. As he scanned the white landscape, he felt the warmth of his blood leaking out through his brow, drawn through the glass and swallowed by the chill atmosphere.

"Recognize anything?"

Beside him, Endryx nodded to indicate the terrain they were flying over. She had placed the copter on one of the tight-beam navigation tracks between L.A. and Northern-most Parish, freeing her from attending to the controls.

He shook his head and went back to gazing at the vistas of snow rolling beneath their progress en route to Victoria Base. In the truncated sphere of the cabin he could hear Endryx tapping at the controls in her forearm, and the silky whisper of lenses sliding into place. The shadow, its legs folded alongside its black carapace—like a spider, thought Schuyler, the way you find them dead and curled up inside an old web—was tucked into the small baggage space behind the seats. He could feel its glass eye examining the hairs on the back of his neck. What was the point of a shot like that? he wondered. Other than the camerawoman's craft having become habitual, almost unconscious; he supposed piloting the helicopter was too much interface with the mechanical world. Fuck of a sprinter she'd make, he thought. Can't be bothered to drive. Only when everything was reduced to video could you get the pure cool abstract that she preferred, a world of artificial horizon and infinite possibility.

"What's to recognize?" he said. He tapped on the curved surface of the glass. "All looks alike to me."

"You're the one who walked over a good chunk of it." She had set up her shot the way she wanted it—the shadow's recording lens extended on a telescoping stalk to the cab's ceiling, so that the landscape passing below framed Schuyler's silhouette whenever he turned round to look at her. Leaning back against the angle of her seat and the steel door frame, she watched him. Pinned in the small space, there was no way for him to escape. "From up here, I guess it's different."

"Yeah, right. Better. You're not freezing your butt off, and there isn't ice whacking you in the face all the time and things jumping out of snowdrifts to eat you. Damn straight, it's different." All the way out from L.A., as soon as the helicopter had crossed the sharp dividing line between the weathermods' zones of operation—desert heat on one side, Arctic snow to the north; from up here it seemed like a thumb's width between them—he had thought of the difference made by perspective. The ice and snow that had cost him, and Cynth, so much to cross by foot, each wearying pace into the razor-edged wind, now glided away under the copter's insulating sheath. And farther north, if they were to go all the way up to the Parish—the step it had taken him twenty years to make, out of the place he'd been born, would be traversed in a couple of hours. That's all it'd take, he thought. There's something to be said for technology. God had been born, at least according to the Godfriends, in the wild cold, in the winter prison. The machine took you above that, reduced the white landscape to something behind glass, as though the copter's shield were a monitor's screen.

"Key Him in," said Schuyler, his thoughts going aloud. "Like special effects."

"What?" Endryx shifted her cramped, angular frame. "What'd you say?"

He glanced at her, then back to the glass an inch from his face. The copter had penetrated a gray cloud, ice crystals chittering against the shield. "Nothing," he said.

Outside the stone walls of Victoria Base, a snowless space: a helipad bared constantly, heat paid for by the Cathedra Novum. The melted snow ran off the concrete with its buried thermals and froze again at the raised circle's edge. As the copter settled its weight down onto its landing struts, Schuyler watched the runnels' steam flatten under the blade wind. A colonial convenience, and grand gesture. Some Church bigwig could fly up here any moment of the day or night to inspect their pet savages' doings, and the pad would be waiting. A flat brand set into the snow. He couldn't imagine any woman of Cynth's blood being much impressed by it. They probably ignored it as easily as the stone perimeter of Victoria Base did.

He stood by on the pad while Endryx unloaded the shadow from inside the copter. It unfolded itself stiffly, as if its metal legs had gone to sleep during the journey. The lens turret swiveled around until it spotted him. He found himself staring again at the face caught in curved glass that was his, now with a plume of breath hiding the nose and mouth.

"You sure they're expecting anyone?" He looked around at the silent walls, fifty meters away. No sign of welcome or even simple recognition of their presence had shown above the white-crested stones.

"I think they got kinda burnt out by the taping crews." Endryx led the way across the pad, toward the high gate. "Not that they ever put out much of a red carpet."

"Get any flash on this?" she asked as they stepped off the concrete edge, boots crunching through layered ice. "Memory traces? Since you have been here before."

He shook his head. The cold—the bite of the air on his face—had awakened some non-specific cellular dread. Didn't haul my ass all the way down to L.A. to go dogging through this frozen junk again; no way, he told himself. Having come close to death in it, his own and Cynth's, he let his skin tighten into armor against the snow drifting into his plodding steps. But the sight of Victoria Base in solid fact rather than in Endryx's tapes kicked over no spark in his mind. I was so screwed up then, he thought as the wall's shadow fell over him. When I was here before. The trek across the snow fields from Eureka Station, and all that happened in his and Cynth's mock death, had shorted out—apparently—his perceptions; he remembered nothing of the Godfriends dragging his chill-fatigued body here. If God had been born into the world in that small pocket of dwindling warmth in the cold wasteland, then the God-friends were right about the world's being a prison. A death sentence or a life sentence; all the same. He trudged on, sunk in cold thoughts.

The Godfriends were expecting them; that became apparent when the gate swung open at their approach. Schuyler watched as Endryx and the young guard inside exchanged brief nods of recognition. Hammered gold ornaments and braided, oiled hair; recognition across only a short span of time. He had seen this one before, perhaps, driving a shattering dagger against his chest. Maybe she had been at the last ritual, with Cynth and the gun. As the Godfriend led them toward the low, sloping cluster of buildings—her quick strides triggering a memory of Cynth loping, wolf-like, across the snow, a long time ago—he noted a pre-fab metal shed tucked against the wall's curve. The Speed Death logo was stenciled on one side. He supposed that Endryx and her crew had stored some of their equipment here, looking ahead to more videotaping. Or else they had just given the empty building to the Godfriends when they were done; either way, a certain presence remained.

Endryx fell back to guide the shadow's angle on him, as the guide took his gloved hand in her bare one. He let himself be led into a building's dark interior, stooping under the low doorway. Behind him, he could hear Endryx and the shadow picking their way through the passage, taping the whole programmed scene.

The dark opened into space and light. A smell of wood smoke, but no fire. A row of heaters, red glow behind metal grilles, around the perimeter of a rough-plastered room. Drag marks, parallel lines in the floor's dust, curving toward other doorways; Schuyler wondered what altars had been stowed away, and whether because of his tainting presence or the prying camera's.

"Schuyler." The reception committee in the center of the room: two mothers flanking a third, the oldest, sitting in a carved wooden chair. He recognized one as the shepherd of the yearly trek of initiates into his warehouse in L.A. The mother superior spoke again, raising her leathery hand from the chair arm: "You've come without bidding."

Properly oratorical; he wondered if they were working from a script. One, as usual, that hadn't been shown to him. At the corner of his eye, Endryx and the shadow were circling the room, working a slow pan. It would all play well with a religion-crazed audience. And that's the point, he reminded himself. No other.

He returned the stern face's gaze. "I wanted to see my son."

Gold ornaments rattled, sliding down the tendons and mottled skin of the mother superior's forearm. "Your wishes don't concern us. Shall you gloat over your lust's issue?"

What the fuck. The room's stifling warmth had him sweating under his jacket. "I thought I had permission."

"The world's permission is not ours."

He glanced over at Endryx, who gestured, palm outward, for him to be quiet and wait.

"However—" The old woman craned her neck to level a crepe-lidded gaze at him. "The child wishes to see you. He was made aware of your coming, and has said that you should be brought to Him."

"I see." He nodded acknowledgment to Endryx; a thin smile crossed the room in return. "Kid's got clout."

"Father-of-God, the child's wishes preserve the breath in your body. As in all of ours."

"Right," said Schuyler. "Whatever you say." Irritation had set in; he felt as some ancient explorer must have, leading his helmeted and cuirassed band across an unexplored continent and having to deal with every podunk mudhut village between the coast and any El Dorado. Should've brought beads, he thought dourly, and trinkets. That's how you deal with these arch-formal–type minds. Tactics requiring going along with the bombast language, rather than just grabbing someone by the neck and shouting,

Cut the crap, where's the fucking gold? Not that that hadn't worked in the past, when the odds had been better. It was definitely not a smart idea now, though, when there was just him and Endryx, and a mechanical spider to videotape the snot getting beat out of them by a bunch of foul-weather amazons.

AUDIO: The mother superior's voice: "The child awaits."

VIDEO: LONG SHOT, EXTERIOR, space defined by stone walls stretching parallel to meet a third. A garden of snow: shrouded stone forms, visual echo to the low, heavy clouds. REVERSE CUT to CLOSE-UP, THREE-QUARTERS PROFILE of SCHUY-LER. The sky's slow roil mirrored in his pupils, cut by the walls' black shape as he scans across the enclosed area, looking for his son.

AUDIO: Metal on stone, a knife blade's quick scrape. Then a child's voice: "Better with the oil. It sings up into the tang."

VIDEO: LONG SHOT as before. TRACK FORWARD, SCHUYLER's motion as he steps forward, toward the clear, high voice.

AUDIO: A girl's voice, older, but also a child: "You can feel it there, along the edge."

VIDEO: PAN ACROSS one of the garden's high stone shapes, its edge disappearing at the right of the frame, revealing the two children sitting on a flat table-like rock, the smooth surface scraped clear of snow. The boy, profile to the camera, sits cross-legged, leaning intently over an array of bare blades, whetstones and handles of yellowed bone, spread over an oil-stained rag. A knitted skullcap covers his head. The girl, a few years older, dangles her thin legs over the flat rock's edge; her hair, not yet bound in the ritual braids, falls across the rough fabric of her cloak.

TRACK FORWARD to CLOSE-UP of the boy. He holds one of the blades up to his eye to examine it, then, aware of his onlooker, turns his serious, self-composed face to a point just to the side of the camera. PULL BACK to reveal SCHUYLER standing quietly, a couple meters away from them.

AUDIO: SCHUYLER, softly: "Do you know who I am?"

THE CHILD's voice, calm as the small, clear-eyed face: "Why shouldn't I? The thing of light-in-glass that isn't you, but is given your face and name every night, looks just like you. You're my father."

In the empty warehouse, he gazed at the image of the child's face on the screen.
"What did you think?" said the other. "When you saw him?"
He didn't turn toward the voice but went on watching the monitor. "Just a kid," he said after a moment. "She was right. That would've been enough."

VIDEO: LONG SHOT, SCHUYLER facing his son.

The Godfriend child, the girl—Schuyler figured her to be around ten, all coltish limbs under the woven leggings and belted cloak, but with the same level, sizing-up-instantly glance of her elder sisters—started gathering up the half-assembled knives and various sharpening tools.

"Your friend doesn't have to leave," he said to his son Lumen. "It's all right with me if she'd like to stay."

The child's somber gaze swung round from the bright metal disappearing into the cloth folded by the girl's hands. She looked up at him as well. "It's okay," she said, her smile demure over a clever trace element. "I'll be seeing you some other time." The bundled knives vanished under the cloak; she slid from the rock and darted away, the black hair a brief flag through the maze of stones.

Schuyler nodded ruefully. He wondered when they started preparing for it, their inheritance, which included his ritual murder at their hands. Children's hands, he thought bleakly, children when they aim the blow, adults—officially, by their creed—afterward. That's the absolute bottom, he knew. Some part of himself he had forgotten had been lifted by the sight of the two children playing—play appropriate to this zone, he supposed—in this space of snow and rock. He didn't come into contact with children in L.A.; there might not be any in the whole city, as far as he would know. All my buddies, the sprinters, male and female alike; we all live in that sterile bachelor territory, where the whole world ends with your own getting snuffed out on the field. No future, like the song goes; because we didn't bother to make one, didn't cut off the necessary piece and throw it on ahead of ourselves.

And now this, he thought as he gazed at the stones the girl had disappeared among, is what my relationship to the world of children has become. They grow up waiting to kill me; the last little bit of play, before they put away childish things.

"It's not as bad as that."

He pulled himself up from his heart's lightless cellar, and saw his son studying him. He supposed the Godfriends had taught him to speak like that, the formal adult phrasing in a child's high voice. A smart kid, even a prodigy, or as much of one as all that worshipful carrying-on could make him. It didn't strike him as a good thing. "Not as bad as what?" he said after a moment.

"As what you think," said Lumen. The five-year-old's compact body leaned back from the cross-legged perch, small hands resting on the bare stone. He was wrapped in a tunic similar to the girl's, but overlapped and bound with scarlet straps. The edge of the knitted cap was frayed, a curly yarn strand dangling over the unlined brow. "They don't all hate you. And they love Me very much. Some of them, the night before the pilgrimage to L.A., cry very deeply over those long-past events which brought Me into this world, and thus require the ritual of your death. Some regard it as a great tragedy, such as *Wuthering Heights* or *Black Beauty*, or other ancient classics eternally popular with adolescent females, here as elsewhere."

The preternaturally wise face, a Buddha transparency superimposed over the face of a real child, and the oddly cadenced words left Schuyler silent. Like talking to—an alien, he mused. If there were any. Coming in on another world's wavelength. That, according to the Godfriends, would be exactly the case. He had come all this way— counting miles, not the copter's shortcut through the hours of passage—to see a five-year-old, his own son. He had found that much. And what else? he wondered.

"They've got books like that up here?" Schuyler couldn't imagine its being part of the Godfriends' harsh curriculum.

Lumen nodded sagely. "A certain underground exists, as always, with teenage girls. The books are passed down, from generation to generation, in the dorms. This is a tradition of time immemorial."

"Really. No shit." He found himself silent again. Here he had come, here was the child, flesh of his flesh—God to some people—that he'd never seen . . . And what was the point? He shook his head, brushing away a trace of snow that had tangled in his eyebrows. Maybe Cynth— steel-and-ice Cynth—had once gone swoony over some old

Victorian novel. Flashlight under the covers, her teenage heart racing; the image in his mind amazed him. What must she've thought about women who swooned and fainted? Talk about alien wavelengths. But what distance was worth crossing to find *that* out?

"That's not what you came for," said Lumen.

"Cool it with the mind-reading act." This being, perhaps, the conclusive proof that it was his own son before him, and not some ringer or preserved midget: he was already getting annoyed with the kid.

"What mind-reading would be necessary, with a face that you write your every thought upon?"

That mollified him. He could accept that, the kid having a line on him, blood to blood. Brushing aside a fresh dusting of ice crystals on the stone, he sat down beside his son. "Why did I come, then?" he said quietly.

Lumen shrugged. "Many reasons. You have a confused heart. And there is little I can tell you that you would understand . . . at this moment." The grave, small face looked up and regarded him; for a moment Schuyler saw his own face reflected in the dark space at the center of the child's eyes, fringed with soft, animal-like lashes. "But you have nothing to fear. That much you should bear away from this place. The Godfriends—" The child's small hand gestured at the walls and the settlement beyond them. "Their love for Me is conscious; they foresee the results of all their acts. You know little; thus My blessing is on you. Ignorance made possible the New. You won't die in darkness and night of the desert. I ordain otherwise."

Schuyler said nothing. A sadness growing in him would drive him out of the stone garden's peace. For a few more minutes he wanted to remain beside his son. A beautiful child; the thought deepened the sadness. Cynth's child. He could see her face, as if another transparency had been laid over the calm expression. That was the line of her brow, the corner of her mouth, when we were in each other's arms. At that moment, in the tent buried in drifting snow, the child had then been as well. The potential changed to actual. And why wouldn't that have been enough? He sat quietly gazing at the small boy while inside he brought his fists against the wall behind his temples. How much New had to be brought into the world? he wondered fiercely. The child couldn't just be a child—they've got to make him into God? The biggest deal of all. So they could have a five-year-old handing out blessings, like a midget evangelist working tent-show revivals centuries ago. So that he wasn't even a child anymore; they had sold the kid his own line.

They can all go to hell, thought Schuyler grimly. All the Godfriends, except one. Who they probably don't even count as one of themselves anymore, but just keep her around as an object lesson in their nutball theology, the same way they've done me.

Lumen read the anger as easily as his father's other emotions. "You may see her," he said. "You know that, don't you?"

"Sure." Schuyler nodded wearily. "Thou hast ordained it, no doubt."

"I ordain all."

"Whatever." He caught his son's gaze and looked full into the large, light-drawing eyes. "Can you tell what else I'd like about that?"

A second, then the child nodded. "That is my wish also."

Schuyler looked around to where Endryx had stationed herself and her shadow, silently videotaping the first encounter between father and son, God and Father-of-God. He had lost track of her presence completely, lost in his own thoughts and the child's un-childlike words. He'd remembered only when the talk had come round to the second goal of his journey here, seeing Cynth.

Two Godfriend guards appeared, taking positions on either side of Endryx. Another one of my son's parlor tricks, thought Schuyler. Maybe he has a whistle only amazons can hear. Endryx coolly inspected the guard standing closest to her.

"Take the woman and the machine to a warm chamber, where she may wait in comfort." Lumen turned in his cross-legged position and tapped his fingers lightly on Schuyler's forehead. "See that My father is taken to My mother."

The guards stepped back to give Endryx room to turn around, back toward the doorway into the stone garden. She stood still for a moment, then nodded, eyes half-lidded above a thin smile. "That wasn't the deal, Schuyler." The red LED in the shadow's lens turret went dead as she tapped the controls in her forearm.

His spread palms protested his innocence. "Talk to the kid about it. What he says, goes."

"Check." She turned and walked, followed by a retinue of machine and Godfriends.

"Say hello to her for me," called Lumen as Schuyler followed his own guide out of the walled space.

The Godfriend that led him was the oldest one Schuyler had ever seen. Older than the mothers; using as a crutch a spear whose head had been carefully swathed in rags, she silently guided him through the Victoria Base compound and outside the stone walls. A path with markers barely visible above the snow curved around the settlement to what Schuyler first took to be a mound of loose stones piled against the wall. As they neared, Schuyler following behind the old woman's slow trudge, he saw the low doorway and the gray mortar filling the hut's chinks against the wind.

The old woman stood outside, her sharp profile turned away, as he pushed open the unpainted metal door, ducked his head and stepped over the high sill keeping out the drifting snow.

He hadn't known what to expect. The small room he

straightened up in, the ceiling a few hand-widths above his head, held warmth and light. There were lanterns at either end and a softly glowing heater, whose fuel line, he supposed, ran back through the wall into Victoria Base. There was also a table with the usual Godfriend sleeping roll folded neatly beneath it, and on its surface, and in a wooden rack on the wall, lay a neatly ordered array of metal-working tools, gold-beating hammers and the like. There were a few scraps of metal in a tray, but no sign of any ornament that had come from under the tools.

Cynth sat at the table, her hands resting on it, watching him as he looked around the stone hut and its fixtures. He said nothing; the room, and the woman's presence in it, had triggered overlays of memory. There had been the hut back at Eureka Station; he remembered that. They had been together there, a small space bounded by snow. And then—for a moment it slipped away, then he had it firm—the last time he had been at Victoria Base, five years ago. Just before they shipped me off to L.A., he thought. And the last time I spoke with her. Until she came to blow me away.

Cynth broke the silence. "I'd offer you something to drink, or anything like that, but I'm afraid I'm given little provision for hospitality here."

He turned round to her. "Did they tell you I wanted to see you?"

She nodded. "I knew you would. Even if they hadn't told me you were coming to this place." She gestured at the other chair across from her. "At least sit down. You have all the time you want."

When he leaned forward over the table, his own hands a small distance from hers, he saw how much older she looked. Older than even the brief glimpse he'd had of her when she'd thrown the concealing hood back, just before the shot had lifted him and pinned him against the warehouse wall. He imagined the same process had happened to him. Veterans, he thought, of our own little history.

"Are you okay here? I mean, do they treat you all right?" He knew he was repeating the same concern, almost the same question, as from five years ago.

She smiled, the slight lift of one corner of her mouth, as before. "You don't ever have to worry about that, Schuyler." One hand gestured at the small room. "Not plush, but adequate. Face it, we both have lifetime jobs. Sinecures. We worked our way into the religion, and now we're props. There're rituals about the Father-of-God, and ones about the Mother. So I'm taken care of. I get by." She studied him for a moment. "Aren't you scared?"

"Of what?"

"That'd you come walking in here, and I'd finish what I started. Kill you."

It struck him now that he hadn't even thought of it. Any of the metal-working tools in the rack above his head, or just her own hands, would be enough. And I didn't come here for that, he thought. To give her a second chance. There had been no subconscious conniving, he was sure, at his own death. I just knew she wouldn't. That's it; I knew there was no danger.

He shrugged. "I wasn't worried. I just wanted to know why. Why you did it in the first place."

Cynth scanned his face, as if searching for something below the skin. "Don't you know? They took you to see our son, didn't they—and you still don't know?"

Carefully, as though some fragile object hung between them that his own words might shatter, Schuyler said, "You tell me."

"He's not God," said Cynth. "Our son's not God. You saw that, didn't you?"

"I'm not sure what I saw."

"You saw a child, who is very clever and lovely. And he has the knack that all children have for reading people's thoughts from their faces. He just speaks what he sees out loud, instead of staying silent. But he isn't God. He's come to believe he is, because he's surrounded by people who tell him so. They worship him, in their way, and he accepts it as his due. But there was no God born to us."

"You know this?" was all that he could say; she had spoken the shared knowledge between them.

She nodded slowly. "The first time he was at my breast, I knew. Who should know better? The Godfriends are wrong, perhaps they were always wrong. They worship a simple child, who should be just loved instead."

Connections formed in his thoughts, forming a rough skein of reasoning. "So you smuggled yourself down to L.A.," he said finally. "To kill me. And prove what you know about Lumen."

"So I intended. But my hand failed me. The Godfriend theology, as it has incorporated you, believes that you are under the numinous protection for having fathered God. They believe no harm can come to you; your son Lumen sees to that."

"They're not the only ones." Perhaps the root of the religious mania that had taken over the Latin American factory dorms was here. Schuyler could imagine some recent account of the Godfriend religion filtering southward and arriving to burst into full flower with the bio broadcasts, and the subsequent sprints. That's how it works, he thought. The article of faith having a certain life and durability of its own.

"The mock assassination the initiates perform every year—the knives shattered on your chest—is not an expression of hatred of you, for having brought God into the world. It's a ritual affirmation of that God's power, that you can't be hurt. If I had succeeded in killing you, they might have realized the truth. There is no numinous protection over you, because your son is not God."

"Why's that so important? That they know?"

"So that the child will not grow up mad." Cynth leveled her gaze at him. "Even in a madness shared by everyone around him. Better the truth than that."

She was right; he knew that. He could make no reproach, if he had ever intended one, over the attempt at his death. That's how a mother should act, he thought. They get the right, for their children's sake. All acts legal, including murder.

"So why not now?" he said. "I'm here. You've got another chance."

Her eyes regarded him, in them both pity and a cold sternness. "He's your child, as well. It's your duty now."

"To kill myself. Christ."

Cynth shook her head. "That would prove nothing."

"Then what would? I came here—" He swung a hand toward the walls of the hut. "I want to know. You tell me."

Now there was only the sadness in her eyes. For both of them. "I don't know," she said quietly.

Then they sat together in the hut, in an interval of time slowed by memory. Silent; outside snow whitened the sky and every point of land.

The guards took him out to the landing pad first. He sat inside the copter, watching through the ice-streaked glass sphere as Endryx and the spider made their way from the Victoria Base gates to the pad.

"That was some cute trick." Endryx brushed snow from her hair as the door sealed itself shut. The copter's blades *whup-whupp*ed into motion as she flipped switches on the control panel.

Her anger, Schuyler saw, had settled down, become an entry in a personal ledger book. Not enough to interfere with business as usual. "What trick?" His stomach swayed lower in his gut as the copter lifted away from Victoria Base.

"Cutting me out of the scene between you and the

woman. Which is why we came up here in the first place, you know."

He shrugged, there being other things on his mind at the moment. Screw it, he thought. He pointed with his thumb at the shadow folded up and stowed behind the seats. "Why don't you just take your contraption here, and round up Larry Monmouth and all the rest of the crew, and make up the scene? The big confrontation between the hero and the would-be assassin. Then you could have the truth any way you wanted it."

She glanced at him, shook her head in disgust, then pushed the throttle open.

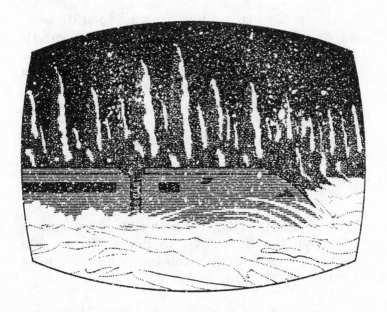

Segment Seven

Working his way through the first six-pack in the case—
the usual preparation for a night's run—Schuyler sat
sprawled in front of his own small video set. The screen a
square blank a few inches from his feet; he regarded it from
a height of miles. Finally he reached down and switched it
on.

For a few minutes he endured the prattle of one of the
indies' color men. Then, sighting over the curve of an
uptilted can, he saw another section of his past begin to
unreel on the screen. No escaping it, he thought as he
slumped lower. Even if I wanted to.

The white landscape, and the train moving across it.

Schuyler tilted his head back, gazing up at the ware-house's ceiling. Screw this—I know what happens next. He got to his feet and loaded the remainder of the case into the sprint car. Maybe there was already some of the bunch out at the Phoenix loading zone. He could hang out with them there until the run. Fuck if I'm going to watch myself get the shaft.

The video, left on, cast its glow across the floor as he pulled the car out and onto the street. The shifting images went through their motions reflected on the metal door when it rattled down into place.

VIDEO: AERIAL SHOT, the train a black line cutting through the snow. CUT to INTERIOR, an unlit compartment. A figure can barely be seen, lying on a narrow bunk.

Dimly, at the edge of sleep, Schuyler felt the train slowing down, preparing to stop. The rhythms that coursed through the steel frame, almost subliminally now, shifted to those that, when he was awake, were confirmed by the drifts of snow nearest to the windows slowing into synch with the horizon. He rolled on his side, eyes opening stiffly, and twitched aside the ragged curtain hanging near his pillow; its scent of stale smoke and dust had entered his dreams more than once.

Through the double insulating plastic layers of the window, barely wider than his face's reflection, he viewed a piece of white landscape. The glare stung his eyes, pupils widened for reception of his dreams' faint signals. They took a few seconds to narrow down to the real world's wavelength. Now where the hell are we? he wondered, pressing his cheek flat against the cold window, trying to look down the length of the track. Probably some other goddamn thing sitting on the line. He knew, even as the thought of another wetblanket or an impediment less animate fell away, that that wasn't the case. Those stops were more sudden, the velocity of the train forcing itself against the brakes, grinding steel against steel. This slowing was a damping of the engine's life, a gradual loss of speed.

He listened for a moment, then turned back to the small window beside him. The snowdrifts were crawling now. Also—to his surprise—there were other features breaking up the white stretching to the horizon. A building of some kind, the snow banked almost to the curved metal roof. As the train chuffed by the structure, not much bigger than one of the freight cars, Schuyler studied the hut's smoke-darkened windows. He pressed his other cheek against the plastic to follow the hut sliding past, and when it was almost gone down the track, spotted a swaddled figure step out into a trail stamped into muddy slush between shoulder-high walls of snow. The eyes above the edge of a knotted rag stared back at him.

The apparition in the snow appalled him. Jesus, thought Schuyler. A thin wedge of alarm crept through the seal of the window, chilling him. Where *is* this? What's between Northernmost Parish and L.A.? Nothing that I ever heard of. A pair of huts, constructed out of the same corrugated sheet metal as the first, crept into view, flanking tarpaulined mounds half-buried in the snow. A brown trail of smoke dirtied the air. The outskirts of Nothing; it made the Parish look like a thriving metropolis. And there're people here, he thought. That was the worst of it.

"What's going on?" Schuyler finished tucking the shirt-tail hanging beneath his jacket into his pants. He had scrambled only halfway into his clothes before heading for the freight car's vantage point.

Cynth spread her hands from beneath her coarse robe. The jeans and military jacket had been exchanged for the fur and leather-strapped gear. "First stop on the line," she said. "I guess. Nobody told me the itinerary."

They leaned out the freight door and looked down the

track. The train inched toward a short loading dock. Beyond
the huts clustered in a semi-circle, the boom of a crane
dangled a blunt hook in midair.

"Doesn't look like much, whatever it is." Cynth lowered
her head and squinted under the haze of brown smoke that
had begun to seep into the freight car. A greasy taste
collected in Schuyler's mouth as he breathed. He looked
around Cynth and saw a group of figures, black against the
snow already recovering the scraped-level loading dock.
More were clambering up the sagging wood framework to
join them in awaiting the train.

The edge of the dock platform drew alongside the freight
car. The train stopped, sighing, and Schuyler found himself
staring into the faces of the small crowd that had gathered
and stood silently waiting. A couple of dozen faces, most of
them muffled like the first one he had seen come out of the
hut on the edge of the settlement. Their eyes, all that he
could see of them, locked onto his with an usettling
voracity. The few uncovered faces were lean, stretched
against the sharply carved bones by the cold, as though
every scrap of flesh beneath the skin had been burned to
keep the heart ticking. Layers of thick clothing bulked the
thin figures. The air's greasy smoke had coated the outer
jackets with a dark film, but Schuyler could still make out
emblems and rank insignia of the Cathedra Novum on the
sleeves.

"Hey, look." Cynth had spotted the grimy shoulder
patches as well. She nodded toward the shabby crowd.
"These are your guys."

Once we were as you are; Schuyler put the words into the
rag-covered mouths. It must be some other Parish or
something, he thought, that I never heard about. More of
that stuff I suppose I should have been paying attention to,
instead of scheming all the time on how to get out. Still, this
was the perfect illustration of why he had been scrabbling so
hard, squeezing the corner of his brow into every corner of

the wall around him, trying to widen it enough to slip
through. The Church had brought these people here; this
was the consequence of faith. Poor fuckers.

Cynth's commanding officer came striding down between
the crates stacked inside the car. "You," jerking a thumb at
Cynth. "Get out of the way. These people got work to do."
The train's crew of freight handlers followed behind her.
"Take your buddy," the thumb swung toward Schuyler,
"for a walk or something. Come on, move it, move it."

Tie-down straps thumped on the car's floor; Schuyler
stepped back to avoid a canvas cover that was whipped off
the pyramided crates. "Okay, we're gone," said Cynth. She
stepped over the foot of space between the freight door's sill
and the loading dock. "Come on, Schuy, before they flatten
you."

The crowd parted to make room for him. "Greetings,
brother," said the closest, nodding slowly as the glazed
eyes wandered back to the train. A silent chorus of nods
bobbed behind the figure. Eesh, thought Schuyler. The
smell of stale sweat permeating synthetic wool clogged his
nose.

"Good-looking bunch, all right." Cynth pulled the edge
of her robe away from the soiled mitten of a pre-teenage
girl. The thin face gaped up at the amazonian figure.

Several of the other pasengers had gotten out of the cars
farther down the platform. They milled about in a tight
clump, or stood motionless, gazing uncomfortably across
the gap—wider than mere distance—between themselves
and the settlement residents.

Schuyler spotted Bischofsky, glum with his beard lowered against his collar. "What's this place?" said Schuyler,
walking up to him. "Looks like hell."

"You might be right about that." Bischofsky gazed
around at the silent figures. "Actually, it's Eureka Station—
if there's a difference. It's another Church dig. Look over
there." He pointed to the crane beyond the circle of huts.

From the platform's angle a pit was visible, with a broken spire rising from stone ruins in the middle. A small bulldozer and other pieces of equipment sat half-buried in snow on an earthen ramp curving down the side of the hole. "One of the research teams came across it six or seven years ago. It's not much to look at, but it's supposedly important. Historically, that is; some indication that it was the original cathedral before it was abandoned and the bishopric moved to Northernmost Parish. The Church wanted me to come out here a while back and look at some window the excavation crew found, but I was able to date the pieces of glass they sent me. It was no big deal, just a fairly late copy of a European original, so they sold the whole schmear off to a museum back East and I didn't have to come out here after all. Thank God."

"This is the crew?" Schuyler tilted his head toward the silent crowd.

"Archaeologists all. Of a sort. Plus the usual support personnel. It's not one of the Cathedra Novum's bigger operations."

"I'll say. Look at this devolved bunch."

"You'd get that way, too, if you were here for five years at a stretch."

"What?"

Bischofsky nodded. "That's how often they bring in supplies." He pointed to the crates stacking up on the platform, the handlers quickly jostling them out of the freight cars. The crowd looked at the jumbled cartons with a palpable air of disappointment, as if growing aware that their deliverance wasn't included in the shipment. "Plus you might not even get rotated out of here after five years. That'd get you down, I think."

Jeez, thought Schuyler. Five years. Five years *here*. Northernmost Parish would be better by far. He watched as a half dozen of the ragged figures, standing separate from the rest of the settlement's inhabitants, and with bulging duffel bags slumped against their feet, handed their papers to the Church official in charge. With the crisp authority of the distant headquarters, he checked names off his clipboard. One by one, moving in the slow trance walk of dreams, the figures picked up their bags and shuffled into the train. That does it, resolved Schuyler. I hit L.A. and it's adiós, Church. Why wait for them to jerk you around like these poor suckers, such jerking around being inevitable, he knew—the nature of the beast.

The lucky few, the exiles returning, having been loaded aboard, the Cathedra Novum official followed them inside, then emerged a bare minute later. Shrieking profanities trailed after him, growing louder until the woman's voice emerged into the open. Lina, her arms held by two Church guards so that her feet treadmilled furiously above the platform, went on cursing the official. The other passengers standing farther down the dock, and the dull faces of the settlement residents, turned toward the screeching. A canvas carryall, Lina's, popped out of the train's door and landed beside her. The two guards let go of her, which allowed her to plant one of her small, rock-like fists in the official's chest. He fended her off with his clipboard until the guards repinioned her.

"You son of a bitch!" The guards' grip lowered her fierce glare to the level of her shoulders. "What the fuck do you expect me to do in a shitpile like this?"

The Church official backed away, raising his hands. "Hey. Don't look at me. This is what your transfer was for. You work it out with the settlement boss what you're gonna do here. There should be an opening for potscrubber in the communal kitchen that your aptitude scales match you up for—we're rotating the old one back to the Parish." A certain malice shaded his words, no voke to keep the proper bureaucratic tone. She had made herself thoroughly disliked in the course of the train's journey; Schuyler watched as the official laid the hard outlines of reality on her. One of the pleasures of the job, he supposed.

Lina's eyes swept across the platform like a marksman's and spotted Bischofsky. She struggled harder against the guards, the spittle of her words falling to ice on the snow-covered planks. "You fucker! You did it! You made 'em put me here—so you could get rid of me! You and your goddamn faggoty priests." Tears now. "If you think you're going off to L.A. without me . . . You just wait. You just wait and see. I'll get there. You aren't getting rid of me." The guards lowered her; she collapsed into a sobbing heap, but with enough venom left to take a random punch at the shin of one of them, before lapsing into a panting, unseeing stare at the patch of dock just under her red-rimmed eyes.

Schuyler turned to look at the effect the scene had had on Bischofsky. The older man's face had turned ashen. In grim silence he watched his ex-wife's weeping. He didn't do it, thought Schuyler. He didn't pull any strings to get her put here. If any strings were pulled, they were pulled behind his back. That was it; that was why the Church let her wangle her way aboard the train in the first place. So they could dump her off here and let Bischofsky get on with his work. What he wouldn't do for himself—prune his life, cutting away the parasites sapping his energy—the Church would. It was all for the Church's glory, of course; Schuyler knew that. The stained glass was what mattered, not the hand working on them.

He wondered how many others were here for the same purpose. Schuyler looked across the gray, huddled figures. The excavation in the distance had a useless, unworked-on look, a mere excuse. Maybe they were all in the way, he thought. Attached to someone of more value, who could be used. And you had to have a place to put them. When you were of no value, this was where you wound up. Or someplace like it.

Bischofsky turned away, his shoulders hunched as he

looked down the steel rails cutting through the white fields. He knows it, too, thought Schuyler. That they've intervened in his behalf; he's become an object to be managed. The hand of God, as the Church likes to think of itself.

"Schuyler. There you are—I've been looking all over the train for you."

He heard his name, turned and saw the Church official with the clipboard striding towards him.

"Good; you're already off the train." The official made a notation on the clipboard. "Got your stuff? That's your bag over there, I think."

Schuyler stared at him. "What're you talking about?"

"You're here." The clipboard gestured at the metal huts. "This is it."

He felt as if things were sliding away from him. The train, the platform and the people on it were still there, but somehow blurred, as if they were hitting some velocity that he couldn't match. "I don't know what you're saying."

The official patiently turned the board around for him to see. The top sheet he recognized as a duplicate of his transfer papers. "Right there," said the official. "Eureka Station. Didn't you read the code before we left the Parish?"

The line of numbers under the official's finger danced before Schuyler's eyes. "You don't understand," he said, looking up. "I'm going to L.A."

Pity softened the official's face. "Did they tell you that?"

"Sure. Of course. They said—" He felt a hollow open from his throat to the base of his stomach, his heart falling through the gaping space. *Next train south. Pack your stuff; you're on the next train south.* That's a good one, he thought. That's real good. The full savor of it curled bitterly under his tongue. This was certainly south of where he'd started from, but being under the same weathermod zone, who could tell? Lembert and the rest of them were probably still laughing about it back at the Parish headquarters.

"What's the deal?"

Bischofsky was at his side; Schuyler was dimly aware of the other's presence. "I'm off the train," he said, somewhat dazed. "They're putting me off the train here." He looked around at the gray, haunted-eyed figures and the half-buried shacks. He wouldn't need five years to commit them to memory; every detail was already burned in like a high-contrast photo transparency, complete black against dead white.

"The fuck they are." A few yards away, Lina looked up at the sound of her ex-husband's voice. She sniffed and smeared the tears around on her face with the heel of her hand.

"Please, Mr. Bischofsky. It doesn't concern you." The official's voice signaled deferential politeness, the tilt of the head a semaphore of helplessness against the common enemy, the powers that shuffled people about on the face of the earth. "Why don't you go back on the train, sir? We'll be pulling out soon."

"No." His brow wrinkled into a scowl. "You're handing this guy a raw deal." He shouted around the official to the freight handlers. "Hey! Put this guy's bag back on board."

"Dolph—" Schuyler held up his hand. "It's okay, man. Really. I knew this was going to happen. I knew it all along."

"Shut up; you're in shock." The bear-like figure's anger was widening, taking in everyone before it. "I told you to put that bag back on the train." The handlers froze in place, staring at him.

"There's nothing I can do," pleaded the official. He turned the clipboard around like an inscribed shield. "It's the orders, Mr. Bischofsky."

"Yeah, right. Sing me another."

"He can't come with us—"

Bischofsky shook his head. "Then I'm not getting back on the train, either."

"Please—"

"Naw, screw it. This place is fine." He nodded, miming a grimly satisfied survey of the settlement. "Nice and quiet. I can get a lot of work done here." A wave to the freight handlers. "Forget the bag. Start unloading my stuff. Every crate. Everything." The men swung their gaze around to the official, waiting for confirmation.

"Come on, Dolph." Schuyler laid his hand on the other's shoulder. "Don't talk crazy. You can't stay here. Lina's going to be here, man." From the corner of his eye, he saw her watching him, alerted by the mention of her name, a sharp caculation apparent behind the reddened eyes. "You couldn't hide from her in a place this small."

"I know what I'm doing. They can't jack you around like this. And I can work something out with Lina." Bischofsky dropped his voice for the last, aware of her anxious gaze. "You know, try it again. I owe her that much." He turned back to the official. "You can haul all that fancy analysis equipment they've got waiting for me in L.A. up here on your way back. They got a generator or something here, don't they? Sure, look." He pointed to a flickering bulb swaying on a wire at the end of the loading dock. "Just tell them I decided I needed a quiet place to work. I fell in love with the scenic beauty of this place. Tell 'em whatever you want."

"I don't think that's really possible, Mr. Bischofsky."

Schuyler caught a slight motion of the official's other hand, a signal toward the train. "Dolph . . . wait a minute—"

But the other figures, the Church thugs, already surrounded Bischofsky, as if the official's gesture had summoned them up from the ground, a true magician's trick. "Get the fuck away from me," said Bischofsky, annoyed.

The official stepped away, quickly grabbing Schuyler's elbow to hold him back. The thugs' backs blocked his view. All he saw was a quick horizontal jerk of one's elbow, and the gray-bearded face suddenly sinking from view beyond them. The thugs turned around, each holding the doubled-over Bischofsky under the arm and steering him toward the train. Bischofsky's shoes plowed lines through the platform's layer of snow.

"Sorry." A final notation on the clipboard, then the official nodded to him and turned away.

The engine's muttering and clouded sighing grew louder. A final drawing shut of the freight car doors, and the platform was suddenly less crowded, as if one overlay with figures painted on had been removed. Schuyler stood on the platform, the settlement's gray figures—my neighbors, he thought; now I'm one of them—behind him. The train started to move, backing slowly back down the spur to the main line. And from there to L.A.; he watched it until it was past the platform, gathering speed and curving away through the white landscape.

The train's noises were at the edge of the loading dock's silence. Around him he could hear the long-term residents shuffling about, climbing off the platform and heading back to their metal shelters. Lina's tears had dwindled to long, dragging sniffles, muffled sometimes as she drew her sleeve under her nose. I suppose there's somebody in charge, thought Schuyler. He bent down to pick up his bag. Hopefully there is; if these people haven't devolved all the way. That's the first step.

"Yo, Schuyler."

He looked up and saw Cynth. She had a smaller bag, made of skins stitched together, with wide straps for slinging it onto her back. "You're not on the train," he said.

"Good. You caught that." She walked up to him and looked down the track for a moment, then back to him. "I got assigned here. Guard duty. Keep these poor devils from getting ate up." She indicated the last of the residents straggling back to the huts. "Much as they'd like to be."

"For how long? I mean, how long you going to be here?"

She shrugged. "Until I'm not here. The Cathedra Novum isn't the only outfit that operates like that."

Schuyler swung his bag up to his shoulder. "Well," he said simply, "I'm glad you're here."

Bischofsky looked up as Wyre, hands full with two paper sacks against his chest, walked into the hangar space.

"Give me some room there." Wyre nodded toward the low table. Bischofsky leaned forward from his chair and stacked up the spread-out reference books, most of them open with slips of paper stuck between the pages. He set them on the floor as Wyre carefully lowered the bags.

"Where'd you go?"

Wyre had pulled up one of the folding metal chairs and was pulling white plastic cartons out of the sacks. "The Thai place over on La Brea." He lifted one of the carton lids and fragrant steam billowed up. "Where'd you put the plates?"

He glanced over at the video murmuring a few feet away. The indie broadcast was on the screen. "Yeah, right." Wyre nodded as he dug a spoon into a carton's depths. "You come off pretty well in this episode. A regular fightin' hero."

Bischofsky looked at him. "You've seen it already?"

"You don't want to eat that part; they just put those in there to poison the ignorant." He settled back with the loaded plate in his lap. "Yeah, I've poked around a little in Endryx's files. You know, the woman in charge of the whole project. I got a line on her."

The other chewed and swallowed, watching the video. "I don't know about her," he said. "Seemed like she was on some weird kick, the couple of times I talked to her."

Wyre shrugged. "She's a mystic. She's looked at the TV screen so long she's fallen into it."

"Mystic, huh." Bischofsky poked at the food on his plate. "Suppose that's what you think I am. I've been looking at the goddamn window long enough."

"Nah. You're way beyond that." Wyre leaned over the table, searching through the cartons. "You're what they call—a holy fool. That's it."

"Thanks a lot, turkey. What does that make you? You're the clown who helps me with the stupid thing."

"I just like watching the wheels go around." He flashed one of his manic smiles. "In your head."

Bischofsky grunted. His wide shoulders stretched the back of his shirt as he went on eating and watching the intersection of his past with Schuyler's.

VIDEO: LONG SHOT, the dimly-lit interior of a storage shed. The space is roofed with the same curved sheet metal as the Eureka Station huts, but much larger; the windows letting in gray, dust-filtered light are high above the two figures standing with backs to the camera. TRACK FORWARD, slowly; the camera goes farther into the semi-darkness and sees the objects beyond the figures. Haphazard piles of stone and rotting crates, the crudely carved filigree of what might have once been the framework for a stained glass window crumbled beneath one toppled stack. CUT to CLOSE-UP. PROFILE of SCHUYLER. His breath steams in the storehouse's cold. He reaches one gloved hand up and pulls off a scrap of paper stuck to one of the crates. He looks at it and the camera sees that it is data print-out, now water-stained and nearly illegible. The gloved hand crumples it as Schuyler looks around at the other shabby pyramids, nodding as if in weary acknowledgment.

AUDIO: The other figure's voice: "We've kinda gotten behind on our cataloguing." A flat statement, with no trace of apology.

VIDEO: The camera PANS around from SCHUYLER's viewpoint, to MEDIUM SHOT of the other figure: one of the gray Eureka Station residents. The look of madness and isolation, the limitless snow fields stretching behind the eyes, is lessened in him. The sleeve of his heavy coat has an insigniaed armband knotted around it, too soiled now to read. Regardless, it is clear that he is some sort of leader, official or otherwise, of the little community.

AUDIO: SCHUYLER, off camera: "You could say that."

VIDEO: The other nods, his gaze trailing away after some private vision.

AUDIO: SCHUYLER: "Am I supposed to just start in on this mess, or something? Is that why they stationed me here?"

VIDEO: CLOSE-UP of the other's face, the dull eyes turning back to SCHUYLER.

AUDIO: The other's voice, slow links in a chain dragged across the littered floor: "You can do whatever you like. I don't think it matters. The Church hasn't taken anything out of here in ten years or so."

"I knew it," said Schuyler. A rueful smile now. "That's when I knew they'd really screwed me." And as an echo, coming from the monitor screen.

VIDEO: CUT to SCHUYLER, a thin smile cutting the

corner of his mouth, the joke completely appreciated now, as he gazes around the cluttered
storehouse.

AUDIO: "I knew it." SCHUYLER's voice almost
breaks into a laugh. "I knew it from the start."

"You can bunk down with all of us." Asch, Eureka
Station's Church-appointed mayor, took in with a gesture
the interior, muggy with stale sweat, of the communal
living quarters. Most of the settlement's inhabitants were
there, appearing to have always been there through glacial
oozing of time, silently clustered around a muttering
television or, separate from the others, staring vacantly
ahead at a broadcast from some inner channel. The space
had the appearance of a mental hospital's day room shortly
after the dispensing of medications. "Or you can—you
know—find a hut of your own. Outside." His hand
displayed its slow tremor as it pointed to the snow-covered
fields beyond the building's window.

"Thanks," said Schuyler. "I'll probably do that. Find
my own place, that is." No way, he promised himself, am I
moving into this snakepit. These lunatics would have me
mumbling and scratching in a week.

"I spotted a couple of empty ones," said Cynth. She had
finished her initial patrol of the settlement's thermal fences,
and had joined up with Schuyler's introductory tour when
Asch had led him out of the excavation storehouse. "They
looked like they'd do all right."

Asch's sad eyes drifted their gaze over to them. "Most of
us like to be together. All the time. It's not so bad that way.
When you're all together. You don't . . . hear the wind so
much."

"I'll take my chances," said Schuyler.

"You can also just come to the dining hall—over there."
Asch pointed to a group of rows of tables, most with dishes

and moldering food left uncleared on them. "Or you're entitled to draw a ration from the storeroom. If you want to. And take it back to your own hut."

A sudden crashing of metal sounded from beyond a pair of double doors. They swung open, pushed by two of the residents backing out of the building's kitchen. Schuyler caught a glimpse of Lina, eyes squeezed shut in the full fury of her tantrum, hurling a skillet against the racks of pans over the multi-burner oven. A kettle of soup, shiny with grease, overturned and splashed the floor with a torrent of soppy rehydrated vegetables. Another resident—like Asch, not completely submerged under his own mumbling fantasies—retreated with the apron and scrub brushes to which he had apparently attempted to introduce Lina.

"Right." Schuyler began edging toward the exit door. A sudden claustrophobia had gripped him. The vacant faces of the inhabitants swung toward him, the tropism of machines geared to a slow pivot, alerted by the climbing pitch in his voice. "Thanks for showing me around. Appreciate it. I'll come back later and check out the food situation. Okay?"

"Over here," said Cynth quietly. She had him by the arm, pulling him. The sudden enveloping of cold calmed him; he was outside, away from the blank, watching faces. The heavy doors of the settlement's communal building swung shut and sucked tight their thermal seal, holding in the musk and animal heat of the residents huddled together.

"I'm okay," he said. "Don't worry." He leaned forward to ease the blood up into his dizzied skull; deep inhalations of the freezing air, cold fire down into his throat, flushed the rank odor of the Station's community from his nostrils. Straightening up, he looked at Cynth beside him. "Jesus Christ." Shaking his head; that was close, he thought. "Did you *see* those people?" The image came of himself, in—how long? What amount of time was left to him, he wondered—however long it took for the brain to dribble out the ears, huddling cozy in the shared warmth and body odor, one of the group, the only thing private the shards of memory and frayed-stitch fantasy that prompted his mutterings. Good for my soul, as they say; Lembert's words wheedled, the unctuous voice attached, into his thoughts. The Church's only priority. Thanks a lot, he spoke to the distant officials. Your concern for my spiritual well-being is deeply moving.

"They've adjusted," said Cynth. "Come on. Let's go find a hut for you." She stepped down into the narrow trench of a pathway cutting through the snow banks.

"Right. They sure have." As I will, he thought glumly as he followed after her. Which was my problem in the first place; or so Lembert and the other Church officials, in their wisdom, had probably diagnosed. If I had adjusted—adjusted myself, set my will to it, turned the right screws in my head—I'd be sitting in the relative comfort of Northernmost Parish. Instead of freezing my ass off *and* going slowly crazy here. So it comes down to the inevitable missing of what you used to have. He lowered his head, bracing himself against the sharp edges of the ice-bearing wind as he trudged behind Cynth, leaving the settlement's communal warmth behind them.

"Here we go."

He looked up and saw Cynth pushing open the door of one of the small, metal-roofed huts. All dark inside; he peered into the space as she swung the beam of a flashlight about the interior.

Inside, out of the cutting wind, Schuyler looked around; the flashlight, propped against the wall, smeared a wide cone of light across the arched ceiling. "I guess it'll do," he said.

Cynth bent down to inspect the machinery in one corner. After a few minutes of prodding, the coils of a heater worked their way from dull gray to a deep red, heading for an orange glow like the hidden sun. She pulled off her gloves and bathed her hands in the heat, a visible shimmer

from the rust-specked grille. Schuyler watched a small
hillock of ice that had collected under one of the windows
turn shiny and sweat a margin of water, dark against the
floor.

"Seals look okay," said Cynth. She pulled the window
tight, shutting out the cold. "You won't freeze."

Schuyler pulled a chair out from the table in the middle of
the room and sat down. The hut's last occupant had left a
rat's nest of crumpled paper and thin pamphlets scattered
about. He pulled one across the table and saw a cheap, two-
color drawing of something out of the Book of Revelations;
multi-headed Beast and a woman whose jewelled crown and
lewd, half-lidded expression was no doubt meant to suggest
the Whore of Babylon. The picture's ink had faded under a
sweating hand. Schuyler pushed it away; the pamphlet slid
off the table's edge and fluttered to the floor, landing with
the same page showing, the binding permanently creased
open. The thought of some poor sucker staring through the
long nights, while the wind and ice trampled on the metal
roof, depressed him. It might have been some other poor
jerk who had started out for L.A. once. Then you wind up
here and start reading that stuff, he thought, and it's good-
bye. There was probably a stash, a regular library of the
stuff, in the communal building; the Cathedra Novum
would make sure of that. Good-bye to your brain; easy to
get religious in a pit like this. That was where the good-for-
your-soul jazz most likely came in.

The aluminum tubing of the chair creaked as he let his
weight sink through it to the floor and the frozen ground
beneath. He had come to a stop, at last. Even before he had
gotten on the train, back when he had still been in
Northernmost Parish, he had been in motion. Travelling, or
scheming on travelling. Comes to an end here, he told
himself. Dead stop.

He looked up to see Cynth watching him. "What's the
matter?" he said.

"You're fucked up," she said quietly. "You've been staring at that book for about ten minutes now. You're not going to make it."

The information registered as a minor fact in his brain. He made no reply.

"Screw it." She looked around the hut. "I'll move in here with you. There's room enough. And somebody's gotta look after you until you pull yourself together."

Her words puzzled him. "You'll do that?"

"Hey, it's my job. I'm a guard, right? Everybody's welfare is my concern."

He mulled it over. "I thought it would be . . . forbidden or something. I mean, your living in the same place with a male."

She smiled. "You know, I really admire your self-confidence. Even under these circumstances, you're right up there. As if we weren't going to be in this dump for more than ten minutes without climbing all over each other." She shook her head. "Believe me. It's not going to happen."

Schuyler watched her turn and begin fiddling with some other apparatus. A bare bulb overhead flickered yellow as Cynth knocked the butt of a folding screwdriver against a control panel.

"Well," he said. "Welcome home."

She looked around at him, her gaze studying his face for a moment, then went back to the quick, sure motions of her self-appointed task.

Segment Eight

"Sure hope this picks up," said Urbenton. He idly scratched himself as he gazed at the central monitor.

Endryx watched the image of Schuyler trudging through snow. "Hang in there," she said. "You'll get your action."

VIDEO: MEDIUM SHOT, two figures standing talking amid the snowdrifts.

"So what happened to the other guy?" Overnight, a storm had laid a fresh layer of white over the settlement, obliterating the thin paths between the scattered buildings. Schuyler stood knee-deep in the soft fresh snow, a few yards

from the hut nearest—a matter of a hundred meters or so—
to the one in which he and Cynth had settled in a few days
before. From the lay of the railroad tracks, visible now only
as a row of wooden posts marking the steel lines buried
beneath, he assumed that their neighbor was the figure he
had first spotted from the train's window. "The guy who
was in there before us?"

Ruskin, the neighbor—if the word applied to a purely
geographical relationship; watching the man's distant-
focused eyes, Schuyler wasn't sure if any other sense of the
word operated here—scratched through his tangled beard.
His head swiveled from side to side under the hood of his
parka. "Him? He wasn't . . . right. Wasn't right at all.
Just started . . . walking, one day. Looked me right in the
eye, when he went past." One hand raised, patting the air
between them and the snow-covered vistas. "Kept on
walking. Wasn't right."

Keen, thought Schuyler. The other way out. In some
ways preferable; at least it's over quicker. Across the snow
he saw Cynth, the fur-bundled figure black against the
glaring white, returning from her early-morning inspection
of the thermal fences.

" 'S a devil," said Ruskin matter-of-factly.

"Huh?"

The other nodded at the approaching Godfriend. "One of
the devils. The new one. They guard this place. 'Cause they
live here. So they're devils."

He stood silent, working the hinge of the little syllogism
in his mind, complete with its unspoken premise. Easy
enough to work backward to the frowzy-bearded wraith's
whole theology. Gnostics everywhere, thought Schuyler;
this guy and Cynth could actually get along together pretty
well.

That seemed unlikely—Ruskin began retreating toward
his hut as Cynth came closer. He scurried the last few
meters, glancing wide-eyed behind him. The door slammed

shut hard enough to shake loose a drift of snow from the edge of the curved roof.

"How's it going?" Cynth nodded at the silent hut. "Making friends among the natives?"

Schuyler grunted. "Guy's a loon. Deep-frozen loon. Like everybody else here."

She tossed back her hood and scanned across the white field bisected by the train of her footprints. "He thinks I'm a devil. Or something like that."

"True enough."

"They all do. Marr—the 'friend I replaced—told me all about it." She shrugged. "Comes with the territory. It's because I'm at home in this world."

"This place?"

"No, jerk." She swept her gloved hand across the view. "The snow. I could walk from here to Victoria Base, if I wanted to."

He regarded the figure wrapped in fur. "You could do that?"

"Given the supplies—easy. Marr's probably getting close to the Base now."

Schuyler ran off the days in his head since they'd arrived at Eureka Station. How long've I been here? he thought. Already starting to lose track. A bad sign. "So it takes about a week?"

"For me. Longer for you—if you could find the way." Her thin smile was tinted by the cold. "Which is why you ain't going nowhere."

"Hm." Schuyler felt the touch, as if of a fingertip on the exact center of a nerve. She had read the direction of his thoughts. "I got the impression you hated this place, too."

"Yeah, but it's my job to stay here. You can't leave without me to show you the way. So you get to stay here, too."

"That's the shits." As much of an idea as had formed in his mind froze into place. He could see his own tracks

plodding through the wide curve of his veer towards the
horizon. Like that other poor sucker, he thought. That
Laughing Boy next door told me about. Time enough for
that eventually, he decided. He wasn't there yet.

VIDEO: LONG SHOT OF SCHUYLER sitting at the
   table in the metal hut. The wall behind the camera
   is "wild"—a part of the set that can be moved for
   the videotaping—so a distance of miles, the hut a
   narrow dimly lit tunnel, seems to lie between the
   lens and SCHUYLER. The camera slowly TRACKS
   FORWARD, drawing the space into itself and
   annihilating it, until the figure at the table fills the
   frame. HOLD. SCHUYLER, with vague, slow motions, works his way through a scrambled mess on
   an aluminum plate. The stamped sheet-metal
   spoon rises from the congealing food to his
   mouth, and repeats: a machine drawing the last
   reserves of its battery.

The change in SCHUYLER has reached this point.
The unkempt beard of the Eureka Station males—
the personal hygiene of minor-league prophets
whose visions were lost in some internal desert—
straggles over hollowed cheeks. The eyes do not
see what is in front of them, the plate, the
cammed motion of the spoon in the hand, or the
surrounding wall; the eyes are along the slow
search towards that point that those of the long-
time residents have found and locked upon.

The shot HOLDS for a full minute.

AUDIO: Silence, except for the wind sifting frost
   through the hut's spot-welded seams.

VIDEO: Sudden light. The screen bursts to white for a fraction of a second, fading to the red-orange of flames. Schuyler's shadow streams away from the burning glare filling the hut's window.

AUDIO: Explosion, sharp then rumbling down through octaves to match the visual spectrum's shift.

VIDEO: Same CLOSE-UP of SCHUYLER as before. For a moment he takes no notice of the distant explosion and flames that have masked him in shifting color. The spoon continues its upward travel from the plate. Then it stops in mid-circuit. The flame reflected red in the center of SCHUYLER's eye sparks the end of the fuse retracted into the skull. The startle reflex jerks his spine into an animal crouch, the spoon and greasy plate scattering to the floor as he grips the table and snaps his gaze up to the window's square of burning light. PULL BACK and PAN to follow as he runs to the door, the chair falling backward from the table.

CUT to LONG SHOT, SCHUYLER's POV. The expanse of snow is illuminated by the red-orange glare. In the distance, flames wrap the Station's common buildings; the steel framework and jagged sheet metal curl into a darker red at the fire's center. A few shapes with sprawled arms and legs blot the snow, motionless silhouettes.

AUDIO: Another explosion, then "What the hell— What happened?"

VIDEO: CLOSE-UP of CYNTH, stopping breathless after a dead run. The flame light washes across her face, glints into matchheads struck at the center of her eyes. PULL BACK to TWO-SHOT of her and SCHUYLER silhouetted by the burning Station, LOW ANGLE, their shadows striped across the snow and wobbling with the churning flames. SCHUYLER turns his head. CUT to LONG SHOT, SCHUYLER's POV: the neighbor RUSKIN stands frozen in the doorway of the neighboring hut, eyes wide as if gazing upon a long-awaited apocalypse.

AUDIO: SCHUYLER calls: "Come on!" over the snapping of metal twisted in heat and the rush of combusting oxygen to the fire's core.

VIDEO: LONG SHOT, SCHUYLER running after CYNTH, already several yards ahead as she sprints across the snow to the fire. SCHUYLER looks over his shoulder as he runs; CUT to RUSKIN, standing in the doorway of his hut: the transfiguration is complete. He doesn't move.

CUT to MEDIUM SHOT, SCHUYLER stops, breathless, and looks down at a dark shape in the snow. CUT to CLOSE-UP of what he sees: a body, arms flung wide, fills the frame. The body is charred black, recognizable as human only by the cross-like shape against the snow. Its chest is broken open, blood steaming into the trench dug by the impact against the ground.

AUDIO: The hiss of the blood's heat melting the snow. CYNTH shouts: "You can't do anything for that one!" The roar of the flames jumps decibels louder as

VIDEO: CUT to MEDIUM SHOT, a wall of flames. The distorted outlines of the common buildings' rooms collapse in on themselves, an X-ray plate crumpling under a torch. Two silhouettes, edges blurred as though the fire behind had frayed the edges of paper cutouts. The figures crouch, shielding themselves from the billowing heat. CUT to MEDIUM SHOT: CYNTH unloads a body from her shoulder. It sprawls in the slush of melted snow between her and SCHUYLER, the charred arms folding like hinged sticks onto the ribs. CUT to CLOSE-UP of CYNTH as she kneels down, her face shining with sweat beneath streaks of black, all lit with dancing red-orange light. She looks up from the body.

AUDIO: "This one—" starts CYNTH. A mewling groan interrupts.

VIDEO: The body arches, spine contracting into a bow, then collapses again. CYNTH leans close, an inch above the ruined face, as if listening for some secret. Then she stands up, as another explosion in the center of the buildings sends a ball of churning orange into the night sky. SCHUYLER pulls CYNTH back from the burning edge.

AUDIO: SCHUYLER's voice barely heard above the wind feeding the fire and the clash of metal falling: "—no use—"

VIDEO: PULL BACK as the two figures retreat. They stop, facing the flames, and the camera PULLS BACK farther to reveal the dark forms, once human, sprawled in the snow around them. Shallow troughs trace where the bodies were pulled from the fire.

CUT to LONG SHOT, the same scene. Hours have passed; the snow fields are gun-metal blue in the first gray light seeping across the blackened debris. Thin lines of smoke trail from the heat-warped steel framework. The metal panels, torn by explosions, saw their jagged teeth through ash-muddied slush. The corpses are arranged in more decorous poses, limbs straightened, a rank of coal-carved figures in a collective white shroud. SCHUYLER stands at their head, gazing off-camera toward the horizon, his collar turned up against the chill wind now that the fire's heat is only enough to melt ice crystals drifting onto the sooty metal.

AUDIO: Silence, then CYNTH's voice: "One missing."

VIDEO: CUT to MEDIUM SHOT, SCHUYLER's POV. CYNTH walks along the black row, ticking them off on a smudged sheet of paper. The faces, or what is left of them, stare up at the sky.

He watched the cool, rational inventory, the counting of the dead. Another world, of ashes cooling in the snow, had appeared from underneath the fire, after the flames had burned through their fuel. Cynth's actions, now as when the flames had been pillaring up into the night sky, were entirely appropriate, he knew. This is what you do, he thought, regarding the Godfriend as she compared the list on her paper to the equally static column laid out on the snow. You calmly add up the figures.

"I still get one missing," said Cynth. She reached the

end of the corpse row nearest to where he stood and looked up from the paper she held. The white was smudged with dark ash from her unwashed hands.

"Did you count me?" said Schuyler. His own manner of calm had settled into his chest; the thought of being included in her calculations—numbered among the dead, he thought, but with an asterisk beside his name—would have been disquieting otherwise. Now it's just business as usual. Especially for a Godfriend, he considered abstractedly; in a theology like that, all deaths would be considered business as usual.

"Sure. Of course." Cynth folded the scrap of paper and tucked it with the pencil into one of the pouches underneath the cloak. She set her hands on her hips and gazed at the charred wreckage of the common buildings, viewing with no enthusiasm the prospect of rooting through the ashes and twisted metal struts for the missing corpse.

"What about what's-his-face. Our neighbor, back out in his hut." That fucker, thought Schuyler. Chicken-shit bastard. The blistered skin along his forearms stung with a surge of angry blood beneath. The thought of Ruskin cowering out there in the cold, nose deep in his sweaty Bible while he waited for a seven-crowned beast to swarm over the horizon like the rubber special effects in an ancient Japanese monster flick, while he and Cynth were getting their eyebrows singed away—that pissed him off.

"Oh, yeah, I got him. Still one short."

"Any idea who?"

"Must be one of the women," said Cynth. She pointed down the silent line. "I'm pretty sure these were all males. And those are the females at the other end. And that's where we're missing one."

They went back into the burned-out buildings. The surrounding cold had leached out more residual heat, so that metal struts and blackened sheet metal impossible to touch before could be pulled away now. They found nothing and

still went on looking, the gray plumes of their breath
chilling with the sweat beading on their foreheads. It's her
job, thought Schuyler as he tugged at a blackened mass of
roof insulation. That's why she can't quit until they're all
accounted for. She was supposed to be guarding the place,
and now they're all dead; whose fault is that? Hers, by
military standards. She was on duty when it happened.
Whatever happened, he thought. They had been too busy
poking about for corpses to determine the cause of the
explosions and the fire.

"Screw this," he announced, straightening up against a
locked-in crick in his lower back. He let the girder end fall
with a muffled whump against the snow. "What's the
point?" he said to Cynth when she turned around from
pulling out a melted bale of plastic-coated cables. "I mean,
if there's somebody buried under all this, what's the point of
digging them out just so we can bury them somewhere
else?"

She looked at him for only a second before going back to
her task. "Knock off, then," she said. "Take a breather."

Thanks, commandant, he thought, stalking out of the
gray, stamped-down slush and out to the clean snow.
Fuckin' drafted. Again. The physical exertion of searching
through the rubble, after the debilitating, muscle-dwindling
months of canned rations and brooding cooped-up in the
tiny spaces of the Station's narrow world, had tired him,
made him irritable. And Cynth's preoccupation about
accounting for all of the Station's residents; morbid's not the
word for it, he thought. Which might be funny in other
circumstances. Or other places—L.A., for instance. Did the
destruction of the Station release Cynth from her duty to
guard it? He pondered that, hoping that religion wouldn't
outweigh practicality. Like it usually does, he thought. A
sudden tug at his stomach to the base of his throat made him
realize how hungry he was. Adrenaline and sheer work, a
long siege of both, from when he had first run out into the

illuminated night from his hut, had eaten up the thin reserve trickling into his blood sugar. Enough with the stiffs, already; he almost said it out loud to the toiling, bent-over back of the Godfriend. Other questions—way beyond how the damn fire got started in the first place—had to be addressed. Like surviving long enough to get out of here.

He walked farther away from the rubble, toward the remains of the fuel shed. The destruction zone included this as well; a good case could be made, Schuyler noted, that the fire had started here. Only a few scraps of splintered wood, radiating in a far-flung star, surrounded the ruptured tanks. And not much of those, he saw; the explosions that had ripped them open had thrown pieces like hot shrapnel all over the landscape. From here, the bulk storage area—five years' worth of volatile propane and hydrogen loaded into the tanks taller than a man—to the utility tanks in the common buildings. Schuyler stood and swung his gaze around, tracing the path carved through melted and refrozen ice.

Knowing where it started didn't help much, he decided. The immediate problem—Cynth's continuing search aside—was to see how much, if any, fuel was left, uncombusted by the explosions and the fierce heat. He worked his way into the thick of the deformed metal, squeezing between the knife-edge teeth of the ruptured tanks. There could be some small tanks buried beneath; he seemed to recall seeing them on the introductory tour that the now-dead Asch had given him.

He poked about and found nothing. Lifting a saw-edged sheet, he saw only more blackened metal beneath. For a moment he hesitated before dropping it, letting the weariness drain along his straightened arms. Then he heard the sound of breathing.

"Cynth!" She looked up from her own search, hearing in his voice the reason for his shout. Instanly, she had scrambled out of the common buildings' rubble and was running toward him with her quick, distance-eating strides.

Cynth grabbed the other edge of the sheet metal he was holding, bent down and listened. The sound barely perceptible from beneath was rapid and shallow, a fluttering of breath at the edge of stopping. Without speaking, they strained against the metal, prying it away and toppling it aside from the mound of the fuel shed's wreckage. Cynth climbed down into the dark space revealed, a narrow triangle formed of the shed's steel struts wedged together. "I got her," called Cynth. "Give me a hand."

Schuyler kneeled down. A slight figure emerged, as though rising from a tomb, lifted by Cynth from below. He slipped his hands under the figure's arms and stood up to raise it further. A small animal moan escaped as the head lolled against his chest. Raw pink tissue showed beneath one side of the blackened face; the hair had been burnt away from the skull. A nauseating smell of cooked meat curled in Schuyler's nostrils.

Lina, thought Schuyler as he looked down at the face against his chest. The open, bloodless mouth sucked in its little gulps of air. Of all of them . . . she'd be the one. I should've known it.

"Come on." Cynth pulled herself out of the pit and grabbed Lina's legs, lifting her horizontal between them. "Let's get her over to the med unit."

The Station's minuscule medical unit, separate from the rest, had been the only part of the common buildings to escape major damage. That had struck Schuyler as something of an irony, all the potential patients being too dead to make use of it. Better if it'd been a morgue, he had thought. More use for that. Now he held the unconscious Lina upright—a tiny, bird-like weight, as though the fire had hollowed her bones—as Cynth switched on the Station's medex capsule. The function lights came on in a row underneath her hand, the whir of the autonomic equipment switching to life. Efficiently, with the small knife from her belt, Cynth stripped off the charred rags from the scalded body, then helped Schuyler lift the breastless, childlike body up into the capsule's hatch. The pallet retracted into the cylinder, the door closing after it, sealing tight.

Cynth went around the side of the capsule and peered in through the circular observation port. Schuyler looked over her shoulder and saw the gentle machinery inside moving over the damaged figure, cleansing and sterlizing the pink tissue exposed when the dirt and charred skin were removed. "She was lucky," said Cynth, tapping the round glass.

"What?"

"When the first fuel tank exploded it split down a seam opposite from her. The metal flattened out like wings and then must've jammed up against the shed's outer wall, with her between. So she was shielded—to some degree—from the rest of the explosions. Otherwise there wouldn't be a scrap of her left."

The medex capsule's smell of disinfectant had replaced the stench of cooked meat, to Schuyler's relief. "That's luck, all right. I guess."

"The only question is—" said Cynth, watching the capsule's operation, "what was she doing in the fuel shed in the first place?"

"Christ, who knows?" Back on the train, Bischofsky had related all sorts of stories about his ex-wife's furtive, rat-like behavior, an account more in the manner of a psych ward's diagnosis than a legal indictment. The list had included hiding things in tiny crevices of their apartment back at Northernmost Parish: odd things, scraps of foil or the tiny sparkling wafer from the inside of a broken digital watch. Rat treasures, a tiny secretive mind at work, busily poking about the corners of the rooms late at night while Bischofsky had lain on his bed staring at the dark ceiling and listening to his wife scurry about on her self-appointed errands. "Like Gregor Samsa in reverse," he had described it to Schuyler. "You know, in the Kafka story—very astute for a bachelor to have written—where the person turns into a giant cockroach? Only in my case, the giant cockroach had the run of the apartment while the normal people hid out in the bedroom." Bischofsky had tolerated it until the smell of hidden scraps of food rotting had finally stirred him to seek psychiatric help for Lina; which course of action had eventually ended the marriage. But not the relationship, thought Schuyler as he gazed at the medex capsule. Not even yet.

"Anyway," he said, "there's no way of finding out."

"These things can be monitored," said Cynth. "Listen to this." She stepped over to the capsule's control panel and flipped a switch under the rows of blinking lights. An appalling sound of ragged breathing, a labored intake and expulsion of air, pulsed through the med unit.

Schuyler looked up, his spine contracting underneath the sound, until he spotted the speaker mounted in the corner of the wall and ceiling.

"It's slower now. The breathing, I mean." Cynth studied the panel's gauges. "The medication's in her bloodstream."

"Great. So who wants to listen to it? Jesus." Schuyler winced, as the breathing sound dragged on.

Cynth pulled a manual from a chrome rack under the panel. "These things have their uses," she said, flipping through the pages. "A little pentothal mixed into the medication flow, and we'll have her singing opera arias."

"Are you kidding? She's out of it. And this thing's programmed to keep her this way. Besides, she can barely breathe, let alone talk."

"She doesn't have to be awake for this." Cynth compared the gauges with a diagram in the manual. "And we only need to pick up a subvoke." She twisted a knob, turning up the gain, and the rasping breaths became thunder beating down from above.

"You know how to work this?" He shouted over the noise from the speaker.

"Standard equipment back at Victoria Base. Somebody

gets hurt bad on a hunt or something, you have to be able to find out what happened to her. This is how you do it."

Schuyler backed away toward the med unit's door. "Whatever you want," he said. "Let me know when you're done." He fled out into the chill, silent air outside.

"Hey, Schuy, catch this." A draft of freezing wind came with Cynth into the hut. Schuyler had spent the last couple of hours inventorying the meager food on hand, the remains of the last draw he had made on the Station's supplies. There wasn't much; he had been about due to restock for himself and Cynth. He looked around from the small pile in the center of the floor and saw Cynth holding out a cassette recorder, marked with the broad red cross of the med unit.

"What's that?" he said. "You got what you wanted?"

"Take a listen." She set the recorder on the table and switched it on, running it ahead to a specific number on the counter.

It took a moment for him to make out the soft, aspirated whisper. Then he recognized it as a ghost of Lina's constant whine. Under the drugs the words rambled and oozed along, free of any connection to each other. This is the pure thing, thought Schuyler as the wheedling voice went on. The unadulterated Lina, with the restraining top levels of the brain removed at last, that had always kept her acting at least marginally human. And this is why Bischofsky split on her; because he saw down to this level at last. The always-hungry little animal.

"Here it comes," said Cynth. "This is the part." She turned up the recorder's volume.

Schuyler bent closer to the machine, his head nearly touching Cynth's over the table. He listened, and heard. The words coalesced into pieces, and then whole sentences. The top of her memory, thought Schuyler. Just before the explosion. The whispered voice went on, until Cynth switched off the recorder.

He looked up at her. "She did it," he said. That's what the words on tape had meant. No confession; he never would've expected that of Lina. Just the last installment of her grievance against the world. "She sabotaged the fuel system. And then it blew up on her."

Cynth nodded. "You heard it too. I guess she thought the stuff would just leak out into the snow or something. And then the Cathedra Novum would have to shut down the Station, and take everybody out of here." The last was close to verbatim from the tape.

Schuyler finished the duet, words that the burned figure in the med capsule hadn't spoken, but which they both knew anyway. "And they'd take her to L.A. So she could latch on to Bischofsky again." Christ. What a fucked-up plan. He looked down at the silent recorder. The plan, he could see, was a micro-representation of Lina's mind. Fucked in the planning, and fucked in the execution of the plan. Some loon who couldn't even handle scraping out pots in the station's communal kitchen, fooling around with high-volatile fuel. And even if she had succeeded in leaking it all out into the snow, what was the point? The Station didn't have a radio or any other means of contacting the outside. Maybe, he thought, Cynth could have hiked out to the Victoria Base and contacted the Cathedra Novum authorities from there. But everybody would have been frozen stiff in their tracks before any kind of help could have arrived. Jesus Christ, he thought, shaking his head in grim wonderment. All that malice and incompetence canned in the medex capusle, medication and anesthetics dribbling into the bloodstream. The incompetence had not, as he remembered Bischofsky hoping back on the train, kept Lina from causing major damage. A couple of dozen people were dead because of her. And us? Me and Cynth? The thought was tagged to the rest, the end of a logical string. Remains to be seen.

"We should go unplug her," he said. "Stupid bitch."

Cynth's thin smile, wearier, appeared. "Should," she agreed. "But I can't let you."

He'd expected that. "Fine. That's your duty, all right. How much farther than that does it go?"

"What do you mean?"

"Now do we start hiking out of here?"

She nodded. "Now we start."

Schuyler exhaled, a knot unlocking in his chest. At last, he thought. He said, "All the way to Victoria Base?"

Cynth glanced at the small pile of supplies in the middle of the floor, then back to him. The smile had drained away, leaving the sadness in her eyes. Sadness that was readable even before she spoke. "As far as we get," she said.

VIDEO: MEDIUM SHOT, SCHUYLER and CYNTH stand in front of the Station's ruins. Snow has almost buried the blackened girders; it continues to fall, drifting onto the two figures' shoulders. SCHUYLER hoists a bulky pack up behind him, and snugs the straps tight across his chest, compressing the insulated jacket beneath. CYNTH is already prepared for travel, her fur wrappings covering another bundle of supplies.

AUDIO: CYNTH: "You talked to Ruskin?"

"Yeah," replies SCHUYLER. "He's gonna stick it out right here. And freeze to death."

"I didn't think he'd come along."

"You know," says SCHUYLER, "he's got a little bit of food cached up there. What's the point of his sitting on them?"

"Forget it." An incongruous laugh in CYNTH's voice. "It wouldn't make that much difference."

VIDEO: CLOSE-UP, SCHUYLER's profile as he turns

away to look at something. The camera's focus shifts into LONG SHOT of the med unit at the edge of the burnt-out buildings.

AUDIO: "How's the patient?" asks SCHUYLER.

"Fine." CYNTH's calm, dispassionate voice. "The medex brought her down to deep process. Her metabolism's running at about a tenth normal. She can go a long time that way."

"She'll outlive us all, won't she? Maybe even long enough for the Church to come by and find out what happened. Take her back to a hospital and put her back together."

"That's the breaks."

Silence.

VIDEO: MEDIUM SHOT, the two figures turn and start walking. PULL BACK until they are two black shapes against the white expanse. The camera TRACKS BACK even farther, the figures blurred by the falling snow. LIFT to AERIAL SHOT, higher and higher, two lines of foot tracks trailing away from the black wreckage, following them until they are lost somewhere below.

"That wasn't too bad," said Urbenton. "A little action, at any rate. But you didn't make enough of the fire."

Endryx was already at the door, letting out the shadow to do the errand she had programmed for it. On the monitors behind Urbenton, the sprinters were approaching the fire zone. "Maybe," she said, "I'm interested in a different kind of action."

When the night's run was over, and he was back in L.A. at last, he didn't try to sleep. With after-images of bursting fire seared into his retinas, Schuyler walked instead through the steel-colored streets, quiet and empty, to Bischofsky's studio. He knew the lights would be on, the bright day of some synthesized latitude and time streaming through the rose window's simulation, at whatever arrangement of color and symbol mirrored Bischofsky's thoughts. And the gray bear would be trudging on through his own never-ending shift, on a field transfixed by light fiercer in its way than fire.

The interior of the studio was even brighter than before. Schuyler's eyes took a moment to adjust from the pre-dawn outside. Standing in the hangar's doorway, he looked across the high-ceilinged space to the rose window simulation. There were more blank spaces in the framework than before: a row of saints silhouetted in white light gazed up at the empty form of a cross, the vacant center of the window. Reds and blues picked out the circumference and the straight edges of shapes; there were now, Schuyler saw, more blank spaces than pieces of glass filtering the light from behind.

Bischofsky sat behind the terminal, hunched forward with folded arms braced against his legs. Reference books, folded open, were stacked around his chair. He looked around and spotted Schuyler. "How's it going?" he asked, his voice heavy with fatigue.

"It's all right." He came over and stood by Bischofsky. A dark sweat stain pasted the other's shirt to his spine. "There's been some stuff happening."

"I heard." Bischofsky nodded. "Wyre told me. You should take a walk, Schuy. Before you get killed, too."

"Suppose so. There aren't many of us left. Though some people think I'm just going to slide through without a scratch."

"You making book on this or something?" Bischofsky managed a smile. "I don't think you're going to find a lot of smart money backing immortality."

"I got lucky. I got the numinous protection."

Bischofsky listened to Schuyler's summary of what Endryx had told him. The gray head nodded at the description of the new religious passion in the factory dorms.

"So what do you think of that?"

Bischofsky shrugged. "I don't criticize other people's ideas. I got enough crazy ones of my own." He glanced up at the rose window, then back to Schuyler. "People want to make you part of their religion, I suppose they got a right. You're a public figure now."

"And numinous protection?"

Another shrug. "Maybe they're on to something. Who knows."

"Too bad for me if they're wrong," said Schuyler. "They can go back to the old-time religion, and I'll be charcoal on the sand."

"What if they're right?" The sharp point of Bischofsky's gaze flashed from underneath the tangled eyebrows. "Stranger things have happened. You should've gotten something for all the shit you went through."

Schuyler turned that one over in his mind. *What did I go through?* He couldn't think of anything special. Or anything, at least, that could be called *through*. There were burn marks on the desert floor, sand fused smooth, from where the small debris of the struck sprinter cars had been hauled away. The sprinters that he had known, talked and drank with, that those black circles memorialized—they could be said to be through with the process, only the details of which had been different for him. Where was their numinous protection? If you're lucky enough—if luck was the word—to have God for a kid, then you get a free pass? "Is that how it works?" he mused half-aloud.

Bischofsky read the thoughts behind Schuyler's face. "You can't tell how it works," he said, quietly and urgently. "It's something to do with light. It's like the world is all heavy and dark, everything made out of iron and lead. And if something outside the world comes into it, *it can't be made of the same stuff.* It has to be transparent and weightless, a different order of being. Light can penetrate the world because it changes nothing; everything penetrates it. For it to be different, for it to have mass and power, would be for light to take on the nature of iron and lead. It would no longer be different; it would be the same as the world and the things in it.''

Nodding, Schuyler bent close to the other's whisper, as though some secret were being protected from those who would overhear.

"And if that light," Bischofsky went on, "wants to accomplish something in this world, it can only do it with the smallest touches. Intangible pressures, tiny blows that can't be felt. Or the tool itself would be shattered, would be destroyed, become its opposite. The ways are not so much mysterious, as the means are below our levels of perception. We can't see the transparent. If we do see it, then we haven't seen it. And the blows that shape us can't be felt.'' Bischofsky's voice went back to a normal level. "So numinous protection—why not. If that's how it works, so be it.''

"Maybe so." Schuyler straightened up. He traced the path of color and full-spectrum white from the rose window to the figure seated behind the terminal. The gray, combed-back strands tangling at the frayed collar took on a blurred mirroring of the window's pattern that slid across Bischofsky's face when he looked up. A premonition fell inside Schuyler, a smooth small stone rolling into its predestined niche. Looking down at the gray-bearded profile, he realized what had hurried Bischosky's words, had made time a sudden and sharp-pointed factor.

They were silent for a few minutes, letting the morning advance outside. "I'll catch you later," Schuyler said finally, laying his hand on the other's shoulder.

Bischofsky nodded, gazing unseeingly at some point
between himself and the window.

VIDEO: LONG SHOT, INTERIOR, SCHUYLER and
BISCHOSKY, beyond them, the bright window.
The younger man, standing, leans over the older,
listening to what is spoken.

AUDIO: (The edge of a distant whisper,
indecipherable.)

Alone in Urbenton's office—Urbenton himself having left
to catch a little sleep after another hot night editing the
suddenly blood-charged sprint footage—Endryx peered
closer at the central monitor. She had watched the live feed
from Bischofsky's studio, and had now run the same small
segment of tape from it over the playback heads four or five
times.
"The old fox," she said aloud as she watched Bischofsky
once again, his face intent as he spoke close to Schuyler's
ear. She had assumed that, in his abstracted obsessive
manner, Bischofsky had forgotten about the shadow being
stationed in the studio—he had always been oblivious to it
before, after it had picked its way in and taken its post. And
Schuyler had appeared not to have spotted it, hidden in the
dark farther into the hangar; not once in this segment had his
eyes turned full upon the long-distance lens.
Yet even with the gain turned all the way up, she couldn't
make out the words Bischofsky had whispered to Schuyler;
only the background tape hiss sounded from the speakers.
"You can't hear what he said." A voice came from
behind her. "The mike didn't pick it up."
She turned, unsurprised, and saw Wyre at the edge of the
glow cast by the monitor. He had made no sound coming
into the studio; that also was no surprise.
"You show up everywhere," she said. "Don't you?"

Wyre shrugged as he walked around the end of the desk. "When you put in the locks," he said, "you get to keep a key. Everybody knows that—at least in L.A." He sat down in Urbenton's chair and ran his hand over the monitor controls. The screens behind him bloomed into light as he flicked the switches, one after another. Endryx could see that he knew the control panel; he had done this before.

He leaned back in the chair. Around him the images of past runs, the sprint cars splitting the desert parallel to the dark horizon, unwound from the archives. "You're logging in a lot of hours," he said. "Very dedicated to your job."

She regarded the silhouette defined by the background phosphors. "It has its compensations." She smiled. "And what about you? Freelancers have to hustle, don't they. Just to stay alive."

"It's the things they don't pay you for. That's the interesting part." Wyre leaned across the desk, closer to her. "Don't you think so?"

"Maybe." She waited for the next step in the dance. "It depends."

He reached and took her wrist, pulling her arm to him. His grip was light, easy enough for her to have pulled away from. She let the narrow span of bone and flesh rest in his palm, the fingers curling against the blue line of her pulse.

Her jacket sleeve was already rolled up. Wyre stroked his other hand across her forearm, as if skin were there instead of the key pad's plastic and metal. He pressed the controls, the tiny LEDs flickering as he fed in a control sequence. She knew he had his own hot-wired control box for tapping into the shadow and its files; this was a different act, an interface of another order. He had learned the tenderness of machines.

The screens behind him switched from the sprinters on the desert to one image: Cynth's face, sleeping.

VIDEO: CLOSE UP, a woman's face, three-quarters

profile. The eyelids are set closed above hollowed
cheeks, in the sleep of exhaustion. Her mouth is
slightly parted, her shallow breath steaming in the
cold. PULL BACK and HOLD. SCHUYLER lies next
to her. He has raised himself up on one elbow, his
head brushing against the snow-weighted fabric
of the tent above him. He watches CYNTH
sleeping.

Still holding her wrist, Wyre turned his head to look at
the screens behind him. "Tomorrow night's episode?" he
said.

He needed no answer; he already knew. "That's the
show."

Wyre drew the one hand away from the key pad. "You
know," he said, "when I first saw all this, the taping and the
reconstructing and everything, all the little detail—when I
first saw it, I thought it smacked of obsession. The kind of
obsession that grows. Like it started out as a job for you,
then it became something different. I thought about it a
lot."

"Really?" She regarded him across her outstretched arm,
as though it were a device separate from her. "Come to any
conclusion?"

He let go of her wrist. The chair slid back as he stood up.
She watched as he laid his palm to the central monitor's
screen, then brought his face against the glass, his profile
covering Schuyler's image, as if he could look down an
angle into the world beyond it.

"I thought," said Wyre, not lifting his face from the
screen, "that maybe you had gotten to love him. Like you
had gotten so far inside, knew so much about him, that you
had to have everything. Image wasn't enough."

She looked up at the half-obscured screen. "I don't love
Schuyler." Her voice stayed level. "Or anybody."

"I know that." He glanced out of the corner of his eye at her. "But you're jealous."

The word made her smile. "Of who?"

He raised his hand and tapped with one finger the image on the other half of the screen. "Of her." His touch rested on the glass above the phosphor dots assembled into Cynth's face.

"Why her?"

"Because," he said, turning away from the screen to look at her, "something happened with her that you can't re-create with your little tapes, and your special effects and all the rest. Something happened back then, out there in the snow, that you can't get inside. And she's there already."

She watched herself rolling her sleeve down over her forearm. "What about you? Who are you jealous of?"

Wyre looked over his shoulder at the screens. "Nobody," he said. "Except somebody who knows more about what's going on than I do."

Endryx stood up and walked around the desk. She brought her face close to Wyre's, letting the glow from the monitor wash across her. The lines of Schuyler's image were cast across Wyre. "Maybe that's not jealousy," she said softly. "Maybe that's who you love." She stepped back, away from the screen and out of the glow of Cynth's image.

He stayed beside the bank of monitors, his gaze following her as she stepped out in the corridor with the shadow.

VIDEO: LONG SHOT, SCHUYLER, BISCHOFSKY, the window.

He stood up and slowly walked away from the monitor, favoring the leg where frostbite had etched the nerves. He gazed out the window but saw nothing, the video's images still unreeling in his vision.

"Do you want to stop now?" the other asked.

All the pieces. As if shattered, he thought. *The clear, curved glass with the darkness behind it, the watching lens. It had struck him as he lay on the anvil of his own past, and the fragments had been neatly bound in the tapes.*

"Do you?" the voice asked again.

He shook his head, making his way back to the chair and the screen.

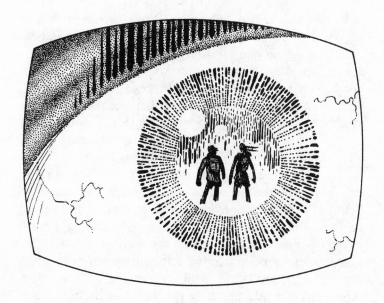

Segment Nine

Another night, another broadcast. Up to the fourth episode; thank God for that, thought Schuyler. It meant that there wasn't much left before this reconstruction of his life would be over. He stationed himself in the chair with the video at his feet, and let it wash over him. Forcing himself to stay in the warehouse and watch. There was little point in going out early to the Phoenix loading zone and doing his pre-run drinking there; by now, enough deaths had accumulated that he would be dogged by ghosts there as well as here.

He watched the simulations of himself and Cynth making their slow progress across the wastes of snow. It was a hard trek, and they'd had little hope. None, actually; they'd known it when they had set out from the Eureka Station ruins. He felt an odd sympathy for the two figures on the screen, trudging with heads down against the ice-laden wind. If he could have helped them, reached into the world built up of electrophoretic dots and sheltered them from the synthetic elements, he would have. Anything to spare them the suffering. But, he reminded himself as he drank, it had all already happened. There's no helping the past.

Their small chances diminished as the two figures went on, bound inside the video screen. A parallel track of Schuyler's own memories began to unreel inside his head as he watched: precious time and energy lost when a wet-blanket had reared up out of a snowdrift and had to be killed, a long process that had left both figures exhausted, unable to go any farther until the next day; the weather turning grimmer and fiercer, only Cynth's inborn line on her birthplace keeping them on a straight, if laboriously slow against the wind, track toward Victoria Base.

And the end: finally, when it came on the screen, Schuyler tilted his head back and closed his eyes. The video was superfluous; he could see it against his own eyelids.

VIDEO: LONG SHOT, a field of snow reaching to the horizon. In the center of frame, a small tent made of skins, half-buried by the wind's burden. HOLD.

They had run out of food two days before. The storm they walked into was the hardest yet. Forward motion ceased; all he and Cynth could do was lie close together under the furs, pooling their body heat and eking out the little bit of fuel for the small catalytic heat unit they had brought with them—sometimes asleep, in uneasy suspension in which they did no more than lose track of time in dulled hunger and exhaustion; more often lying awake, listening to the wind outside the tent.

"I'm sorry," said Cynth. A whisper; their faces so close together, the fur's edge pulled above them, that no more was necessary. "Maybe I should've made you stay back there. Back at the Station."

He took in her words and breath, mingled with his. "So I could turn into an icicle next to old Ruskin?" He managed a smile. "Forget it. I'd rather somebody found me here. So they could look at me lying here and they'd say, well, at least he got this far."

Cynth nodded, and brought her forehead lightly against his. For a moment they stayed that way; he could feel the brush of her lashes against his. Then another warmth opened.

Because we're dead, thought Schuyler. He lay with his arms around Cynth, her head against his shoulder. That's why she did it: let it happen, because taboos and all things forbidden are in present time, when there'll be time afterward to pay the price. When you're already dead, all things are allowed.

She slept, her breath slow and soft against his chest. He looked up suddenly, searching the curve of the tent a few feet above them. He heard nothing, not even the wind. That was it, he realized; the storm outside had ended. Gently, he slid away from Cynth, unsealed the tent flap and crawled out. He stood up in sunshine made blinding by reflection from the new snow.

Schuyler saw them then, a row of figures silhouetted black against the horizon. He stared, and they were still there, coming closer, working their way across the landscape. "I'll be damned," he said aloud. A party of Godfriends—he could make them out now.

He spun around and pulled open the tent. "Hey!" he shouted. "They found us." Cynth looked at him for a moment, then turned over onto her shoulder, away from him and the flood of light.

"Over here!" Schuyler waved his arms at the approaching figures. They took no notice of his shouting; they continued their steady advance across the white fields. Finally, they were close enough for Schuyler to count and make out their faces: six of them, led by a fierce and grim-faced elder. As the Godfriends approached, Schuyler ran to meet them, sinking up to his knees in the soft snow. "How did you—"

Two of the women grabbed him and pulled him to one side, letting the rest of the party march past him without a glance. He hung between them, able only to watch as Cynth was dragged out of the tent and held up before the elder.

He shouted and started to struggle, but was unable to break free from the two Godfriends as the elder raised her staff. A blow from it sent Cynth sprawling in the snow, a red weal across her face.

"What the—" Schuyler strained against the hands holding him back. Cynth lay as through broken against the snow, red leaking from her mouth and nose. The elder's voice jerked his gaze around to her.

The elder looked down at Cynth, who lay without motion. "Most wretched of women," she pronounced, with a bitterness that Schuyler could taste in the blood from his own bitten lip. Yet an undercurrent of pity cut through the anger. "God is within you, and in the world."

They let him see her. He asked to see her, and they took him to her cell.

"Hello, Schuy." Cynth sat on the edge of the thin-cushioned bed. "I was hoping you'd come."

The door closed behind him, and he could hear the footsteps of the Godfriends who had brought him retreating down the corridor. She looked different; in the glow of the lantern set on the floor, it took him a moment to see why. He could see more of her face, the cheekbones visible back to her ears; the dark hair that had been pulled taut to form the thick braid between her shoulderblades had been shorn away. Unoiled, the inch-long hair remaining was light brown. Younger, thought Schuyler as he rested against his hands on the shut door for a moment. That's what it is; she really looks like a child now. The warrior shtick is over. No fur or leather bindings, with which he saw her always in his mind; now she wore a simple loose shift reaching to her ankles, made of the same rough cloth as the blankets on the bed.

"How they been treating you?" She looked thinner to him, as though the pregnancy were somehow diminishing her. Maybe that's just that burlap sack that stuck her in, he told himself. Like some old movie image of the fallen woman. Seduced and abandoned. Barefoot even—her feet were white against the cold stone floor. Flipping perfect, he thought bitterly.

"Not bad." She smiled, triggering a chain of connected memories inside him. "They have. to," patting herself under her breasts. "I'm part of the religion. now. Right inside. Practically a sacrament." Her hand repeated the same motion on the bed beside her. "Come on, sit down. What, you think you're going to get into trouble or something? Kind of late to start worrying about that."

"I guess so." He sat down beside her. He figured they wouldn't have much time together, and there wouldn't be another time. Probably ship me off to L.A. tomorrow, he thought. My part's done. In the so-called cosmic scheme of things. "So what's going to become of you?" Thus cutting straight to the important matters.

She shrugged. "No big deal. In nine months I have a kid. The kid is God. I mean, after that, what more can happen?"

"And they will take care of you? That's what I'm worried about."

"Oh, yeah. No problem." She gazed around the small space. "This isn't plush, but it's only temporary. As soon as I need all the little creature comforts for a smooth delivery, they'll start showing up. We're talking several months of major coddling. If God has to come into the world, they want him to be nice and healthy when he shows up."

"And you?" said Schuyler. "I mean, afterward?"

"You don't have to worry. They may despise me—all that 'most wretched of women' stuff—but they'd never hurt me. You don't mess around with the Mother-of-God." She smoothed a fingertip along his brow, a small caress, flicker of memory. "That's why you don't have to worry for yourself, either. You get off the hook the same way, Schuy. Being Father-of-God gets you some special dispensations."

The words stopped, and silence filled the room. Schuyler saw now the small, intricate curves of her ears. He had only seen the lobes and bottom arches before, the rest hidden by the taut, glistening hair. Tiny smooth scars showed where the hammered gold ornaments had been removed.

He touched her hand. Circuits of memory, the weight of snow pressing upon a small dark space, a pocket of warmth in the cold world. "Why'd you do it?" The other important matter, the question that had puzzled him since the realization of what had happened had shot through him, light with a hard edge. Because what she had done—making love with him—he knew, had been done with complete foreknowledge. She knew what was going to happen, he told himself again, studying her peaceful eyes. Everything—the shame, the complete betrayal of everything she believed. Most wretched of women—that's what she starts with inside herself. Every day from now on. "You did it for me?" he said. "To save me? Was that it? Why?"

"Poor Schuy." Always that pity. That the thin smile had changed to signify. "It wasn't for you. Nothing to do with you."

"Then why."

"You don't understand. Not yet. You still don't understand."

He heard the footsteps outside, approaching. Only a few

moments to say anything at all. "Will I?" All that he could think of to ask.

Cynth looked up at him. "No," she said simply. "Probably not. That's the chance you take."

"Then you take a chance," he said. "Just tell me." Her gaze didn't move from his eyes. "All right." Her voice fell lower, into its last secret. "If it had just been a matter of resisting that love, denying its way into the world—I was able to do that as long as I had my sisters to turn to. For their love. But I was chosen to be made alone." She glanced at the door as a key turned in its lock, then back to him. "If I had been able to love you, just be there with you, I wouldn't have been alone, and I could still have kept God from his sacrifice. But when I was alone, I was too weak to resist that love. Because it was the love for the whole world."

Steps had sounded across the floor as she spoke, and he felt a hand grasp his arm, pulling him up from the bed.

At the doorway, he looked over his shoulder as the guard led him outside. Cynth still sat where she had been, gazing across the empty space without seeing it.

VIDEO: MEDIUM SHOT, a man and woman in a small room of stone walls.

He opened his eyes when he heard the color man's high-speed rattle begin. The episode—that little section of his past—was over. Again. Once was bad enough, thought Schuyler. He shook his head as if trying to drive away the confusing remnants of sleep.

Time to go, he told himself. He stood up, fighting a tremor behind his knees, and headed for the car. It was always time to go.

One other waiting when he pulled into the Phoenix loading zone. From a distance, across the flat fused sands, he recognized Cassem's machine. And sitting upon the fender, in her easy but sharp-scanning perch—a predatory bird, thought Schuyler; a sparrow hawk on a wire—Cassem herself, flanked by a beer carton and her co-pilot, Iode. Her child-like feet, clad in striped canvas sneakers, dangled well above the desert floor.

"Yo, Schuyler." She toasted his arrival, lifting the beer in her hand. "Welcome to the remnant with guts. That's us."

He killed the engine and leaned out the side window. "Maybe a couple more will show up."

"Not likely." Cassem tossed the empty away, reached for another. "I talked to 'em all, back in L.A. All that's left, anyway. They've called it quits. Better a live dog than a dead sprinter." She drank and leaned back across the sprint car's hood. "Can't say I blame 'em."

Iode's saw-edged voice piped up beside her: "That's because they all got *brains*. Which if you had, we'd be sitting in L.A. right now."

"I can dig it." The other co-pilot's voice had triggered Amf, sitting in the passenger seat next to Schuyler. It called, volume all the way up, to its electronic brother. "We're gonna get our circuits fried to atoms, so these turkeys can go on playing hotrodders."

Schuyler left the squawking metal box on the seat. Leaning against the other car's fender, he helped himself to what was left in the carton. "Smitty and Raebel too? They cut out?"

Cassem nodded. "Schuy," she pronounced grandly, "we are the last of a dying breed." Beside her, Iode muttered a sarcastic agreement. "When we go, there'll be no more like us. I drink to our glorious passing. Names writ in water, or some other suitable liquid." Her laughter drifted away across the night desert as she drew herself up, suddenly thoughtful. "At least for me, that is. You, Schuy, have a name. That's cool. A measure of immorality."

"What do you mean?" Though he already suspected.

"Come on, come on." She waved the can around, spilling foam on her wrist. "Don't you watch the color spots? The indie updates? Come on, you don't have to play modest with me."

"I take it they've been talking about me."

"Riots, Schuy. Riots." She lay back on the hood, resting the beer on her stomach, and speaking up to the bright pinpoints of light. "Those Latin Americans have all gone nuts for you. You and your kid. Savior come to kick the collective ass of foreign exploiters. And other good reasons for rampaging around and setting fire to stuff." She propped herself up on her elbows and looked at him. "Numinous protection, huh?"

He grunted. "They talked about that, too, did they?" He could imagine the indie satellites' color men going on. With their smarmy smiles and inch-high dazzling white teeth, he thought. Enough to make you sick.

Now she sat up and rested the hard, sharp point of her chin on his shoulder, so that he could smell the warm alcohol on her breath. "Kinda means," she said, carefully separating the words, "that I'm screwed. Doesn't it?"

Schuyler considered for a moment, then nodded slowly. "Since you're not in on it. The numinous protection, or whatever it is."

"Oh, well. That's how it goes." She pulled away and sat looking across the desert, the curve of her spine parallel to his. "I wonder what happened," she mused aloud. "What changed. We were all having such a great party, larking around and not getting hurt. Did everybody just run out of luck at the same time? Is that it? Or did somebody on the other side get tired of playing around, and pulled out the stops on us."

"I don't know," he said simply.

"Suppose it's the sort of thing that if somebody did know—somebody behind the scenes—they still wouldn't tell you."

He nodded. Inside himself he realized that this was the last time he'd ever sit beside Cassem like this. In Phoenix or anywhere else; that was all over. The paring-down process, whatever its point or method, would continue as long as anybody cared to stick their necks under the blade. Ruthless, until only he was left out on the field. That much of the plan had been revealed. He drank to drive grief numb. I won't see her again, he thought; after we pull away from here. Like the others, dead or wised-up. This tough cookie—he glanced round at her, but she didn't notice, wrapped in her own contemplations. Tough in a different way, not like the Godfriends, amazons striding across the snow. Like a sleek-furred, sharp-toothed animal—a ferret or something like that. Sliding through every hole and other opportunity, catching its small prey. And dedicated to its survival; always surviving, he thought. Until the animal decides otherwise, for whatever reason. But always its decision.

A noise of metal, the ringing of footsteps on the treads leading down the hatchway to the buried factory ruins, broke into his thoughts.

"Here comes our loads." Cassem picked up the carton in both hands and flung it away, the empty cans arcing through scattered trajectories.

VIDEO: AERIAL SHOT of the night desert. Two sprint cars trace parallel lines across the blue-lit sand.

"Finally," said Urbenton, gazing at the central monitor. "Now we're getting down to the really good stuff."

Endryx leaned back in the chair on the other side of the desk. She had sat in silence through Urbenton's usual litany of groans and cracks about the latest bio broadcast; it, and the grumbling remarks, had ended only a few minutes ago. Now he was engrossed, leaning toward the banks of monitors as though he could dive through the glass like a pool of water far below, editing the live feed from the induced visual field out on the desert. But in fact, her silence was easy to maintain. Just wait, she thought, watching the smooth back of his head. She had him on the point of her superior knowledge. Like a bug—I can study him at my leisure. Soon enough, he'll find out.

"Back to the real classics," she said. "Two cars, speed and wide-open spaces."

"You bet." Without taking his eyes away from the screen, he reached behind to the desk's control panel. On the monitor, the shot cut to a ground-level tracking of the sprint cars, one several meters away from the other. The sand blurred beneath the wheels, while the blue-outlined mountains in the distance crawled slower. "I always thought the visual frame was too cluttered with all those cars going at once. You *gotta* keep it simple for max impact. That's all there is to it."

Maybe a little more than that, she thought. But you wouldn't know. She searched around the chair for her cigarettes. "Impact," she said. A point of yellow light, then smoke clouded above her. "Aren't they about to hit the fire zone?" She already knew.

Urbenton nodded, zooming the shot closer so the near driver's mask filled the monitor.

VIDEO: CLOSE-UP, mask with lensed eyes, hands on the wheel. PULL BACK to reveal the car's motion against the landscape. The viewpoint drops out of synch with the car, resulting in a SLOW PAN along the length of smooth metal.

AUDIO: The car's engine suddenly going up a notch, the whine shrieking to a higher note.

VIDEO: The car picks up speed, leaving the viewpoint behind. PAN 90 DEGREES, tracking it as it vanishes into the flat distance. HOLD; for a moment, nothing but the empty desert floor. Then, from behind the viewpoint, blurred metal fills the frame like a hammer to the eye. As quickly as it hits, the second car dwindles after the first.

AUDIO: Fading engine noise, a rough singing of metal, then silence.

VIDEO: The viewpoint TILTS UPWARD, away from the sand. The horizon a jagged line across the bottom of the frame, the star-filled sky taking the rest. HOLD FIVE BEATS. Then a slow line of white fire traces diagonally across.

He saw it coming, out of the dark sky. Up at the edge of the windshield, a scar of light. Cassem had pulled ahead, pressing to the metal's tolerance, farther away than he had known her to lead ever before. His eyes, and the car's scanning devices, could just track her at the limit of their fields. Before they had hit the fire zone, he had realized why: she wants it well witnessed, he thought. By me, if no one else.

The streak of the pursuit satellite's missile lengthened, gaining speed. Inside the close space of his own car, the perception of time slowed; he was barely aware of Amf's stream of nonsense words, triggering his own perceptions of the dangers overhead, readying the necessary evasion patterns to roll down his arms and into his hands on the wheel. For a lengthening moment all he saw were two lines in the distance before him, one parallel to the ground, one now perpendicular and burning to the intersection with the other.

VIDEO: LONG SHOT, across the desert; in the

distance, the front angle of the lead spring car. HOLD; the car speeds toward the viewpoint, filling the center of the frame. At the same time, the white streak of light slants down from top-left frame toward the car. For a moment, the driver's mask can be seen through the windshield, the missile's glare throwing sharp-edged shadows against the hands on the wheel. Just as the car is about to overrun the viewpoint, the frame explodes into light.

AUDIO: The field pickup overloads into roaring white noise. It fades, then the hissing of air feeding combustion is heard.

"Got it." Urbenton leaned back in his chair, contemplating the flames on the monitor screen. "The best set-up yet. That's what you can do, when you get the elements cut down to just what you need."

Endryx said nothing. You're right, she told the other silently. First you cut things out; then you do what you want.

VIDEO: MEDIUM SHOT, a burning shape on the night desert. Roughly a car, or the remains of one; pieces—a shredded tire, twisted scraps of metal— lay scattered about, emitting coils of smoke. Beyond the burning car, the second vehicle, painted orange by the flames, sprays sand as it stops hard. SCHUYLER, pulling off his mask, runs to the side of the wreckage, as close as he can approach through the heat.

CUT to CLOSE-UP, over SCHUYLER's shoulder, of the burning car's interior. Through flames, a small shape can be seen, a blackened torso reduced

smaller than a child's. It falls away from SCHUY-
LER, disappearing into the consuming bright
space.

PULL BACK to SCHUYLER straightening up, the
heat pushing him away from the wreckage.

PULL BACK to LONG SHOT, a figure watching the
flames that silhouette him and smear his shadow
across the orange-lit ground.

PULL BACK and HOLD, where the burning car is a
small source of light in the night desert, the
watching figure barely visible against it.

He found Endryx, again, waiting for him when he got
back to the warehouse. Schuyler got out of the car and
leaned against it, the light from the spider's monitor spilling
across the floor toward him. He could see what was on the
screen: a tape of the bio broadcast. The episode he'd
watched before leaving for Phoenix. On the screen two
figures trudged through wind-driven snow.
    Turning around in the chair, Endryx looked at him. The
white landscape from the monitor slid across the side of her
face. "Hard night," she said. "Down to you now."
    He nodded. "Down to me." He pushed himself away
from the car and headed for the kitchen area. All the alcohol
in his blood had been boiled away by the flames. He came
back out, beer in hand. "You watched it?"
    "Sure. Part of the job."
    Against the cool glass of the monitor he laid his hand, the
electrophores' light leaking around his fingers. "And this?"
he said. "This part of the job, too? Can't watch it enough."
    That, he supposed, being the nature of a recreated past.
Once it's been summoned out of memory, made real, or real
enough, then there was no getting rid of it. A stone. The
common luxury of forgetting had been denied him.

"Always room for improvement," said Endryx. "Maybe I'll do a re-edit for the next time around."

"By popular demand." He prowled around the warehouse space, drinking. It didn't slake his thirst but fueled an anger, as if a fragment of the burning car on the field had lodged in his chest and been carried back here.

She stood up and walked over to the blank wall a few feet from him. Leaning her shoulders against it, she tilted her head back and looked at him. "Wouldn't you like another chance at the past? Most people, that's all they want." One hand reached to her other forearm and worked the control pad.

From the corner of his eye Schuyler saw the shadow stalk away from the monitor, shifting to a new position directly opposite them. Endryx pressed another button on her arm, and the wall against which they stood was bathed in light. He squinted into the bright central spark of a projection lens in the machine's thorax. Looking down, hands spreading wide, he saw the pattern of snow painted across himself. A few feet away, Endryx was outlined by the thin darkness behind her back. Her face and breasts were a white landscape.

A caress of the arm, and the tape inside the shadow sped to another section. The light washing across the wall was dimmer now. The inside of a tent; he recognized it, from both memory and the broadcast. The shot held, freezing the segment of time around them.

Two profiles on the wall, as if the two bodies pressing together for warmth in the tent had been lifted vertical and placed there. Endryx stepped closer towards him, staying close to the wall, her face sliding beneath the projected image of Cynth's. She stopped when the two profiles were in exact overlay. "How much of the past do you want," she said softly.

From where he stood he could see the image of his past self, flat against the wall, looking back at the two women in one space. One in the image's real time, the other in a future unseen. The real time a simulation, a construct; the future a present moment longing to be in the outlines of that artificial past.

"What do you want," he said.

"Does it matter?" Her gaze set and fell into his. "I made it real for you. It wasn't real until now." Closer. "It's real when you can get your hands on it. Make it what you want. It's just memory otherwise. I deserve something for making it real. I should be there with you."

He laid his shoulder against the wall. "Now we've entered the world of the dead." Ahead, he saw the angular distortion of his past face.

"If you say so." Her voice even quieter.

He stepped forward, letting the projected image overlap his present face. Now he and Endryx, their breaths mingling, were the same distance from each other as the other Schuyler had been from Cynth. The parameters of each time met.

"They weren't dead. They're not even dead now." He felt Endryx's hand reach and touch his cheek. "But we became dead." The revelation spilled from his mouth. "We became the past they lived in, so we died in it." In her eye he saw the tiny reflection of the projected scene, and knew it was in his as well.

She said nothing. Distance and light closed between them, and at the center, coldness.

She was sleeping, or at least as far as he could tell. Schuyler slipped out from under the blanket and padded across the bare concrete floor, gathering and pulling on his clothes. His spatial memory guided him among the room's dark objects. One spot of light he noticed missing, from where it had hung suspended before: the red light on top of Endryx's shadow. He supposed the device's special low-light lens was in position on the turret, like a military sniperscope, seeing and recording all, operating on the usual preset that kept him in its focus. At some point she must have turned the machine off, hitting the appropriate button on her forearm. An unusual display of modesty on her part; he wondered what it meant.

Dressed, boots pulled on, he paused to check the regular, slow sound of her breathing. Then he leaned in the open window of his sprint car, patting the seats until he found Amf. With the silent box in his arms, he let himself out and headed down the unlit alleyway.

As he'd expected, light spilled up the stairs from the doorway of Wyre's basement workshop.

"What brings you around?" Wyre pushed his stool a little distance along his workbench to make room for his visitor. He laid down a soldering iron and glanced at his watch. "I would've thought the last American automotive hero would be resting up for his next performance."

Schuyler dragged another stool up to the bench. "You caught the sprint broadcast?"

Wyre nodded. "I'm sorry about Cassem. She was a genuine trip. Talking to her was like putting the jumper cables to your own head."

"Maybe you can get that put on her gravestone. If there is one." Cremation, he thought, has taken care of those formalities. He lifted the square metal box of Amf up onto the bench between them. "Got a problem here."

"Malfunctions?" Wyre raised an eyebrow. "I gave the little bugger a complete overhaul while you were in hospital."

"Something . . . different." Schuyler ran his hand over the unpainted metal. "Something strange is going on. Either I'm cracking up—hell of a time for it—or . . . I don't know. Something."

"Like what?"

Schuyler told him. When he finished describing the voices, reciting verbatim all the words that had incised themselves in his memory, Wyre picked up the metal box and tilted it toward himself.

"Weirdness. You got that down, all right." Wyre studied the speaker grille, as if the internal workings and the glitch inhabiting them were visible through the mesh. "Voices, huh? I am much intrigued."

"What do you think's going on?"

A shrug. "Who knows. Leave it here with me and I'll check it out." Wyre picked up his soldering iron and used it to point to Schuyler's forehead. "If, however, the problem's up there—sorry. Those circuits I don't do."

"Nobody does." Schuyler slid off the stool and headed for the steps. "Thanks. I'll swing by later."

At Bischofsky's studio, he stood unnoticed in the hangar's entryway and saw that Endryx's shadow was here. She sent it out, he thought as he watched it videotaping Bischofsky working at his terminal, when I was in no position to notice. Or else it had just put into operation some preset that she'd already programmed in. That would indicate another layer of calculation, and sense of timing, on Endryx's part. She could get in some more footage for her next project, while he was asleep. Or maybe—the thought renewed his unease, the feeling of being one step behind—she even figured I'd come round here. So she could get footage of both Dolph and me, for whatever follow-up project she's got in mind.

He scanned across from the shadow's inobtrusive position against the side wall, past Bischofsky hunched over the terminal, one of his thick reference books in his lap, to the glass wall. Another step, or several more, had been made in the progress already started: the hangar's space was filled with light brighter than before. The rose window was almost all blank spaces now. From his angle at the entryway he couldn't make out the symbols or geometric shapes formed in the simulated glass, but they were no more than lines traced in luminous blues and reds.

Bischofsky looked up from the reference book to gaze at the window. Schuyler, hidden from the other's sight, watched silently. A feeling he'd had before, back at the night's start when he'd been sitting with Cassem, struck his heart and weighed it down. For a moment he hesitated, wanting to step into the glaring light shed by the rose window, to walk up to Bischofsky and lay his hand on the bear-like shoulder. Then he turned and walked back out to the dark street.

When he got back to the warehouse, Endryx had already left. Even before he switched on the lights, he knew; the sound of her breathing was gone from the space. Off on her rounds, he thought. Or back to wherever her usual resting place is. Mission accomplished. He laid himself down on the empty mattress and closed his eyes.

Segment Ten

Urbenton was asleep when she let herself into the studio. Endryx had never before seen him like that. The corpulent body lolled in the swivel chair behind the desk, one hand heavy and motionless across the deactivated editing controls. His pink, slack face rolled to one side against his shoulder.

She watched him for a moment. Gotta sleep sometime, she told herself. After she'd left Schuyler's place she'd caught a few more hours herself, the result being this displacement in clock time, and catching Urbenton in the low swing of his wake-sleep cycle. It was actually daylight outside the studio's constant semi-lit gloom, although the only sign of it was the desert landscape between Phoenix and L.A. baking in heat glare and carved into various angles to fit the monitors behind Urbenton. He had a big night last night, she thought; she felt almost a kindly pity toward him.

The chair creaked as it swiveled a few degrees to bring him facing her. A slitted gap appeared under his eyelids. "What are you doing here?" At some point during her appraisal he had become awake, perhaps minutes ago.

"Business." She sat on the edge of the desk, closer to him than at any time before, past a certain barrier that had been erected to accommodate her presence in the studio. Urbenton scooted the chair a few inches back, as if physically repelled.

"Later." His eyelids folded down again. "Come back tonight, before the sprint feeds. We'll talk about it then. Whatever it is."

"Speed Death wants me to take over the sprints."

That brought his eyes open. "What are you talking about?"

"The audience stats," said Endryx. "Speed Death thinks we're on the edge of a major breakthrough, a permanent alteration in the target audience's percept systems."

"So?"

"So they don't want a cold mix-down anymore. They want to do a live feed to the indies . . . from the field."

The nighttime animation blossomed in his face, pumping blood to the pink skin. "From the *field?* What're you talking about?"

She waved a hand at the wall of monitor screens, each containing its segment of live, motionless desert. "Controlling the induced visual field—from *inside* the field. With this." Now the hand tapped against the control pad set into her forearm. "Now that the, ah, visual elements have been reduced so much—right?—it's no problem to track one car live. Especially if the edit's on the spot, right with the action. There's room enough for me and a six-viewpoint minidisplay riding along with Schuyler. That's all it'll take."

Urbenton shook his head, a disgusted smile reflecting the world's follies. "They're out of their minds. New York office has let a bunch of factory workers on a religious binge warp their judgment. What do you know about editing a sprint? Even when it's down to a one-man deal—you got zilch eye for action."

Endryx shrugged. "I know enough. And it's what they want to go with. They already bounced it off the indies and got a solid confirm order."

The smile widened, slanting as he looked up at her. "Then they're out of luck, aren't they?" He pointed to her forearm with its underside of buttons and LED readouts. "It'll take at least three weeks to wire you up to handle the field. An induced visual field ain't no walking Bolex like you usually got clanking around behind you. That's real-time throughput, not sitting around watching tapes you shot yesterday. We're talking major neurosurgery, right up into the optic processors in the brain." Urbenton leaned back, tasting the win. "By the time you get set up, Schuyler'll probably be fucking dead. Or those dingey Latin Americans will've gotten some other dumb craze lodged in their video-warped heads. Where's your live-from-the-field then?"

You poor sucker, she thought as she gazed at the round, triumphant face. She said nothing but pushed her jacket sleeve farther up, past her elbow. She punched in a control sequence.

Urbenton detected, from light flickering at the corner of his eye, simulated movement behind him. A dreadful knowledge moved across his face, even before he swiveled around to look at the monitor screens.

The cut-apart desert shifted and moved, every phosphor-dot section panning, tracking, zooming, as though following the trajectories of cars and missiles washed out and made invisible by the brilliant sunlight. Flash cut of stunted cactus, striated rock outcroppings, and the distant wall of mountains, every night's witnesses. Endryx punched another sequence on her forearm, and all the shots froze, then slowly lifted into overhead aerial shots. The desert floor dropped away as the viewpoints rose higher in the field. The sigmoid curve of a dry river bed showed in the central monitor, then it dwindled and was lost to sight. One by one the screens blanked, vision collapsed to fading dots, in time with the tapping of one finger on the control pad.

Urbenton looked around from the dead screens. "You were ready all along," he said flatly. "When they sent you here. You were wired for the field from the start."

Compassion was easy, and cheap, at this point. "That's the line," she said, with a sad smile. "I'm on it, you're off it."

"Jeez. From the fuckin' *start*." He shook his head. "So the bio broadcasts, and the audience reaction down in the factory dorms—Speed Death knew, didn't they? They did market research, didn't they? They got that stuff fine-tuned, to the nth. Nothing catches them by surprise." Urbenton's tone had shifted to grudging admiration.

"Nothing," agreed Endryx.

"Ah, well." He gazed around the studio, inventory of good-bye. "It was a good gig while it lasted. Pure and heady—like wine for the eyes. Screw it. Now I can go back to New York, at least. Tech a game show, or something."

"Speed Death'll keep you on."

A nod. "I suppose." Urbenton looked back at the blank grey screens. "But you know who I feel sorry for?"

Endryx began rolling down her sleeve. "Don't worry about him."

Urbenton went on gazing at the screens, as if they still showed the angles of waiting desert. "Because he's in the plan. But he's not in on it. Is he?"

She shrugged. "He doesn't need to be."

The point of his smile sharpened. "Neither did I."

* * *

When he came back, Wyre's workshop was dark. Schuyler left the basement door open behind himself as he searched for the dangling light cord. A wedge of the street's late afternoon sunlight fell across Amf, power off, sitting on the workbench. A piece of paper had been taped to the metal box.

"Wyre? You here?" Schuyler dropped his hand from the light cord. He'd always assumed that Wyre had a bed and the other normal equipment of living tucked away here; peering into the shadows cast by the bare overhead bulb, he detected no sign of the other's presence.

The paper taped to Amf turned out to be several sheets covered in a thorny, schematic-looking hand. The last page had Wyre's name scrawled across the bottom.

S—

Wd've hung around and ld ths on you, but am too fcked-up. As you'll prbly be whn you're done w/ this. We've been scrwd. Royally. & I'm sorry—1st they ran the # on me, thn they used me to run the # on you.

Schuyler lowered the paper and looked around the room, as if searching for the rest of a joke's machinery. Maybe Wyre was watching him at this very moment, hidden behind a peephole in the wall from the lens of one of the devices on the workbench, and barely able to hold in his laughter. The fucker, thought Schuyler. He hoped that's what was happening, what the multi-page note was the set-up for. Because if not part of a joke, then the chord sounded by the scribbled words—*sorry*; when had he ever heard the cocky Wyre use the word before? Never—then it was too weird. Desperate and sad. Schuyler straightened out the pages and reluctantly went back to reading.

Voices were in Amf, all rt, not yr head. I made cntct w/ them. They wre coming in on a tight-bnd override sgnal tuned to the co-pilot's speech prcsr board—essntly mking a radio out of smthing that isn't a radio—lot of telehack logic intrrpts & reroutngs invlvd—if I'd ever bothrd to build any shieldng into the co-p's, it wldn't have been pssble at all. Plus they were sneakng their sgnal in undrnth East Coast military scan & jammng, which accnts for it fadng in & out like that.

Sgnal comes in frm an undrgrnd orgnztn based in Brazil. Revolutionry grp—apprntly cntrl some key sectors outsde the major cities. Either news of ths has been suppressd or no one up here gves a shit to begin w/. But the grp knows abt us—they know more abt us than we do:

1—The sprints are a fraud. (This main content of their signl.) Never any 'talent' by which sprntrs eluded satellites' missiles. Satellites not lftovers from the war—actually latest military tech—rev grp provided Pentagon access codes to prove this. I got into the files & grp was rt—satellites have secretly been replcd & updatd every 2 yrs. Co-pilots a fraud, too—ability to predict missiles hits an illusion. Illusion supprtd by missiles carefully aimed—until recently—to miss the sprntrs. Specs Spd Dth gave me to bld co-p's with were bullshit. Babble produced by co-p's just that—nonsense. Satellites actually track evasive manuevers by sprntrs, then direct missiles to avoid them. Simulation test provided by Spd Dth a double fake—sim'd hits geared to match up w/ evasive manuevers, pass/fail based

on hidden sgnal from Spd Dth. Even the RH
chips are fakes—'European' buyers are front-
men for East Cost govnmt & military, creatng
artfcl demnd. Rev grp has docs & access codes
to prove all above.

"That's cute, Wyre." Schuyler's voice echoed in the
basement. "Real cute." He rolled the pages—condensed
words, condensed thoughts—and tapped them in his other
palm. Glad he didn't stick around to tell me all this
himself—what would I've said to him? *Gosh! No shit! How
interesting!* There being no appropriate reactions to the
revelation that everything in one's life is a fraud; even if that
revelation matches an unvoiced suspicion that had been
growing from a general theory about the universe to a
specific accusation. Wyre had been lucky enough to get the
truth deciphered to him in private; he had extended the
privilege to Schuyler.

He unrolled the papers and went on.

2—Reasn for above: plan on part of industrial
forces to curtail grwing influence of revolu-
tionary org's among Latin Am factory wrkrs. New
religious mvmnt carefully creatd segmnt of
plan. New religion centrd around wrshp of yr
son Lumen—divrts attn, enrgy of factory wrkrs
from rev org's. The apprance of you having so-
cald 'numinous protection' has been generatd
to prove Lumen's divinity. Plan is workng—new
religion at fever pitch amng Latin Am factory
wrkers.

Rev org found out abt Spd Dth plan—other
sprntrs to strt gettng hit, not you because of
'numinous protection,' etc—then tried to contct

*you through signl override on Amf in ordr to
dissuade you from going thru w/ part mapped
out for you by Spd Dth. Religious propaganda
plantd by Spd Dth in factory dorms has promotd
you as linchpin of new religion—you drop out,
it falls apart.*

*End msg summary. Up to you what to do
abt all this. Catch you later.*

—W

For a moment Schuyler stood lost in thought, folding and then sharpening the crease in the pages. Then a noise penetrated, drawing his gaze back to focus on the room and its objects: a phone ringing. It went on, one rattling burst after another, until he managed to locate it on the cluttered workbench.

"That you, Schuyler? I was hoping you'd be there, man." Wyre's voice on the other end.

"So what's the punch line?"

"Punch line?" said Wyre. "What're you talking about?"

Schuyler tossed the pages on the workbench, as if Wyre were on the other side. "Am I supposed to believe all this shit?" he said into the phone.

The line was silent for a moment. "We can talk about it later," came Wyre's voice finally. "Right now you gotta come down to the hospital. The one you were in."

"Why." He'd had enough weirdness for now; what he wanted was the comfort of his own enclosed space.

"Dolph's here. He's had a stroke. Serious."

It hit him, not as a surprise, but a confirmation. Of what he'd felt, standing in the studio's doorway. For a few seconds Wyre's voice went on squeaking in his eyes, words unheard, then he nodded.

"Right," said Schuyler. "I'll be there."

* * *

"How bad is it?" asked Schuyler. He and Wyre leaned against a wall of one of the hospital's corridors, arms folded and watching the bustling, purposeful movements of white-coated figures visible through the next set of glass doors.

Wyre shrugged. "Don't know. When I found him on the floor of the hangar, his eyes were still open. But I don't think he could really see anything. The paramedics came and ran a quick response scan, but there weren't any results. I imagine we'll get something here pretty soon."

"Hm." He shifted his position, sliding his shoulder blades to a new spot on the wall. Watching and waiting. There were chairs in a waiting room around the corner and down another hallway, but by unspoken agreement the two of them had taken up their station here, at the closest point the hospital guards—one, in Cathedra Novum security uniform, was stationed just past the glass doors—would let them get to the stricken Bischofsky.

Hospital time, that strange mixture of waiting and dread, and waiting for the thing one dreads, was familiar enough to Schuyler. A track he could fit into, if not with ease, at least with custom. Having been recently submerged in it—the body's memory of surgery ached in his reconstructed chest. The body's folly, not wisdom, he knew. It felt comfortable, safe, back at the warehouse where it had been wounded; nervous, fearing more pain, here where it had been salvaged. No smarter than the rest of me, he thought as he went on watching the glass doors. Meaning the entity behind his eyes. Got this one ass-backwards, too, didn't you?

One of the chief features of hospital time: everything else in one's life, in that world outside the oyster-colored, disinfectant-smelling walls, becomes one of the old maga-zines scattered across a waiting room table. Matters of life-and-death importance on the outside change into topics for time-shuffling conversation, words to move the slow min-

utes along until the diagnostic verdict—the real issue, the
only issue—is pronounced.

In that mode, flatly, looking past Wyre to the glassed end
of the corridor, Schuyler spoke: "Did you really expect me
to believe all that stuff?"

Wyre didn't turn his parallel gaze around to look at him.
"You mean the note I left back at my workshop? Taped to
Amf? Believe it if you want to."

"That's not the question."

"You want to know, is it true?" Wyre closed his eyes and
shook his head. "Hey, I fiddled around with Amf's boards
until that Brazilian revolutionary group came in loud and
clear. And I plugged in those military access codes they
handed out over the signal. Man, I saw the files. Both the
Pentagon's and Speed Death's. Everything the group said
was in there, was in there."

"That's still not the question," said Schuyler. "It's not
whether I believe them. It's whether I believe you."

That brought Wyre's gaze around. He scanned the
other's face for a few seconds before speaking. "Why
shouldn't you believe me?" His tone as flat and neutral as
Schuyler's had been.

"You built all the co-pilots, and now you say they don't
work, they're all frauds. That's interesting. And when did I
start hearing the voices coming in? After you brought Amf
to me here in the hospital. Stuff like that."

"So you think I'm in on it? Running a number on you?"
He shook his head in disgust. "Fuck you, jack. I'm the guy
they made a complete fool out of. Speed Death fed me their
little sealed units and I plugged 'em in, sent 'em out—and I
didn't know shit about what they really did. They could've
had a chimpanzee stuffing their boards, for all the difference
it would've made."

"Sorry," said Schuyler bitterly. "Sorry about your
wounded professional pride."

"Forget it. That's not the problem." Wyre looked down

the corridor. "Know what the hard part is? I just wanted to be one of the people who knew what was going on. I wouldn't interfere, I wouldn't care who was getting screwed over. Just as long as I knew, man. Just as long as I was on the inside." He shook his head again. "Then it turns out they were screwing me. I was all the way on the outside, with the rest of the suckers."

"Skip the dramatics," said Schuyler. "I didn't say I didn't believe you anymore. Maybe I'm just not believing anything anymore."

Wyre shrugged. "Why don't you just put things to the test? Everything you've been told by me or anyone else. Numinous protection, Brazilian revolutionaries, whatever. Just push 'em, and find out if they're true."

"How would I do that?"

"Hey," said Wyre. "You're the one going out on the field every night. You figure it out." He fell back into silence, watching the glass doors.

What was that supposed to mean? thought Schuyler. *Figure it out.* A test of numinous protection, co-pilots, all of that. The only drawback being that if you put those things to a test, and they failed—then you're talking death. Not that he greatly cared any longer; it still seemed like an extreme proof.

Wyre pushed himself away from the wall. "You know who I think I just saw?" He pointed to the glass doors and the activity going on behind them. "I think I saw Lina." He looked round for Schuyler's reaction.

"That's weird." He thought he had recognized the small, furtive figure of Bischofsky's ex-wife. "What's she doing here?"

The burly Church guard on the other side of the doors stepped in front of them to prevent their going any farther. Wyre ignored him, peering around the uniformed bulk. "Hey!" he shouted down one of the branching corridors. "What the hell's going on?"

Schuyler saw one of the white-coated doctors, walking with Lina—her frozen wax face unmistakable—turn and look back at the shout. Lina then raised herself on her toes to whisper something in the doctor's ear, who nodded and headed toward them.

"I'm afraid you'll have to leave." The doctor pointed with a clipboard to the glass doors. "Mrs. Bischofsky has asked that no one be allowed to see her husband."

"Husband?" Wyre's voice went up in pitch. "Mrs. Bischofsky, my ass. They've been divorced for years. Fucking hate each other's guts."

The doctor scowled at the clipboard. "We've got her listed as his wife, and thus his next-of-kin."

"She did it," said Schuyler, shaking his head. Somehow, with that rodent ingenuity, always looking for its opportunity. Easy enough to imagine how—she had always kept herself listed in the phone directory as Lina Bischofsky. Some hospital clerk, looking to get all the paperwork filled out, had probably called and notified her about Dolph's stroke and asked her what her relationship to the patient was. The little, scurrying brain always looking for its shot had claimed to be his wife, and that went down on the form. The false information having entered the hospital's records, it became the operational truth. That's how it works, thought Schuyler.

"Call up the Church headquarters." Wyre was shouting now. "This is bullshit. She's got no right to do this. We're his friends."

The doctor looked them over for a moment, then nodded. "All right," he said. "We'll get it straightened out. In the meantime, just be patient, okay?"

Wyre muttered something and glared down the corridor at Lina.

"But you can tell us how he's doing, can't you?" asked Schuyler.

A shrug from the doctor. "We're still running tests. He's

in a coma, but we haven't determined the extent of the stroke damage yet." His voice softened. "Look, it's going to be a few hours. Why don't you come back in a while, and maybe we'll know something then."

"That fucking Lina," said Wyre darkly as they headed for the hospital's exit and the nearest bar. "Should've wrung her little chicken neck when we had the chance."

Segment Eleven

"Did they tell you anything at the hospital? About how Bischofsky's doing?"

Schuyler shook his head to Endryx's questions. "Not too much." He went on with his regular preparations for the night's business while Endryx, leaning against the sprint car's fender, watched him. "The last Wyre managed to extract out of the doctors was that Dolph's on full life-support systems. Respirator, the whole shot."

"Doesn't sound too good."

"Could say." That being the prognosis with strokes, or other cerebral 'events,' as the terminology went. Brain tissue was the one segment of the body that couldn't be

227

successfully rebuilt; once the bone fortress was breached, cracked from outside or betrayed from within, the damage was done and couldn't be undone. Minor or severe, thought Schuyler. More a matter of assessment rather than treatment.

He finished the sandwich he had been walking about the warehouse with, then picked up Amf from the floor and switched it on. "Ready for action?" After the hospital, the bar with Wyre, and the hospital again, he had gone back to the basement workshop to retrieve the device.

"Sure. Why not?" The familiar sour synth. "Let's go get killed. Nothing better to do around here."

He switched it off and went over to the car, leaning past Endryx to place the metal box on the passenger seat.

"Speed Death wants some changes made," announced Endryx.

Schuyler straightened up. "Like what?"

"I'll be going along with you. Tonight, and every night. On the sprints."

"What for?"

She tapped ash onto the bare concrete. "Tonight's the broadcast of the last bio episode, and all the other sprinters are dead or departed. It's a new world out on the field. Speed Death and the indies want a new view of it. No more taping the sprints, editing 'em and putting 'em on the air canned. They want a live signal from the field. Action as it happens." She touched the control pad in her forearm. "So I'm coming with you. On-the-spot edit and trans. You drive, I send."

"Hm." He mulled over this change. "Pretty presumptuous of you and Speed Death. How do you know I want anybody riding along with me?" Which he didn't—he had been looking forward to being by himself, just laying miles down on the flat desert, far from all human contact.

"Schuyler." She ground out the cigarette against the fender. "Don't make me push on this one."

"All right." He held up a placating hand. "Whatever they want." Another thought struck him, a memory trace of talking with Wyre in the hospital corridor. "As a matter of fact . . ." he said slowly, then looked up at her. "It's cool. They're right. I think you should come along."

"I'm glad you see it that way," said Endryx. "Because it can't be any other way."

Schuyler leaned against the car and nodded. "I suppose not. Once something's on track, it can't get off until the end."

At the hospital, Wyre maintained his vigil in the waiting room. The doctors had put him on indefinite hold for any news about Bischofsky. With nothing better to do, he tuned in Schuyler's bio on the waiting room video.

Soon enough he found himself watching his own image explaining the business of being a sprinter to a five-years-younger Schuyler. "Shit," he muttered. What was the point to this? He switched it off, preferring the blank screen to the dead past.

Little conversation between them all the way out to Phoenix. He drove, and Endryx in the passenger seat beside him worked her forearm control pad, setting up viewpoint angles the length of the field, smoothing out transitions between one shot and the next. A panel of six electrophore displays had been mounted on the dashboard in front of her, with a cable snaking between the seats to the shadow folded and tucked behind them, the way it had been in the copter. Glancing over from the real desert scrolling past the windshield, Schuyler could see the same empty landscape, star-lit, chopped into sections. Waiting for him, he knew. On the way back to L.A., on the sprint, between him and the pursuit missiles overhead, a sort of life would be injected into the dead terrain.

"Ready to roll?" At the Phoenix loading point, the moles

had finished tucking the boxes of RH chips into the sprint car and had scurried back underground. Schuyler smoothed the steering wheel's curve and looked at Endryx.

"Sure," she said with a small smile. "Let's hit it."

He turned around in his seat in order to reach behind and switch on Amf. Looking up, he saw something different on the shadow's lens turret.

"What's the blue light for?" Beside it, the red one he had always seen lit before was dark.

"That means we're transmitting to the indies." She nodded at the small displays in front of her; the central one, a ground-level view of the desert stretching to the moon-outlined hills, showed a blue dot in the bottom left corner. "That's the signal they're getting. Then when the broadcast starts, and they re-transmit the signal straight on through to the audience, a green light'll go on." She pointed to the third plastic bump in the row on the shadow's turret. "That'll indicate that the signal I'm sending is going out live, no delay, to anybody tuned in. Your many fans, among others."

"So we'll be in real time," said Schuyler. He started up the engine. "Then everybody'll know."

"What'd you say?" She leaned toward him, trying to hear over the noise.

"Nothing." He pulled the car away from the loading area and headed toward the field and L.A. beyond.

His decision back at the warehouse, and the approach of the point where the decision would become action, relaxed him as he drove. The feel of the drive relaxed him, too: the easy sliding of miles underneath the wheels, the slow pivoting of the distant mountains as the line was re-cut across the desert, the glow of the sensor gauges against his hands; the familiar rituals of motion. The car's progress was echoed in the angles shown on Endryx's display panel. From above or at angles to either side, electrophore images of the car tracked across their segments of the field.

"I think we're about to hit the fire zone," said Endryx. She had caught the shift in the sensor gauges as the alarm LEDs blinked on.

"Could be." Schuyler leaned back, arms straight to the steering wheel, and rolled the loose muscles across his shoulders. "Could very well be."

"Your ass," called Amf from behind his seat. "It fuckin' *is*." It lapsed into the usual silence preceding its rapid stream of nonsense words.

He saw the first streak of light in the distance overhead, the lining up of the pursuit satellites for position as they tracked the car into range. The calm possessing his arms and chest become a cool joy as the firing zone approached. Reflected in the windshield, he saw a green spot of light appear beside its blue twin; on the display Endryx leaned forward to watch, the same light appeared in the central screen.

"You ever think about things?" he said lazily. He took one hand from the wheel and pulled the goggles from his forehead and dropped them to the car's floor. The lower half of the fire-mask remained a loose silver cloth around his throat. He pressed the accelerator, speeding the trajectory so that the zone ahead wouldn't recede in the time slowing inside the car.

"What are you talking about?" Endryx didn't look up from the electrophore displays. Her fingers tapped across her forearm, working the field's angles, cutting from wide angle to tight zoom, aerial to ground level, as she fed the live edit to all the watching world. The shots grew shorter, a faster building rhythm to match the growing streaks of light overhead. "Pay attention to what you're doing."

"Fuck it. Why bother." He left one hand on the wheel, not even holding it, letting the weight of his arm guide the car through a drifting curve. Behind him, he could hear Amf's chatter begin. He shut it out, listening instead to the motor and wind against glass and steel. Somewhere to the left and falling behind them, the first of the night's missiles pounded into the desert floor, washing a bright glare through the rear window. "Aren't I on the track already? If I'm under numinous protection, what's it matter what I do?"

Endryx glanced up from the displays. "What do you mean?" The edge of her own growing surmise was visible in her face.

"Just ready for the test." More explosions sounded around them, bathing the car's interior in a jittering white-out, all edges blurred and shimmering. Beside him, Endryx looked like two eyes set in a match flame. The shaking of the ground under the missiles' hammering traveled up through the momentary contact of tires on sand, buzzing into his wrist upon the steering wheel. "That's all."

He saw the one he was looking and waiting for. In the distance, above the field: a streak of light arcing toward the desert, its approach just visible at the upper edge of the windshield. He could calculate where it would hit easily enough; the barren sand underneath the missile was already lightening as it dropped. The steering wheel slid back into his grip, and he turned toward the spot. Another calculation pressed the accelerator further, to draw the two speeding lines—one horizontal, one vertical—to their intersection.

"What are you doing?" Endryx's eyes widened as she looked around at him from what she saw in the windshield.

He looked at her but said nothing. The car filled with light.

A second before he felt the missile's impact, the flat of Endryx's hand hit his jaw, pushing him against the door. Her other hand grabbed the wheel and swung it hard around. The car skidded sideways toward the impact point. For a moment the car's momentum lifted it up on two wheels; then the explosion of the missile hitting the ground pushed it away.

The side windows shattered, spraying the interior with

silvery bits of safety glass. Schuyler felt the missile's shockwave batter his chest. The seat straps tightened as the car rolled over, pulling Endryx away from him and back to her side. The night desert suddenly appeared above him, then he was blinded by something warm and wet dribbling from his forehead.

Silence beyond the high-pitched ringing in his ears. Schuyler tasted salt in his mouth but could see again. He fumbled for the catch of the straps; when they came loose, he slid down onto his shoulders. He pushed open the crumpled door and crawled out.

The car was upside down, wheels askew and still spinning. Scorch marks from the missile hit rayed a black flower on the sand underneath, the center several meters distant. He rested on his knees for a few seconds, then got up and worked his way around to the other side of the car, resting his hands on the heated metal for support. Endryx was already pushing open the other door when he reached it.

"Jesus, are you fucking crazy?" On her feet, she faced him beside the overturned car. One side of her face was swollen with a darkening bruise. She pointed to the crater fused in the sand. "You were trying to get us killed."

Schuyler touched his forehead, sticky but no longer bleeding. "So much for numinous protection," he said. Glancing in the car, he saw the shadow, apparently undamaged, secure in its tight niche behind the seats. The blue light on the lens turret had gone off. She probably switched it off, he thought. Just before we hit. A certain professionalism there. He supposed the indies' color men were on the air right now, apologizing for some technical breakdown interrupting the live signal from the field.

She studied him, her eyes down to knife slits. "You know," she said finally. "Somebody told you. You couldn't have figured it out yourself."

"Your ass." He waved off the points of her hard gaze.

"What's to figure out? That somebody like you isn't going to come out here unless they know beforehand they're not going to get snuffed? That's easy enough. I just wanted to know why you were so sure."

"And now you do."

He nodded slowly. "Everybody connected with Speed Death must've gotten a big laugh out of us. Running around on our little playground here, thinking we had some hot-shit talent that kept us from getting blown away. Or 'numinous protection'—that's even better. And all the time you were just shooting around us. Just so you could run some number on a bunch of ignorant Latin American factory workers. Make 'em think some kid sitting up in the snow is the new Messiah." He turned away in disgust and looked across the desert. "Great—you guys have got a lot to be pleased with yourselves about."

Endryx walked around and stepped close to him, her face a few inches from his. "I don't know how they got through to you and told you all this, but they didn't tell you everything. You want to know the rest? You're expendable, Schuyler—that's the rest of it. If we have to, we can fake your coming out here and doing these runs. Just like we did with your fucking bio—we can put Jerry Monmouth in one of these cars and put your face on him easy enough. Those factory workers down south have got true religion. They won't be able to tell the difference." She brought the tip of one finger lightly against his chest, as if daubing the center of a target over his heart. "So if you don't want to cooperate, that's fine. You're about to find out how little numinous protection you got."

He met her gaze and held it for a moment before nodding. "I didn't say I wouldn't cooperate," he said softly. "I just wanted to know. Right? You could've saved all of you a lot of trouble. You didn't have to run any number on me." He hesitated, looking away as if the outlined hills had the words written on them. "I just wanted to be on the inside, for a change. Just a little ways."

She tilted her head to study him. "Maybe," she said.

"Hey." He spread his hands and smiled. "I'll make you a deal. I screwed up when we went up to Victoria Base, I know it. You want to go up and try it again? Whenever you want. Just say the word—I'm cooperative."

Endyrx pursed her lips, considering the offer. "Fine," she said. "We'll go up tomorrow. After this screw-up tonight we're going to have to throw our loyal audience a bone pretty soon."

Schuyler folded his arms and leaned back against the car. "Somebody's coming out for us, I suppose."

"That's right." She joined him, looking west toward L.A. and waiting. "That's the star treatment."

He nodded. Soon enough, he thought. One line had ended; she didn't know yet that they had started on another one, the ending of which was just as predetermined.

Maybe it's over by now, thought Wyre. He tuned the video in the empty waiting room to the indie broadcast. Slouched in a tattered vinyl sofa, he endured the color men's hyping of what was to come. "I know it's going to be live," he found himself talking back to the screen. "Get on with it."

The desert between Phoenix and L.A. finally appeared. And with it the solitary car pursuing its line, and shortly thereafter, following the time-honored schedule, the streaks of light in the sky, moving into position for their parts in the play. Wyre rested his chin on his shirt front, letting the images of speed and motion wash over him.

VIDEO: TRACKING SHOT, the car curving through the field of falling missiles and bursts of light. It suddenly veers and tracks a straight course toward one of the lines coming down from the night sky.

The screen went blank, dead gray. For only a second, then one of the color men popped up, as though pulled from a slot at the base of the monitor. He started talking, a smooth flow of words, none of which Wyre heard.

Wyre nodded to himself. "He did it," he said softly. "Wonder what he found out."

He realized that he had spoken aloud and that someone had heard him. Turning in the chair, he looked up and saw one of Bischofsky's doctors.

A note was taped to the warehouse door when he got back to L.A. Schuyler waited until the Speed Death flunkies who had retrieved him and Endryx from the desert were vanished around the corner of the alley before he went inside and unfolded the sheet of paper.

Standing in the empty, oil-stained space that usually held his sprint car—it had been abandoned on the field, there being plenty of replacements available for it in L.A. now— Schuyler recognized Wyre's spidery handwriting.

S.—DOCTORS TOOK DOLPH OFF LIFE-SUPPORT SYSTEMS TONIGHT. THEY RAN THREE BRAIN SCANS ON HIM, FOUND NO "ACTIVITY" (THEIR WORD FOR IT). BREATH-ING AND HEARTBEAT STOPPED ABOUT AN HOUR LATER. SORRY.—W.

He stood for a while under the swaying overhead light, then folded the note carefully and stowed it in his jacket pocket. When he stepped out into the street, the buildings' shapes just visible around him in the first dawn light, he left the warehouse door open behind him.

At Bischofsky's studio—empty now—Schuyler found the chair overturned behind the terminal. He set it upright, then turned and looked up at the rose window.

All the spaces in the framework were blank now. Nothing

but pure white light poured across the floor of the hangar. The final analysis, the last arrangement. The last thing the great bear-like man had seen before the red curtain had come down inside his skull.

Schuyler stood gazing at the empty window while the light outside slowly grew and inched in from the doorway.

Segment Twelve

He watched the snow passing beneath them. Endryx, at the controls of the copter, spoke to him a few times. Schuyler heard the words bounce about in the tiny enclosed sphere but made no reply, not even turning away from the drop into air that began at his elbow to look at her. She gave up eventually; they flew on toward Victoria Base in silence. Once he saw the red recording light of the shadow, from its perch behind the seats, reflected in the curved glass, one of its lenses swiveling into position to tape his contemplation of the white landscape.

The stone walls came into view, and beyond them the snow-bordered square of the landing pad. As the copter settled onto the heated concrete, rocking on its struts, Schuyler pulled himself upright in the seat, roused from wordless thought.

"Here we are," said Endryx. The shadows of the blades on the pad started to slow around them.

"Here we are." He nodded in agreement.

She unbuckled her seatbelt and pushed open the door on her side. "Come on. We don't have all day."

"Wait a minute." Schuyler reached over and lightly touched her arm. "I've got something I want to show you."

His voice, as though issuing from a speaker at the end of a mile of thin cable, halted. "What?" she said, watching him.

He reached into his jacket pocket and pulled out the weight of metal that had ridden in it all the way from L.A. "This." His fingers fitted around the grip's curve, and he raised the gun between them.

Endryx drew back against the cabin's door. "Where did you get that." Her voice was controlled and even as her gaze jumped from the blued steel muzzle to his face.

"Back at my place." A line ran from his thumb above the grip, along the metal's flank, and into a point between her breasts. "Kicked under a pile of trash. It's the one Cynth used on me. Everybody was too busy covering up what happened to search for the weapon. So I found it when I came out of the hospital." He held it unwavering. "And kept it."

He could see the workings behind her eyes, the calculating of distances and possibilities; to flee, to grab, any motion inside the sphere of glass. "Now what?" she asked flatly. She locked her gaze with his, but he could still see her one hand moving carefully toward the control pad in her other forearm. He knew he'd have to cut it short.

"You killed my friends," he said simply. "You and the rest. Speed Death. First you made us think we'd all live forever and we could just go on running and never get hurt.

The nights on the field wouldn't end. Then you put them down when you were ready." He raised the gun, drawing the line between them tighter. "One by one."

Her hand darted to her arm, jabbing at the control pad. The shadow lurched forward, the lens turret swinging around, but the high seat backs held it from reaching Schuyler's upraised arm. He saw the device's motion at the corner of his eye, but didn't look away from Endryx's face. The first shot deafened him, reverberating inside the sphere. Each one that followed became softer to his numbed ears, as though his hand and the jolting weapon in it were farther and farther away from him.

The interior of the copter smelled of smoke and broken flesh when he stopped. Endryx's contorted body slumped between the bottom edge of the seat and the pedals on the cabin's floor. He loosened his grip on the heated metal and dropped it down beside her, then pushed open his own door and stepped out onto the concrete.

He found that the Godfriends were waiting for him, but not as before. At the gates, an old woman, perhaps the same one who had been his guide before; she wordlessly led him inside the Base. The streets and pathways were deserted, as if a somber holy day had been decreed. Schuyler followed the aged Godfriend past the silent buildings.

In the stone garden, at the center of the encircling walls, Lumen sat and watched him approach. The Godfriend withdrew, somewhere in the darkness of the final corridor; alone with his son, he stood and laid his hand on the child's shoulder. The small face looked up at him, the snow drifting down from the gray sky and catching in the soft lashes.

"Hello." A child's voice. Of course; two syllables, quiet and soft. But in them he heard Cynth's voice and, distantly, his own, as if coming back to him on some line routed through a past he could barely remember. Snow and the desert, in potential and in the fact of dead event. His heart battered, Schuyler held his hands back from gathering up the small form and crushing him to his chest.

"You knew I was coming," said Schuyler. "Didn't you."

"Yes." Lumen touched the hand on his shoulder. "It's all right. They know; they won't stop you. I told them your wish was mine. Everyone has said good-bye already."

Hand in hand, they left the stone garden. Through the silent building and the empty streets beyond it, at last through the open gates. The snow had begun to fall thicker, mounting layer after layer upon the drifts. Schuyler lifted his son over the highest of them, setting him down again where the path of the landing pad was still visible.

Lumen watched him remove the shadow from the copter and set it down on the concrete. The child gave no more than a glance to the corpse slumped inside the cabin, the unseeing face pressed against the transparent curve.

The machine, its thin legs still folded up around its body like a dead spider, sat on the pad, unmoving. Schuyler drew another metal construct from his jacket pocket, this one smaller and lighter than the gun. He turned the soldered box, the object of his last visit to Wyre's basement workshop, over in his hands. Wyre had scribbled out a list of instructions for bringing the shadow to life.

It responded to the box's signals, standing upright as if a string attached to the turret had been drawn up into the sky. Another series of switches and the preset lock on Schuyler was triggered; the small red light came on, and he saw his face reflected in one of the lenses as it swung around and focused on him. The snow drifted across his face, catching in his eyebrows and hair.

"Are we ready to go now?" said Lumen.

Schuyler referred back to Wyre's notes and worked the control box some more. The blue light beside the red pulsed on. Now the signal was going straight to the indie satellites and through them to the factory dorms in Latin America.

Let them make of it what they will. "Sure." Schuyler took him by the hand again and led him to the edge of the landing pad, the shadow following after.

The walls of Victoria Base fell far behind them, just visible over the tops of the highest snowdrifts. Schuyler looked back, past the shadow doggedly picking its way after them and transmitting all the while, and saw the stone hut set against the wall, but couldn't see if any figure watched their progress from the dark window.

Then Schuyler and his son were alone in the white world, distance and the falling snow having erased the Godfriend settlement, the copter on the pad and any other sign of human existence. Except for the shadow toiling on, following the object of the program triggered deep inside its circuits. Schuyler felt a certain sympathy for the device, lifting its delicate metal struts high to clear the banked snow, holding its turret level to gaze upon him. It was there, he thought as he watched it catch up and switch lenses from long-distance to close focus. It had been a sort of companion, coming along on the journey that had reached this point. They each had their programs to follow, which had intersected here. It had its own faith.

He sat down on his haunches and looked close into the child's face, brushing the clinging snow away. "We're here," he said. He lay down, his back against a drift's gentle slope, and drew his son to him, bundling the small warmth with his own inside the jacket. The shadow took its position a couple of meters away, training its lens down at them, so that he could see in the dark glass both their faces, Lumen's resting on his shoulder.

Soon enough, he thought. Far away, other eyes were watching this scene, this image of a father dying with his child. The snow would slide through their veins until it reached their hearts, and then make them part of its world, reducing their blood's temperature to that of the surrounding ice. Then they'll know, thought Schuyler. They'll all know.

As is their right; they'll see a dying child, then a dead child wrapped in the arms of his dying father. Speed Death won't be able to lie about us any more. No God.

Lumen shook his head, his snow-flecked hair brushing against his father's neck. "No," said the child. "They'll still believe. They know more than you do."

He looked down at his son. "What'll they believe?"

"My divinity. And your betrayal of Me." The child whispered, keeping his voice below any level the shadow could catch. "You become Judas in the story which they will tell to each other. Which is the seal of their faith. They'll come to believe you became a creature of the same entities which oppress them, and that you were seduced by lies and money to kill your own son, and thus drive away the light that you once helped bring into the world."

Schuyler listened to the quiet words coming from the five-year-old's mouth. Vaguely, he noted that he could no longer sense anything below his knees. "Then," he said, "they won't believe the truth. Because they still won't know it."

"They'll believe that which will make them angry, and righteous in their anger. And that anger will destroy their oppressors. Where their oppressors were, light will be. You will have accomplished what you were foreordained to help Me bring about."

He drew in a great breath of the cold air, chilling his lungs underneath the child's weight. "But I don't believe it." He brought his hug tighter around the small body. "The Godfriends told you that you were God. But your mother knew the truth. And I know it."

Lumen pressed his face against his father's chest, as if preparing for sleep. "It doesn't matter if you believe," he said softly. "Light can blind; would you have done what was needed if you could see the truth?"

He could think of no answer. He lay under the white blanket the wind drew over them, and watched the dark circle of the lens gazing at them. Under his hands he felt the slight tremors of breath and heartbeat stop. He brought his fingers to the delicate mouth and nose under the closed, snow-fringed eyes; no trace of warmth touched his skin.

With one hand, he balanced himself as he knelt. He carefully laid the dead child in the bed of his outline in the snow.

Tottering, he managed to stand up. The third and final death he had planned faded from his thoughts. He was beyond that now. His bloodless legs barely lifted his boots out of his prints in the snow as he started to walk, bracing himself on the storm, head lowered to the ice driving against him.

Then he stopped and looked back. The outline of the shadow was visible through the laden wind. He couldn't see if the blank glass held him or the child in its vision.

Closing

The last tape ended. He sat for a moment watching the blank screen, then reached down and sorted through the pile. He found the one he wanted and dropped it in the playback unit.

On the screen another space formed. A space lit by the colors of a rose window. Time and memory. And in it two figures: his past, and the broad-shouldered, gray-bearded friend.

VIDEO: CLOSE-UP, BISCHOFSKY speaks something close to SCHUYLER's ear.

"You can't hear what he said." The voice comes from behind him. From the other whose presence in real time keeps passing out of mind. *"The mike didn't pick it up."*

It doesn't matter. He leans close toward the screen, hearing the whisper recorded only in the heart.